Broken Boundaries

D.C. KILE

To the girlies who like their fictional men a little bit older and a little bit forbidden. This one's for you.

CHAPTER 1

Aspen

"ARE you sure you want me to go to this? I feel like I'm intruding."

In truth, I don't want to go. I've been hoping my boyfriend would change his mind about me attending lunch with him and his dad ever since he asked me to go. I even gave him an out yesterday and reassured him that it would most certainly not hurt my feelings if he would rather it be just him and his dad. Some quality father-son time. He shot that down immediately.

"Yes, babe," Zach shouts from the bathroom. "Now that we live here, you'll be seeing a lot of my family. You'll have to get used to it."

It's not that I don't want to see his family… It's just I've never really been good at families. Probably because I never really had a traditional one growing up. My grandma watched over me, but I've always been a bit of a wanderer, never really fitting in anywhere or with anyone. It's even harder with Zach and his family because I want them to like me so badly that I end up making every interaction awkward.

I sigh and look around our new bedroom. We moved into this apartment four days ago, the first day of June, and we still have boxes to unpack.

"I know. It's just that we have so much to do. I have to find a job, and—"

"And you're not going to find a job in the one hour it takes to have lunch with my dad. Plus, it's a free meal, which we need since neither of us has money coming in at the moment." Zach walks out of the bathroom with a big smile on his face, knowing that he's got me. A free meal would be nice. We've been eating grilled cheeses and ramen noodles for the last few days while we moved.

"Yeah, you're right."

He extends his hand to me. "Come on. You know I don't want to go alone. Especially not with him."

Zach has never had a great relationship with his dad, which is another reason why I'm surprised he agreed to lunch on our first week here in Blue Haven.

I grab Zach's hand and let him lead me out of our small one-bedroom apartment. Instead of heading to one of our cars, we take the sidewalk because in Blue Haven, Georgia, most places are close enough to walk. Our apartment is very centrally located—just a few steps off Main Street.

It's going to take me a while to get used to living in a small town like this. I grew up in Florida and then moved to Savannah right after high school. I spent two years there before I moved to Atlanta and have been there ever since. After growing up in a not-so-great part of Florida, I thought

I would feel more alive in a big city. But then I met Zach two years ago, fell in love, and he somehow got me to agree to move back to his hometown with him after he graduated from Georgia State University.

I hate to admit that I didn't have much else going on at the time. In Atlanta, I was working at a hotel. My plan was to get into management, but I hadn't made much progress on that front. When Zach told me he was moving home and asked me to come with him, I agreed. I figured it wouldn't hurt to try small-town life for a little while. He always made Blue Haven sound so magical. Truthfully, however sad it might sound, there wasn't really a reason for me to stay in the city without him.

Blue Haven is cute. It looks like your typical small town. Main Street is like every small-town TV movie I've ever seen, with a few restaurants, a general store, a grocery store, a coffee shop, a bakery, a library, and city hall. It's a busy little area, or as busy as it can be with such a small population. Unfortunately for me, none of these cute little places is hiring. It seems people hire those they know, and then those people never leave. I probably should've looked into the job market before I completely upended my life, but I've always been more on the spontaneous side.

Zach opens the door to Melvin's Tavern and ushers me inside. Contrary to the name, it's actually one of the nicer restaurants in town and not what I would consider a diner. Every table has a white tablecloth on it with a candle and a flower centerpiece. There's not a sticky menu in sight.

The hostess leads us to the table by the window that Zach's dad reserved.

Zach and I sit on one side of the table, leaving the other side open for his dad.

"So, what is this lunch for?" I ask as I peruse the menu while we wait.

"I don't know. I think he just wants to check in. Probably so he can say he did the dad thing or whatever."

"Hmm." Zach and his dad… tolerate each other. Their relationship has always been a little rocky, from what I can tell. His parents separated when Zach was really young, and he spent most of his time with his mom, so he didn't get to develop a close father-son relationship with his dad.

It got even worse when Zach decided to go to college instead of working at the Calloway family business: Moonlight Ranch, the shining star of Blue Haven, Georgia. I can't blame him. I don't think that I'd like to be stuck on a ranch for the rest of my life either.

But at least his dad makes some sort of effort, like scheduling this lunch. I don't even know if my dad is dead or alive. That's a thought for another day, though.

The front door opens, and a man walks in. I've met Zach's dad maybe twice over the last two years, and there's no denying the man has a presence. It's especially noticeable in this small restaurant on a random Thursday when he smiles at the hostess, and she practically melts.

Brooks Calloway looks like an older version of Zach: dark hair, dark eyes, muscular build, and a perfect smile. The difference lies in Brooks's sun-kissed skin from working outside all day, the black cowboy hat that he's worn every time I've seen him, and the giant buckle on the belt around his waist. I don't think Zach even owns a belt… or a cowboy hat. Brooks Calloway looks like a real-life cowboy, and unfortunately for him, his only son wants nothing to do with that life.

"Hey, kid. Sorry, I'm late," Brooks says as he stops in front of our table.

Zach stands and gives his dad an awkward side hug. I stand because I feel rude staying seated, which is dumb. It's not like I expect a hug from the man.

"All good, Dad. We just got here."

Brooks tips his head in my direction. "Aspen. Good to see you again."

I can't tell if he actually means that or not, but I smile and say, "You too."

Brooks takes off his hat, and the three of us sit down. I focus back on the menu even though I decided I was going to order the turkey club about five minutes ago.

"So, how's the apartment?" Brooks asks with his signature country twang. I always thought Zach had a strong Southern accent, but it's nothing compared to his dad's.

"It's good. Thanks for getting me in touch with Matt. It's perfect for us."

Zach puts his hand on my leg and smiles in my direction. I smile back and wonder if it's awkward that Zach is touching my leg in front of his dad. Is this a normal thing for people to do? Here I am with my overthinking again.

Brooks nods. "Good. Good. Yeah, it's not much, but it'll be a good spot to start off in while you get up and running."

"Yeah, we're almost done unpacking," Zach supplies. I

don't jump in to say that's a lie. Our place is still full of boxes and half-unpacked suitcases.

"Sorry I couldn't help you move in. It's busy season at the ranch," Brooks explains. While I know summertime must be busy for him, I also wondered if he didn't help us move in because he knew Zach's mom and her new husband would be helping us. Zach has mentioned that the two of them don't really get along, and I've heard a few of the snide remarks his mom has made about Brooks.

"It's fine. We didn't have that much."

The server comes by and takes our order, and I sit quietly listening to the two men talk until Brooks decides to aim a question in my direction. "Aspen, how're you liking Blue Haven so far?"

"Oh." I clear my throat and shift in my seat, trying to figure out how to not shit on his hometown without completely lying. "It's an adjustment, but it's cute."

"You always lived in Atlanta?" he asks. His eyes are laser-focused on me as he waits for an answer, and it's a little unnerving.

"No. I'm from Florida originally."

"Ah, your folks still there?"

"Um, I don't know. Maybe?" I haven't spoken to my mom in over a decade. Not since she left me with my grandmother and ran off with the supposed love of her life. And my dad…? Never knew him. Apparently, I met him once. I have a singular picture of the two of us buried in a box somewhere, but that's the extent of our relationship. "I grew up with my grandmother. She's still there."

Brooks nods and thankfully doesn't ask any follow-up

questions about my family history. His attention is pulled from me to his phone, which is lighting up on the table next to him. He sighs.

Zach notices too. "Everything ok?"

"Uh, yeah," Brooks answers. "Kinda. My assistant/morning desk receptionist quit on me yesterday. Something about a cross-country road trip with her boyfriend. Harper is filling in today. and she's trying to write the job posting but has about a thousand questions."

Zach slowly lowers his fork and looks at me with a big smile. Oh no. I can see on his face exactly what he's thinking. My eyes go wide, and I shake my head to try to stop him, but he doesn't listen.

"Dad, Aspen's looking for a job. Maybe you could hire her."

"Zach!" I whisper-shout. How embarrassing.

"What? You just said that you needed to look for a job."

Yeah, but not with his dad on a freaking ranch.

"You need a job, Aspen?" Brooks asks.

I close my eyes for a second to collect myself before I turn to him and say, "Yes, but please do not feel like you have to hire me because I'm Zach's girlfriend. I have no problem looking around for jobs."

"What experience you got?"

Shit. Guess he's going to humor me. "I most recently worked at the Westin in Atlanta. I worked at the reception desk. I've also been a server, a bartender, and a sales associate. I've tried pretty much everything."

"Can you start tomorrow?"

Wait. What? "I, uh…"

"Yep. She can," Zach answers for me.

Brooks waits for me to answer him, though. "Sure. Yes. That'd be great."

"Good." He nods and focuses back on his food.

"So, that's it? Do I need to do an interview or anything?"

He shakes his head. "If my son trusts you, then I'll trust you."

This is going to be terrible. Not only because I have no idea what happens on a ranch, but because I'll be working for Zach's dad. The same dad that he's complained about fairly regularly over the two years we've been together.

But it's a job. One that I desperately need since I used a lot of my savings on this move. I've searched a few websites for open positions in the area, and the options are slim to say the least. Hopefully, this job pays well. I'd ask, but honestly, I'll take what I can get for now. I'll just work at the ranch until I can find something better.

We finish our lunch, and Brooks pays the bill. On our way out, a few people call out to him to say hello. It seems like everyone here knows each other. That never happened in Atlanta. Most people kept their heads down and headphones on.

Outside, Brooks stops on the sidewalk in front of a big black truck that says Moonlight Ranch on the side.

"Zach, it was good to see you. Let me know if you need anything, alright?"

"Thanks, Dad."

"Aspen. See you in the morning. Nine o'clock."

"Ok. Where do I go? Do I ask for you?"

"Head to the front desk. Give 'em your name, and they'll get you set up."

"Alright. Thank you. I won't let you down," I tell him, although I'm not sure why. I have no idea what this job entails, and I might end up being absolutely terrible at it.

"I'm countin' on it."

He climbs into his truck, and without another glance in our direction, he's gone.

I immediately turn to Zach.

"What was that?" I ask.

"What was what?"

"Um, you practically forcing your dad to hire me. All you've ever done is tell me how he's a terrible father."

He has the audacity to shrug. "Just because he's a bad father doesn't mean he'll be a bad boss. That ranch is his life. He treats his employees better than he treats me. And I'm sure the pay will be good. The ranch makes more money than everywhere else in town."

"Still would've been nice if we discussed this before you put me on the spot like that."

"Noted for next time," he says, playing it off like this is not a big deal and I shouldn't be upset. "I just wanted to make sure you had something lined up, and that job woulda gone quick once it was posted. When I start the police academy next week, I'm going to be gone a lot. I don't want you to be bored."

I exhale a deep breath and try to release some tension. I know Zach meant well, but the execution could've been better. Working on his dad's ranch was not part of my plan, but he's right. I do need a job. I've never done well with just sitting around.

"I know. It just took me off guard. I don't want people to think I only got the job because I'm your girlfriend."

Zach laughs. "Babe, this is a small town. Everyone has a job because they know someone. That's just how it works around here."

Well, I guess I'm officially a Blue Haven resident now. Add one more to the population number on the town sign.

CHAPTER 2

Aspen

WHAT DOES one wear to work on a ranch?

I run my hand along all of my newly hung clothes and try to decide what would be best. The internet was no help. I scoured the Moonlight Ranch website, and all I found were pictures of land and horses and cabins. No photos of employees to be seen.

I finally decide on black dress pants and a white blouse. This is usually what I would wear for an interview, but I figure it'll work for today since I'm meeting the rest of the staff for the first time. I want to make a good first impression.

"You look nice," Zach says, coming up behind me in the bathroom. He's just rolled out of bed, but I've been up for awhile trying to prepare myself for today.

"Thanks. Do you think this is ok?"

He shrugs. "I dunno. Looks a little fancy for the ranch, but I'm sure they'll give you a shirt or something."

That's entirely unhelpful. "Should I change?"

"No, babe. You look good."

I sigh and take one final look in the mirror. I've done my makeup and made sure my curls are as tamed as they can be in this humidity.

"You're going to do great, babe. Stop stressing."

"I know, I just—I just don't know what to expect."

"You worked in the heart of Atlanta for years. I've heard some of your horror stories. This is going to be a cake walk for you."

"Alright, well, I better get going. I don't want to be late."

"Have a good day, babe. We'll go out to dinner tonight to celebrate."

I smile. It'll be nice going out just the two of us. It's been a stressful few weeks with the move. While we've been together almost every day, we've been busy packing, unpacking, calling utilities, and cleaning. We haven't gone on a date in weeks.

"That sounds nice."

He gives me a quick kiss and then disappears into the shower while I grab my purse and keys and head out to my car.

Moonlight Ranch might be the only thing in Blue Haven that isn't walkable from the town center, but it's not that long of a drive before I'm passing under the iron arch welcoming me.

I park in the lot in front of the giant lodge and take a few calming breaths before I get out of my car and walk in. The lobby smells like butter and syrup, which I assume is coming from the restaurant off to the side. It's packed full of guests enjoying breakfast.

I zero in on a large wooden desk, which I can only assume is the front desk. I wait in line behind a guest who is asking for directions to the stables. When she moves on, I take a step forward and smile at the woman behind the desk.

"Hi, I'm Aspen. Today is my first day. Mr. Calloway told me to get here at nine."

"Oh, thank god!" the woman exclaims. "I was worried Brooks had gotten my hopes up for nothing. I'm Harper, the Director of Hospitality here at Moonlight Ranch."

"It's nice to meet you!"

"Let me get someone to cover the desk, and we'll get started." She picks up a phone and asks someone to come to the lobby.

"So, how do you know Brooks?" she asks while we wait for her relief.

"Oh, I'm dating his son. We just moved here, and Mr. Calloway was nice enough to offer me this position."

"Just to warn you now, he hates being called Mr. Calloway," she informs me. "It's been awhile since I've seen Zach. How's he doing?"

That's right. I guess everyone here probably knows Zach. "He's good. He just graduated with a criminal justice degree and will be starting the county police academy next week."

Her eyebrows raise as if she's surprised by that. "Huh. Good for him. Oh, here comes Jazz."

A woman who looks around my age bounces up to the counter.

"Jazz, this is our new hire, Aspen. Aspen, this is Jasmine. She's a lead housekeeper, but she's cross-trained to help at the desk too in case you ever need it."

"Oh, ok, good to know. It's nice to meet you, Jasmine."

"Call me Jazz," she corrects me with a smile. "It's nice to have a fresh face around here. Let me know if you need anything!"

"Thanks."

Harper motions for me to follow her down a hallway to her office. She grabs some papers from her filing cabinet and sits down across from me.

"Alright, so what did Brooks tell you about the position?"

"Oh, um, nothing actually."

She rolls her eyes. "Yeah, that figures. Well, you're going to be working as his assistant and have morning desk duty. It's usually slower in the mornings up until checkout time, so you'll have plenty of time to do whatever Brooks needs, which honestly isn't much. You'll have access to his emails. You'll respond to ones you can and flag the rest that he needs to respond to. You'll schedule meetings and make sure he shows up to them. He's terrible at checking his schedule. There also might be a few miscellaneous tasks that he doesn't have time to get to. It sounds like a lot, but it's really not too bad."

I exhale in relief. I can handle this. "Ok, that sounds good."

"Good. Your schedule is Thursday to Monday—off

Tuesday and Wednesday. Weekends are busy here, so it's all hands on deck."

"I'm used to non-traditional schedules."

"Perfect. Here's the new hire paperwork. Go ahead and start filling this out, and I'll go grab you some shirts. You can pretty much wear whatever you want to work. Most of us wear jeans and T-shirts, but we provide two Moonlight Ranch shirts. Just make sure you have your name tag on, especially if you're wearing a normal shirt. What's your size?"

I tell her, and she nods, leaving me alone in her office to complete the paperwork. It doesn't take long for me to get everything completed and signed before Harper is back, handing me two T-shirts and giving me a tour of the ranch before we start training.

She takes me through the lodge, pointing out the restaurant, the gift shop, the game room, and the event space. Then we head toward the back of the lodge and out the door just as Brooks pulls up on a UTV.

"Mornin', ladies."

"Hey, Brooks," Harper responds for us. I stand next to her, smiling awkwardly. I clasp my hands behind my back and then drop them immediately. Why am I standing like a soldier?

"Where're you heading?

"I'm giving Aspen a tour of the property before we start training."

He nods and turns his attention to me, giving me a once-over. I definitely shouldn't have worn this blouse.

Everyone is way more casual than I could've ever expected. "I can do the tour."

"You sure?" Harper asks.

"Yeah. I'm sure you've got plenty to do. I'll take her around and bring her back to the desk when we're done."

Harper lets out a relieved breath. "Thanks, Brooks. I'm swamped." Then she turns to me. "I'll see you in a little bit, Aspen. You're in good hands with Brooks."

"Oh, ok."

"Come on, Aspen. Let's get going." Brooks motions for me to get in the UTV.

Once I'm seated, he takes off across the massive lawn. Behind the lodge, there's a pool that's already filling with guests. We pass the pool area and head toward the cabins.

"We've got two types of rooms out here: the cabins and the cottages. The cabins are smaller and give more of a camping feel. The cottages are more like villas. They have separate bedrooms and full kitchen and living areas."

"It's nice that you have different options," I say, looking at the small wooden cabins as we drive by.

"Our goal is to appeal to all families, but we understand that some people don't enjoy basic camping."

"I'm afraid I'm one of those people."

He chuckles. "Something you and my son have in common, then. I could never get that kid to go camping with me once he got to a certain age."

We drive further and come up to the stables. Brooks parks the UTV outside, so I assume we're doing a more in-depth tour.

I follow him through the big doorway. There are probably twenty stalls in here, all filled with beautiful horses. It also smells like it's filled with twenty horses, and I try my best not to grimace. Brooks doesn't seem to notice the smell at all. Must be something you get used to. Hopefully.

"Beck!" Brooks calls out.

A man comes out of a small office toward the back of the stable. He's dressed similarly to Brooks in worn-in jeans, a Moonlight Ranch T-shirt, and boots. The only difference is that Beck is in a backward baseball hat while Brooks has his signature cowboy hat on.

"Hey, man."

"Beck, this is our new hire, Aspen. She's taking over Shelby's position."

"Ah, ok." Beck wipes his hands on his jeans before he holds one out to me. "Nice to meet you, Aspen. I'm Beckham, but you can call me Beck."

I shake his hand. "Nice to meet you."

"Beck is our stable manager. He's got a few guys who help out and do the trail rides with guests. Beck's been with us for about ten years now. Probably knows more about this ranch than I do."

Beck laughs. "I don't know about that, boss. Maybe a close second. You ever ridden a horse, Aspen?"

"Um, no actually. I haven't." I'm embarrassed to admit that in front of two men who have very obviously been around horses for their entire lives.

"Well, we'll have to get you out here one day. Let me know when you have time, and I'll walk you through it. You'll be riding in no time."

One of the horses snorts next to us, making me jump a

little. She's a beautiful brown horse who looks like she wants to get out on the trails right now.

"That sounds great, Beck. Thank you." I hope they can't hear the wobble in my voice. As beautiful as the horses are, they're huge. Which is a little intimidating for people who haven't been around horses much, a.k.a. me.

Brooks pats one of the horses on the nose before he leads me back out to the UTV.

"Take Beck up on that offer," Brooks says as we drive away from the stables. "He's a great teacher. Very patient. He does all the kid rides, too. He's got a little girl. They live on the property."

"Oh, I didn't realize people lived here."

"Just me and Beck. His house is on the edge of the property. We'll pass by mine in a bit. It's by one of the lakes."

"How long have you lived here?"

"My whole life. My parents lived in the house I currently live in. When I was old enough, I built a small cabin right next to theirs, where I lived until they retired and left this place to me. I renovated their house and moved in. Zach never mentioned it?"

"Oh, um, no. I don't think he did."

"Hmm. He used to stay with me in the cabin a lot. When he was really young, I'd set up a tent out back, and we'd camp. He always got so excited when he saw our sleeping bags ready to go. Once he got to be around ten or so, he stopped wanting to do that."

His voice sounds sad as he reminisces. I feel bad for Brooks. He doesn't seem like a bad guy. I wonder if he just had a hard time being a father at such a young age. I don't know exactly how old Brooks is, but I know he doesn't look over forty. Since Zach is twenty-two, I imagine Brooks was probably a teenager when Zach was born. I can't imagine having a kid at that age. Hell, I can't imagine having a kid now at twenty-four.

"I'll have to ask him about it."

"Yeah. Yeah, do that."

The tour continues as we drive by two lakes where guests can fish and canoe. Brooks's house sits a ways behind one of the lakes. We don't get too close, but even from a distance, I can tell it's stunning. It reminds me of one of those log cabins you see in the movies with giant windows, a big wrap-around porch, and beautiful landscaping all around. It's obvious a lot of work has gone into the house. It's like a mini mansion.

There is a little bit of space between the big house and the little house that Brooks says he lived in when Zach was younger. It's a nice little house, but the size difference is kind of funny. There can't be more than one bedroom in the smaller house. It almost looks like a shed compared to his house.

The tour of the property wraps up with Brooks pointing out the start of some hiking trails around the base of the mountains. He tells me a few that are his favorite, and I nod along, knowing that I'll probably never hike them myself.

When the main lodge comes back into view, I'm actually disappointed that the tour is over. It wasn't as bad as I thought it would be spending my morning with my new boss. It's obvious that Brooks loves this ranch. Hearing him talk about the land and how passionate he is about it all makes me excited to work here. It also wasn't as awkward as I thought it would be with just the two of us. With Zach being the only thing we have in common, I expected a lot of silence between us. But the conversation flowed nicely and professionally.

When I meet Harper back at the front desk, I'm smiling and thinking that maybe this job won't be so bad after all.

CHAPTER 3

Aspen

"THERE SHE IS," Zach greets me from the couch as I walk into our apartment. "How was your first day?"

I put my purse and keys down on the counter and try not to notice all the boxes that are still unpacked. "It was good. Learned a lot. The ranch is beautiful."

"Yeah, it's not bad."

Not bad? Between the land, the lakes, and the mountains, it's all stunning. Moonlight Ranch could potentially make this city girl like living in the country. I don't feel like arguing with him, though. He's got his own reasons for not liking the ranch, and I try to remember that.

"What did you do today?" I ask, grabbing a glass of water.

"Eh, not much. Finished unpacking my clothes. Grabbed some groceries."

"Cool. Hey, how come your dad didn't offer us the cabin by his house instead of helping get this apartment?" I've been thinking about it all day. Not that I particularly want to live on the ranch. At least the apartment is in town and makes it feel like I'm not in the middle of nowhere. It just seems odd that Brooks wouldn't have at least offered it.

"He did," Zach says, like it's obvious. "But I don't want to live so close. And I know he'd just try to get me to work there if I was that close."

"Would it be so bad to work there? It seems like a nice place. Give you a chance at a good future." I try not to sound too annoyed that he conveniently forgot to mention that offer. It's something we should've discussed together. I would've understood his reasoning, but it would've been nice to be involved.

He sighs and looks back down at his phone like he would rather talk about anything else than this. "I don't want that life, Aspen. I told you that. The ranch is his thing, not mine. I don't want to take over his stupid family business."

"Right." I can't help but think about how sad that must feel for Brooks. His only son doesn't want to continue on the family legacy that he's worked so hard on. I wonder where the ranch will go when Brooks decides to retire.

"And trust me. You don't want to live in that shit-hole cabin."

"Really? It seemed nice."

Zach looks up from his phone. "Did he take you in there?"

"Well, no, but we drove past it on our tour of the property. He says he has a lot of fond memories with you there, like camping out back when you stayed with him. Until you stopped…"

Zach huffs a laugh. "Yeah, we had to camp because that place is smaller than this apartment. It was fun at first, I guess, but it got old quick. It's just one big room. There was no privacy. I hated being there."

"Oh." Honestly, it sounds kind of charming to me, but I didn't go inside, so I can't say for sure. I guess I need to trust Zach on this. "Well, I was just curious."

"You'd better change. We're having dinner with my mom tonight," Zach tells me, changing the subject abruptly.

"I thought we were going out to celebrate." I'm so concerned with the change of plans that I don't have time to be offended that he told me I need to change. I think I look cute.

"We are. I talked to Mom earlier, and she wants to take us out to celebrate your new job."

"Oh." I can't hide my disappointment. "I was hoping it'd be just the two of us."

He finally gets off the couch and walks over to me and wraps me in a hug. "Sorry, babe. We'll go out just the two of us another night. I didn't want to hurt her feelings."

He didn't want to hurt her feelings, but he had no problem disappointing me. I take a deep breath and try to shake off the irritation. I've had a long day, and I'm sure he didn't mean anything by it.

"That's fine. Maybe next time just talk to me before you commit us to something?"

"Sure, babe. I can do that."

He kisses my head and releases me from the hug. "Go get changed so we can go."

I nod and head to our room to throw on a casual

sundress. One I know Zach likes. I touch up my hair and makeup and then meet him back in the living room.

"Where are we going for dinner?" I ask as we walk down the sidewalk of Main Street.

"It's this place called Roadside. It's a little bar and grill. You'll like it."

We walk two more blocks before we're standing in front of a small building with a crooked sign out front that says 'Roadside.' I try to be optimistic because Zach seems to think I'll like this place, but my optimism fades as we cross over the threshold.

I was expecting (or maybe hoping) for a nice little restaurant. What I get is a bar with a few tables and a large dance floor in the back. The air smells of sweat and alcohol. Don't get me wrong, I'm used to being in bars. I've bartended at a few different places in Atlanta, but this place looks like it's on its last leg. I'm also a little nervous about the quality of food.

I wonder what about this place makes Zach think I'll like it.

Lacey and Jason, Zach's mom and stepdad, wave at us from a table in the back corner. Zach takes my hand and weaves us through the people waiting to get to the bar. We take a seat across from them at the table.

Lacey has always been nice to me, but I've gotten a sense that she doesn't particularly like me. I'm not sure what it is exactly, just the gut feeling you get when you can tell someone is being fake with you. I've never mentioned anything to Zach about it because he has a really good relationship with his mom, and I don't want to stir up any issues. It's probably all in my head anyway.

"So glad you guys could make it!" Lacey says.

I smile politely like my grandmother taught me. "Thanks for the invite."

"Oh, of course. We wanted to celebrate your first day at work. It's not always easy to find work in a small town. I'm just sorry you got stuck working for Brooks."

Jason huffs a laugh next to her. I guess he's not a fan of Brooks either.

"Oh, it's not too bad. Everyone seems really nice at the ranch." I pull a sticky menu out from behind the napkin dispenser. I know that Zach's mom and dad don't really get along, but I'm not here to get in between their drama. Especially since Brooks is my new boss.

"I'm sure they are." She chuckles. "They're probably all brainwashed to love that ranch as much as Brooks does."

"He's proud of his property. You can't really blame him, can you?" I ask, suddenly feeling like I need to defend a man I barely know simply because he's not here to defend himself.

"I can blame him for a lot of things," Lacey says.

I feel her eyes bore into me like this is a moment for two women to bond over their hatred for a man. But I don't hate Brooks. I have no reason to. And I'm not going to bash him simply because they have a history I'm not involved in.

"I'm just grateful to get a steady paycheck," I say carefully. "Zach is the one who suggested me for the job in the first place."

"Right. Of course. And we're happy for you. It'll be

good for you to have a job while Zach is becoming a police officer."

It'll be good for me? Am I a child? I don't know if she realizes that 1) I'm two years older than Zach and 2) I paid for almost all his expenses and bills while he was finishing up his last year in college. I don't need to be told how to be an adult.

But again, I don't want to cause any trouble, especially at the dinner table. So I keep my mouth shut. "Yeah."

We order our drinks and food. I go with the cheeseburger. Not exactly what I was hoping for as a celebratory meal, but it'll do. It also seems like the safest option in this place. After we order, Lacey turns her attention to Zach.

"How has it been being back home? Have you seen any of your friends yet?" she asks.

"Yeah. I've seen a few of them." Huh, that's weird. He hasn't mentioned that to me. Not that he has to tell me everything, but I would've thought it would come up in conversation. "Had lunch with Cory and Anders today."

Why wouldn't he have mentioned that when I asked him what he did today? It just seems odd. But I know now is not the time to bring it up.

"Oh yeah? How are they doing?"

"Good. Anders is getting into real estate," Zach tells us. I have no idea who Anders is, so I just nod along.

"You know, that's probably a good idea for him. That boy was always very convincing. I bet he'd be a good salesman," Lacey laughs.

"Cory is with Melinda now."

The laughing stops abruptly. "Oh." Silence. "Are you alright with that?"

Um. What? What the fuck is happening? Who are these people?

Zach shrugs. "Yeah, I mean, he texted me a while back and asked if it was alright. I'm certainly not going to be the reason to stop them. Besides, I've got Aspen now." He turns and smiles at me, but I get an uneasy feeling in my stomach.

"Sorry, who are these people?" I ask, not able to hold in my curiosity anymore.

Zach opens his mouth to answer, but Lacey beats him to it. "Melinda is Zach's high school sweetheart. Lovely girl. I'm surprised he never mentioned her."

Why on earth would my boyfriend mention his ex-girlfriend to his new girlfriend? He said things about an ex before, but I don't remember him saying her name. And honestly, I don't care to know. She's an ex for a reason, and that's good enough for me.

"I guess she wasn't an important topic of conversation," I murmur.

"And now she's dating Zach's best friend. Crazy how that works out," she says as if she's actually amused.

"Yeah, I'm happy for them," Zach says. Of course he is. Why wouldn't he be? He's moved on, so she should too.

Thankfully, the conversation steers away from this topic. When our food is dropped off, I eat as quickly as I can so we can get out of here before any more of Zach's past decides to pop up unexpectedly and make this celebratory dinner any worse.

CHAPTER 4

Brooks

I HATE SITTING AT A DESK. I hate emails. I hate paperwork. I hate meetings. All the admin stuff… yeah, I hate it. Granted, I've handed most of that stuff off to Harper because, for reasons I'll never understand, she loves that shit. I'd much rather be out in the lodge talking with guests or out at the stables helping with trail rides. Hell, I'd even love to renovate the guest cabins myself. Working with my hands has always been a skill of mine.

But occasionally, I do have to do some work that involves this stupid computer. Unfortunately, Harper can't do everything. Some things still require my input. So, that's what I'm doing this morning. Reading through emails that are waiting for a response from me. I've been putting them off for almost a week, so it's time. Figured I should knock it out early so I can spend the rest of my day doing… anything else.

There's a timid knock on my office door, and I look up, ready for a welcome distraction.

"Yeah?"

The door opens, and my new employee, Aspen, walks in holding my favorite coffee mug.

"Good morning, Mr. Calloway." She sets the mug down on the corner of my desk. "I brought you your coffee."

"Mr. Calloway is my father. Everyone calls me Brooks." She nods. "And you don't have to bring me coffee. I don't mind getting it myself."

"Oh, Harper said—"

"I know what Harper said, but I can get my own coffee."

She cocks her head, and I can see the confusion in her eyes. "Did your old assistant bring you coffee?"

"Well, yeah, but you're—"

"Then I'm also going to bring you your coffee. I don't want to be treated any differently just because I'm Zach's girlfriend."

I chuckle. "Well, alright then."

She looks much more casual today in her jeans and Moonlight Ranch shirt. Her curly hair, which was down and wild yesterday, is pulled back into a braid today. I was a little worried that she wasn't going to fit in around here. Since Zach is so anti-ranch life, I assumed that she would be similar. But she's looking the part already after only one day.

"Is there anything you need from me this mornin'?" I ask. I know she's still deep in training with Harper. It might be a week or two before she's ready to handle things on her own.

"Yes, actually. I wanted to remind you of your meeting

with the mayor in an hour. He'll be calling promptly at ten."

"Aw, damn." Add meetings with the mayor to the list of things I dislike.

"Would you like me to reschedule it?"

"Nah. I'll just get it over with. He wants to go over plans for the Fourth of July, but we do the same damn thing every year. I don't know why we need a whole ass meeting to discuss it."

She tries to hold back her laughter at my outburst, but she can't hide her smile. "Oh, right. Is there anything I can do to help?"

I don't really need her help, but since she's offering. "Yeah, you'll need to sit in the meeting with me. Take notes on what we need to get done before the Fourth. It'll be a good virtual introduction to the mayor of Blue Haven, also. He's always been a good partner with the ranch."

"Yes, sir. I'll be back in here a few minutes before ten then."

"Good."

"Anything else?" she asks.

"That'll do it."

She nods and turns to leave my office. Not even five minutes later, Harper is bursting in and taking a seat across my desk. She doesn't bother knocking anymore.

"Hey, Harp. How are you doin' this lovely morning?"

"Overworked and underpaid," she states flatly.

I roll my eyes. "You're the highest-paid person on this ranch."

She laughs. "I know. I just like hearing you say it."

"Of course you do."

"Listen, you know the Reynolds family is checking in this afternoon?" she asks.

"I wasn't aware, but I'll make sure to track them down." The Reynolds family has been coming 'round the ranch every year since I can remember. They used to bring their kids, and now their kids bring their kids. Those are my favorite kinds of guests. The ones that love the ranch so much that they come back over and over again.

"Good. You ready for the meeting with the mayor?"

"Is there something for me to be ready for? Same shit, different year." The town wants my money and my staff to help with the celebrations. It happens every year for every holiday. You'd think the town treasury was directly linked to my wallet at this point. But if I don't do it, I'm the bad guy.

"True. Well, in other news, the new girl seems promising."

Thank god. The last thing I want to do is have to start interviewing. When Zach mentioned Aspen needed a job, I was glad to jump on the opportunity. I trust my son to be with someone who has enough common sense to do this job. Hiring Aspen has hopefully earned me some points in Zach's eyes, too. He used to love hanging out with me and being at the ranch, but the older he got, the more he pulled away from me. I thought it was just a teenager phase, and that I just needed to give him time and space. I mean, I was a kid once. I remember not wanting anything to do with my dad. I came around, though. Unfortunately, I'm still waiting for Zach to do that. With any luck, now that he's back in town, I can try to fix whatever is broken between us. It would help if I knew what that was, though.

Aspen was also a blessing because I needed to get Harper relief for the desk fast. She's got enough to do around here besides checking people in.

"That's good to hear," I tell her.

"Yeah, she picked everything up quickly. Seems really smart and motivated. I think she'll fit right in."

"Good. She told me yesterday that she's never ridden a horse, so we need to change that quickly."

Harper laughs. "Got it. I'll add it to the list: teach the new girl how to ride."

"Get her a time slot with Beck. He can teach her."

"Alright. You going into town tonight?" she asks. Occasionally, we meet up for dinner or drinks. Both of us being over thirty and single doesn't give us a whole lot of options around here, unfortunately.

"Wasn't plannin' on it. You need a wingman?"

She huffs a laugh. "No. I'm out of food at home and dreading going to the grocery store."

"I made pulled pork last night. You're welcome to come get some. Got tons of leftovers."

"I might take you up on that." She stands from her chair. "Alright. I gotta get back to it. Good luck with the mayor."

———

I get at least forty-five minutes of silence to answer emails and finish my coffee. At two minutes to ten, there's a gentle knock on my office door before Aspen walks in and takes a seat. She puts her notebook and pen on the corner of my desk as if she's worked here for years. I like that. I like that she's confident. I've had plenty of associates act like they're terrified of me, which always confuses me. I'd rather us all be one big family.

"Ready?" I ask.

"Yes, sir."

Before I have a chance to say anything else, my phone rings. Eli Cunningham's name pops up on my screen, and I sigh before sliding to answer and putting it on speaker.

"Mornin', Mr. Mayor."

"Brooks. It's a fine mornin' if I do say so myself." Eli and I went to school together. All thirteen years of it. I've known him my entire life. He's always been a little bit of the nerdy type, but even I have to admit, he's a pretty good mayor. He loves Blue Haven, and the people love him. So as much as I dread having these little talks with him, I know they're necessary.

"That it is. I've got my new assistant with me today. Her name is Aspen."

"Aspen?" Eli asks, more to himself than to us. "I don't think I know an Aspen. Are you new to town?"

I look over the desk at Aspen. "Yes, sir. I am."

"Oh!" Eli is way too excited about this. "Welcome to Blue Haven: the best town in the state of Georgia."

Aspen lets out a quiet chuckle as she says, "Thank you. I'm glad to be here."

"You'll have to come on down to city hall soon. I'd be happy to give you a tour of the town. Welcome you properly."

Aspen looks terrified by that suggestion, but she agrees nonetheless.

"Alright, let's get down to business, shall we?" I say. "Got a busy day today."

"Yes. Right. I won't keep you long," Eli says. "Just wanted to go over plans for the Fourth of July."

"You mean you wanna know how much money I'm gonna give you?"

"Well, yes, Brooks, but you don't need to say it so crudely. I'm only looking out for the town. They've come to expect a certain standard for these town celebrations. Unfortunately, without raising taxes, your generous donations are the only way we can keep it up."

"Don't get your panties in a twist, Eli. You know I'm going to *donate*."

"As you know, the Moonlight Ranch donations cover the food trucks, the 5k, the DJ, and the activities for the kids. You should feel proud that you're contributing to so much joy."

Miraculously, I manage to hold in my laugh. "Don't need you telling me how to feel, Cunningham. Tell me what you need, and I'll write the check."

Eli goes over the breakdown. Unfortunately for me, he's very thorough in covering exactly where the money will go. He goes on and on with his quotes and which vendor the city has selected. If he expects me to question him on his math or sources, he's got the wrong man. But I let him talk because, after all these years, I know he just needs to get it out.

"Sounds good, Eli. I'll drop the check off this afternoon."

He sighs in relief as if he expected me to say no. I've never rejected anything this town has asked me for. My father didn't either. The Calloways are rooted deep in Blue Haven, and I plan on keeping it that way for as long as I can.

"Alright. Thanks, Brooks."

I hang up the phone and notice Aspen frantically writing things down on her notepad. "Sorry, I didn't get some of the numbers. He went so fast."

"That's alright. I don't really need it." Guess I should've told her that earlier. I'd like to say I had a good reason for her to sit in on the call, but honestly... I didn't. Just kind of wanted her to be in here.

"Oh."

"I'll come grab you after lunch, and you can come to city hall with me. Get your meeting with Eli out of the way."

"Alright. Can't wait. I'll be at the desk." She stands from her chair, and I watch her walk out of my office with her little notebook. She's cute. It's easy to see why Zach likes her.

And the good news for me is that she really does seem eager and motivated to work. I'm really hoping this works out.

I grab my phone and shoot Zach a text.

Me: Hey, wanted to check in. How's everything going? Anything you need?

Of course it goes unanswered, and I'm left wondering if our relationship will ever mend.

CHAPTER 5

Aspen

"YOU'RE SO LUCKY," Jazz whines after I tell her I'll be leaving with Brooks in a minute to go to town.

I chuckle. "Why? You want to go to town? Don't you live here?"

She laughs. "No, you're lucky you get to go with Brooks."

"Why?" I ask again, even more confused now.

"Are you kidding me, Aspen? Surely your eyes are working, aren't they? Brooks is hot."

"Oh," I say, finally understanding what she means. "He's my boyfriend's dad. I haven't really looked at him like that."

"Well, you're missing out, honey, because Brooks Calloway is a gorgeous man to look at."

"I'll have to take your word for it. Isn't he like forty? Kinda old for you."

She shakes her head and smiles. "He's not forty yet, and besides, age is just a number."

My laugh comes unexpectedly. "Well, he's all yours. Count me out of that competition."

She winks. "Good to know."

"Are you good to watch the desk until we're back? Shouldn't take long."

"Yes, ma'am. Just got one more cabin to clean at three."

"Got it. We should be back by then."

A guest walks up to the desk, and Jazz shows me how to check them out and then how to email the invoice for their stay. As soon as we're done, Brooks appears at the desk, asking if I'm ready to go.

"Yep. Do I need anything?"

"Nah. Just you."

Jazz lets out a small exhale when he says that. I turn to her with wide eyes to tell her goodbye. She wriggles her eyebrows at me as I follow Brooks. I shake my head and stare forward. Unfortunately for me, I'm walking behind Brooks, and my eyes inadvertently glance down his body.

Damn, he does fill out a pair of Wranglers well.

My cheeks heat, and I try to look anywhere else besides my boyfriend's dad's ass. Oh my god. It's only been two days, and Jazz is poisoning my mind already.

Brooks opens the door to his truck for me, and I have to grab the handle and hoist myself up to get into it. I don't miss his quiet chuckle at my struggle.

He keeps the radio on during our drive so we don't have to talk much. Brooks seems like a nice guy, but I don't take him as someone who appreciates small talk.

Blue Haven Town Hall is smaller than I thought it would be. The brick building is two stories and could easily be confused for a storefront instead of a government building.

I follow Brooks inside to the clerk's desk.

"Hello, Ms. Dorothy," Brooks says with his Southern twang as he shoots her what can only be described as a flirty smirk.

Ms. Dorothy looks to be on the cusp of eighty years old, but she still blushes when she looks up to see Brooks. It seems Jazz was right, and I've completely missed Brooks's appeal.

"Oh, hello there, Brooks. How're you doin' today?"

"Better now that I get to see you."

She waves him off. "Oh, stop. You find yourself a girl-friend yet?"

He laughs. "Since I saw you last week? No, ma'am. Still married to the ranch."

"Well, honey. Your face ain't gonna be this pretty forever. You better find someone right quick."

He laughs again. "Noted. Is Eli around? Here on official holiday business."

"He is. Let me make sure he's available." Dorothy picks up her phone while we wait.

When she hangs up, she looks at us and nods. "You can go on in."

"Thank you, ma'am. Oh, and Ms. Dorothy? This is my new assistant, Aspen. You'll be seeing her around."

I wave awkwardly as she greets me when I pass her desk and follow Brooks down a hallway. I am on sensory overload these last few days, meeting so many new people. I have no idea how I'm going to remember them all.

Brooks doesn't bother knocking as he walks into an office at the end of the hall. A man, who I assume is Eli Cunningham, stands behind his desk.

"Brooks! Good to see you. Ah, this must be Aspen."

I step around Brooks and reach my hand out. "Yes, Mayor Cunningham. It's nice to meet you."

He smiles at me as he shakes my hand. "You as well."

He's younger than I expected. Maybe I just assume all mayors are old, I don't know. But he looks like he's about Brooks's age. He's wearing a suit, which is the first one I've seen in Blue Haven.

He releases my hand and gives Brooks a strange look, to which Brooks responds with an annoyed eye roll. I have no idea what the hell is going on, so I just stand there feeling (and probably looking) very out of place.

Brooks grabs a check from his pocket and puts it on the mayor's desk. I couldn't believe the amount of money the town is requesting from him. Zach has never mentioned how much money his dad has, but from the number on that check, I can safely assume he's doing pretty well financially. Which makes me wonder why Zach and I were living in a shitty one-bedroom apartment in a questionable neighborhood in Atlanta when he could've just asked his dad for a little help. I would've asked my parents if I knew where the hell they were.

"Thanks, Brooks. The town appreciates you."

"Yeah, yeah. If you need anything else, call Aspen," Brooks announces as he turns to leave the office. This was a faster trip than I was anticipating.

"Do you have a piece of paper? I can write down my

phone number." Eli grabs a stack of Post-It notes from his very tidy desk and hands them to me with a pen. I quickly write down my number and wave goodbye before I jog after Brooks, who didn't bother waiting.

"What took so long?" he asks when I finally catch up to him.

"It was like five seconds. And I had to give him my phone number," I explain. I thought that would've been obvious.

Brooks stops walking and looks at me. "You gave him your number?"

What? Did he forget the last thing he said? "You just told him to call me if he needs anything."

"He can call the desk at the ranch."

"Ok, and what if I'm not at the desk? It's just easier. We should probably exchange numbers, too. Just in case," I suggest.

"Yeah, probably." He unlocks his phone and hands it to me. Alright, I guess we're doing this now. I put in my number and then send myself a text so I have his.

As I'm handing him his phone, someone comes up behind Brooks and claps him on the shoulder.

"Brooks Calloway. How the hell are ya?"

I look behind him to see a sheriff decked out in all his gear.

"Donovan," Brooks greets him.

"What are you doing here?"

"Chattin' with Cunningham. You here to file some more useless citations?"

I suck in a breath at Brooks's insult. I've never heard

anyone talk to an officer like that and not get in even more trouble. But unexpectedly, Donovan laughs. "Somebody's gotta do it."

Donovan's eyes shift to me as if he just realized I'm standing here. "Well, hello there. I don't believe I've had the pleasure of meeting you yet. I'm Sheriff Donovan Lewis."

"I'm Aspen, Brooks's new assistant."

"Yep. And we're just leaving," Brooks announces, placing his hand on my lower back to usher me toward the door. "Watch where your eyes go, Sheriff. She's also my son's girlfriend."

Donovan chuckles, making me wonder where his eyes went and how I missed it. "Alright, but if you ever need anything, Aspen, you have my number."

"Do I?" I murmur.

"He means nine-one-one. He's an idiot," Brooks explains.

"Oh my god. He's kind of young to be a sheriff, isn't he?" He can't be much older than Zach.

Brooks sighs. "Blue Haven is a small town. Not many people want to police people they've known all their lives. Donovan's grandfather was the sheriff. He trained Donovan so when he finally retired, Donovan was easily voted in."

"Ah." So, small towns are weird. Got it.

Brooks leads me to his truck. It's a little easier for me to get up this time since I've done it once already. Once we're settled and he's backing out of his spot, I say, "Well, that was an interesting trip into town."

Brooks chuckles again and glances briefly in my direction, his dark eyes amused. "Yeah, I'll bet. A lot different from Atlanta, huh?"

"That's for sure. Thanks for letting me tag along, though. It's nice to see the town. I'm still getting used to it."

"Zach hasn't shown you around?" he asks, letting one hand hang loosely over the steering wheel as he drives. I'm not sure what it is about that, but I have to look away.

"Um, not really. We've been to the store, and we had dinner with his mom at Roadside, but that's about it."

He huffs a laugh. "Oh yeah, how's Lacey doin'?"

Bitter. Rude. But I don't say those things. "She seems fine. I think she's glad Zach is home."

He cocks his eyebrow. "She tell you you shouldn't be workin' for me?"

"Not in so many words…"

"Yeah, I'm sure."

"Do you guys not get along?" It's obvious they don't get along, but that seemed like a better question than diving straight into their drama when it's really none of my business.

"You could say that. She's still mad about things that happened over twenty years ago. We both made a lot of mistakes when we were younger. If she wants to take out her anger on me, that's fine. She gave me my son, and I'm grateful for that."

This family has such a confusing dynamic. I've yet to figure out why Zach doesn't like his dad. Everything I've seen so far, which, granted, isn't much, indicates that Brooks has been a very present father. He's willing to do almost anything for his son. I don't think Zach realizes how lucky he is.

"What about your folks? They get along?" Brooks asks, changing the subject.

"Uh. No, not exactly. I don't know my dad, and I haven't seen my mom in years, so…"

"Ah, jeez. Sorry. You mentioned your grandma the other day. I'm an idiot. Forgive me."

"It's alright. It's a normal question to ask. I just unfortunately don't have a normal family."

He nods, but doesn't say anything else until we're pulling into the parking lot of the ranch. "Well, I'm glad Lacey didn't turn you off of workin' here. I know it's only been a few days, but you're going to be a strong asset to our team."

"Thank you. I appreciate that." I'm also glad I took this job. As much as I didn't want to get the job because of who I am to the boss, I'm glad I didn't let that get in the way. From what I can tell, no one treats me any differently because of it. "I've got to go relieve Jazz. She has a cabin to clean or something."

He chuckles. "Yeah, watch out for that girl. She's trouble." But the smile on his face makes me believe it's not a real warning.

"Noted. Have a good afternoon, Brooks."

"You too, Aspen."

I walk toward the lodge as he walks around the side of the building. I'm not proud to admit that I take one more glance in his direction to get a look at those Wranglers.

The cowboy look might be growing on me.

CHAPTER 6

Aspen

ZACH SITS PROPPED up in our bed while I get ready for the day. He should be getting up too, since he has to be at the police academy soon, but I'm not his mother, so he can be late if that's what he wants to do.

It's been a week since I started at Moonlight Ranch, and so far, I actually enjoy going to work every day. I haven't had one terrible guest interaction since I started, which is such a breath of fresh air after working in a busy city for the last few years. And my coworkers are wonderful. It's been kind of fun.

Zach seemed to think I was crazy when I mentioned how much I like it. It's almost as if he wanted me to hate the job he forced me into. I don't know what his deal is lately. I know it's stressful moving and starting a new job, but at least he knows people here. It's even more stressful for me. I moved to a town where I don't know anyone except him, simply because he asked me to.

"Do you know how to ride horses?" I ask as I blend my eyeshadow.

He chuckles. "Yeah, babe. I do. You don't?"

"Nope. Your dad wants me to learn, though."

"You don't have to do anything he wants you to."

I look over at him. "He is my boss…"

"Yeah, but your job description doesn't require you to ride horses, does it?" he asks. I don't have to look at him to know he's smirking right now.

"No, but I think it'd be a good idea to learn. He said I can ask Beck to give me a lesson or two."

Zach finally climbs out of bed and makes his way to our bathroom. He stands behind me and wraps his arms around my waist. "I can teach you how to ride if you really want to learn. But you did a pretty good job riding last night." He winks at me through the mirror before he kisses my cheek.

I ignore his sex comment and add, "If you were to teach me, it would require you to come to the ranch."

He makes a face and shakes his head as he drops his hands and walks toward the toilet. "Nah then. Beck can teach you. He's good."

"I don't understand why you don't like the ranch. Or your dad, for that matter."

"I told you. My dad loves that ranch more than anyone or anything else. He always put the ranch before me. He wanted me to take over one day, just like he did when my grandpa retired, and I don't want that. And he treated my mom really shitty."

"How did he treat your mom?" I ask carefully because I can tell he's getting annoyed.

"He didn't give a shit about her, just like he doesn't give a shit about me." I want to argue because I don't believe that's true, but I keep my mouth shut as he continues. "He broke up with her when I was a baby. Didn't even want to try to work on their relationship."

"Weren't they just kids when they had you?"

"Yeah, but mom wanted us to be a family. She wanted to work on it, and he just gave up. Didn't even try."

"But he still wanted to be in your life, didn't he?"

He shrugs. "My mom was always there for me. I only saw my dad every other weekend. It was like hanging out with a stranger. Mom hated it when I left for those weekends, so I decided to stop going. She needed me more than he did."

"Oh," is all I can say because, again, I don't think that's true at all, but it's not my business. Zach is an adult and can make his own decisions, no matter how wrong I think they might be.

"You think I'm the bad guy, don't you?" he asks, coming up beside me again to wash his hands.

"No. Your feelings are valid. I'm just trying to understand." Because I would do anything to have a dad, even if he only hung out with me every other weekend.

"Families are complicated. I know you don't really understand that." Ok. Ouch. I swallow down the hurt from that comment because I know he didn't mean to hurt me, but it still stings.

I nod and drop the subject, not really wanting to get into an argument before work. I finish up my makeup and then give Zach a kiss goodbye.

"What time do you think you'll be home tonight?" I ask. The past few nights, I've been getting home before him. He's been exhausted, so I wanted to try to have dinner ready for him tonight.

"Actually, Mom wants me to come over for dinner. You wanna come? I'm sure she won't mind."

Why wouldn't she just invite both of us? That seems odd. But I'm also grateful because I don't actually want to go. "Oh. No, that's ok. You enjoy the time with your mom."

"Alright. I'll text you later." He kisses my cheek, and I head to work.

———

"Good morning, Brooks. Here's your coffee." I place the coffee on the corner of his desk. He looks over at me from his laptop.

"How many times have I told you that you don't have to bring me coffee?"

"How many times have I told you that I'm going to do what your previous assistants did?"

He chuckles and reaches across his desk to get the coffee. "Touché."

"Do you need anything from me today?" I ask.

"Not at the moment, but that could change."

So far, he hasn't needed me to do too much. I review his

emails each morning and respond to the ones I can. Harper doesn't even have to sit with me while I do it anymore. I've answered one call from the mayor, who wanted to know how many people were booked at the ranch so far for the Fourth of July holiday. I was pretty proud that I was able to answer that question without having to ask anyone for help. I've even started handling the desk on my own. I do check in and outs. I've scheduled hikes and trail rides. I even offer suggestions in town. For that part, I do have to consult the list Harper and Jazz compiled for me since I still haven't been around town much.

Overall, I feel like I'm doing a pretty good job.

"Alright. I wanted to see if it was ok for me to schedule a time with Beck to teach me how to ride. I can do it on my lunch break."

His face lights up at my question, which surprises me. "Absolutely. You don't need to use your lunch break, though. Just schedule a time with him, and we'll find someone to cover the desk. Hell, I'll cover it if I have to."

I laugh. "I can't imagine you behind the desk."

"Hey, I've had to do it a time or two. My dad always told me that if I wanted to be a good leader, I needed to make sure I understood exactly what I was asking other people to do. So, I know how to do just about everything at this ranch."

"That's pretty cool, actually."

"Now, I never said I was good at it, but I can manage if I have to. So schedule a time with Beck, and we'll figure it out."

"Ok, thank you."

"Of course. Has, uh, Zach mentioned anything about stopping by the ranch? It's been awhile since he's been here."

He looks so hopeful that I don't have the heart to tell him that Zach doesn't want to be anywhere near this place, so I tell a little white lie. "He hasn't mentioned anything, but I can ask."

Surely I can convince Zach to stop by for a few minutes. We can even plan it for a time when I'm here so I can be a buffer.

Brooks nods, and I excuse myself so he can work. At the front desk computer, I add my name to Beck's schedule for tomorrow. There's an open spot at one, which is perfect. It's after check-out time but before check-in.

The first half of my shift passes by quickly. Harper stops in to check on me once, but for the most part, I've become pretty self-sufficient.

Around midday, Jazz stops by. It's becoming our little routine. She hops up on the desk and lets her legs dangle. I love that she doesn't care what anyone thinks about her. She seems completely sure of herself. Her energy has drawn me in, and I hope we'll be good friends.

"My dearest Aspen. How art thou today?" she asks in the most Southern Shakespearean accent I've ever heard.

I laugh. "I'm even better now that you're here."

"Yes, I do tend to have that effect on people."

"You'll be happy to know that I scheduled my first riding lesson with Beck." I told her the other day that I've never ridden a horse, and she proceeded to tease me, telling me I needed to learn since I work on a ranch now.

"Ugh, he's so hot. I wish he could give me riding lessons, if you know what I mean."

I'm embarrassed by the loud cackle that explodes out of me, but I swear I never know what she's going to say. "Yeah, I think I know what you mean. And I'm starting to think that you think everyone is hot."

"That's not true. Have you met Danny?"

The name doesn't sound familiar, but I may have just forgotten. "I don't think so."

"Yeah, well, he's not hot, trust me on that."

"I'll take your word for it."

"So when are you doing it?" she asks.

"Doing it?" I ask, confused. My mind has officially crossed over to dirty territory, and I can't remember what we were discussing.

She cocks an eyebrow at me. "The riding lessons?"

"Oh, right. Tomorrow afternoon."

"Cool." She leans back and looks down at the ground behind the desk. "Please tell me you have boots."

I look down at my sneakers and realize that's what she's looking at. "Oh. Um, no, I don't. Do I need them?"

"You don't *need* them, but you kinda need them," she explains.

"That makes no sense."

She sighs. "What are you doing after work?"

Well, I guess I'm not doing anything since Zach won't be home. "Nothing."

"Cool. We'll go to town, get you some boots, and then we'll have dinner. Girls' night!"

I smile. "I'd love that."

She hops off the desk. "Cool. I'll come up here after I finish my last cabin."

"Alright." She starts to walk off, but I stop her. "Hey Jazz?"

"Yeah?"

"Thanks for this."

She smiles. "Anytime, sunshine."

The rest of my shift passes quickly, probably because I'm so excited to do something with a girlfriend. I had a few friends in Florida, but when I moved to Atlanta, I had a hard time meeting people. I wasn't in school, and the people I worked with weren't there to build friendships. Then, when I started dating Zach, all my spare time went to him. It's been a long time since I've done anything for just myself.

True to her word, Jazz walks toward the desk right as the night shift person comes to relieve me.

"Perfect timing!" Jazz says as I grab my stuff and follow her out to the parking lot.

"I can drive if you want," I offer, heading to my car.

"Cool."

We're just about to get in when I see Brooks and Harper walking in the direction of his truck. Harper is laughing, and Brooks is smiling at whatever they were just talking about. My curiosity gets the better of me. "Hey, Jazz. Are those two a thing?" I nod in their direction.

She turns her head to see who I'm looking at. "Brooks and Harper? Nah, they're more like brother and sister."

I can't look away as Brooks slings his arm over Harper's shoulder and pulls her in close. "Doesn't look like it…"

Jazz laughs. "No, really. You should hear them together. There's no romance there."

I'm not sure that I believe her, but it's really none of my business anyway, so I force myself to look away and think about my first girls' night in my new town.

CHAPTER 7

Brooks

BLUE'S DINER is busier than usual for a Thursday evening. Likely because school is out and summer is in full swing. With the longer days and the warmer weather, the people of Blue Haven are out doing things. No one wants to be stuck at home cooking on such a nice day. Which is exactly how Harper and I ended up here after work.

The season is in full swing at the ranch. The days are busy. We've been booked solid for the last month. It's exhausting, but it's a good problem to have. The ranch has been in my family for generations, and there have been plenty of seasons where we could barely afford to keep it running. I never want to see it get that bad again. Not while I'm in charge. I want to make sure that the ranch is set up well enough so that when I pass it on, it'll be a smooth transition, just like it was when I received it.

Now, if only I knew who I would be handing the ranch off to. I trained for almost thirty years to take over for my dad. When Zach was born, I felt sure that he'd follow in my footsteps, but I can't even get Zach to text me back these days.

Harper and I manage to find a booth toward the back of the restaurant. My stomach growls from the scent of the fresh french fries being delivered to the table next to us. I skipped lunch today, busy fixing a fence on the backside of the property, so I'm more than ready to dig into one of Blue's burgers.

Harper grabs one of the menus from behind the napkin holder and looks at it like she doesn't know everything that's on that thing word for word.

"Why're you looking at that? You know you're getting the chicken tenders," I tease.

She glares up at me. "I thought about trying something new."

I lean back in my seat and cross my arms over my chest. "Oh yeah? What're you thinkin'?"

"Well, I was looking at a… salad," she says slowly.

"Girl, quit playin'. You've never ordered a salad a day in your life."

She sighs and rolls her eyes before she closes the menu and puts it back behind the napkins. "You ruin everything."

I laugh. "No, please. Order your salad. I can't wait to watch you eat that while I dive into my nice juicy burger."

"You're an asshole, Brooks Calloway."

"Yeah, you've told me that before."

This is how we are. She's one of my very best friends and one of the best business partners I could ask for. One of the best people I know, too. We tease each other because it's easy between us. It'd be even easier between us if there were some sort of romantic spark. Unfortunately, there's not. We've discussed it before because being close friends in a small town always opens you up to unnecessary rumors. But neither one of us was interested in more than a friendship.

"Oh, look. It's the girls," Harper says suddenly, her face lighting up as she waves at someone.

I have no idea who *the girls* are, so I turn in my seat to find Aspen and Jasmine standing at the front of the diner.

Harper waves them over. Jasmine takes Aspen's hand and pulls her in our direction.

"Hey!" Harper greets them. "What are you two up to?"

"We just went shopping," Jasmine answers. "Have y'all ordered yet?"

"Nope."

"Good. We're joining you," Jasmine declares and motions for Harper to scoot over. "There aren't any seats left, and I'm freaking starving."

"Jazz," Aspen whispers with wide eyes. "We can't just invite ourselves."

"Come on, they don't care." She looks at us. "Do y'all care?"

Harper and I both say "no" in unison, and I scoot over to make room for Aspen. She hesitates for a moment before she sets her bag down on the floor and scoots in.

She's in the same white T-shirt and black jeans she wore at work, but she's taken her hair down, letting her curls go wild. I like them like this. And being this close, I can smell the vanilla scent of her shampoo.

Whoa. Why the fuck am I noticing what her hair smells like?

My back goes rigid, and I quickly try to find something —anything—to focus on besides that little blip in my brain.

"So, what were you shopping for?" I ask quickly and hope I don't sound as uncomfortable as I feel.

"Well, Jazz insisted that I needed boots in order to ride a horse."

"It's a fact," Jasmine adds. "Also got her a matching belt. You'll feel more confident if you look the part." She winks at Aspen, and I can't help but chuckle. Jasmine is something else. She has no filter and says and does whatever she wants. But she's a good person with a big heart, which I assume is why she appears to have taken Aspen under her wing.

"Are y'all ready to order?" A server finally stops at our table.

Aspen looks around, a little panicked. "Oh, I haven't looked at a menu yet."

"Do you like burgers or chicken?" I ask.

"Burgers."

"You'll like the burger then. Fries or onion rings?"

"Fries."

"Alright, we'll have two Blue's burgers, both with fries." Aspen smiles at me, and for some reason, it makes me feel all warm inside, like I've done something right. I barely manage to smile back at her before I have to look away.

Harper orders her chicken tenders, and Jasmine gets a chicken sandwich.

"Are you girls excited about the Fourth of July celebration?" Harper asks, making conversation with the table. She's good at that. That's why she's the one who deals with most of the guests at the ranch. She's a people person.

"Should I be excited?" Aspen asks tentatively.

"Oh yes. Blue Haven goes all out for the holidays. Didn't Zach tell you?" Harper asks. I'm glad she's the one who asked and not me.

Aspen shakes her head. "No, Zach didn't tell me much of anything about Blue Haven, actually."

That's disappointing. Zach was always eager to get out of this small town. I thought going to college in a big city would help him scratch that itch. I thought it worked. But then he came back here right after graduation. Figured he missed it. Maybe I was wrong. Wouldn't be the first time when it comes to him.

"So you moved here without knowing much about it?" Jasmine asks. Her question could be construed as rude, but I think everyone at the table can tell she's just curious.

Aspen shrugs. "Yeah, I mean, he asked me to move here with him. I didn't really have anything tying me to Atlanta. I thought it would be a fun change. In hindsight, I probably should've done a bit more research. I don't know if I would've been able to find a job if there hadn't been this opening at the ranch."

"Well, maybe that means you were meant to be at the ranch," Harper suggests with a soft smile.

"Yeah, maybe it does," Aspen agrees.

I agree with them. It does feel like Aspen is supposed to be here with us at the ranch. She fits in wonderfully with the team, and I'm glad Zach suggested her for the job. I'd tell him that if he would ever text me back.

"So, what happens at the Fourth of July celebration?" Aspen asks.

Jasmine and Harper go off, telling her all of the things. I was worried Aspen would think it was kind of cheesy, but she smiles through all of it, from the pie-eating competition to the sack races and the parade. I think she's going to fit in just perfectly here.

"Where's Zach tonight?" I ask carefully once our food is delivered.

"He's at his mom's house for dinner."

"You didn't want to go?"

"I wasn't really invited," she says quietly. "I think she wanted to spend time with just Zach. I'm not sure she likes me very much."

Harper scoffs. "I'm not sure that woman likes anyone."

I'm glad that comment came from Harper and not me. I try really hard not to talk shit about Lacey, but she's gotten worse to deal with over the years. I'm sure she'd blame me for her attitude. I was sixteen when Zach was born. I was in no state to take care of a baby or make long-term decisions. Lacey wanted to get married. I didn't. I realized we weren't compatible after Zach was born. I tried to make it work, but it wouldn't have been good for any of us if we had forced the relationship. I might have been young and stupid, but I knew enough to understand that.

That didn't mean I didn't do my share. I paid her child support. I spent as much time with him as I could. I was at every doctor's appointment, every school event. I did everything I thought a father should do and enjoyed doing it. But I was still made into the bad guy.

I actually enjoyed having Zach with me at the ranch. Yeah, my mom helped me a lot when he was younger, but it was kind of like having a little best friend with you all the time. I thought he enjoyed it too, but I guess I was wrong.

After we eat, we all order milkshakes to go, and when the check comes, I don't even let the ladies think about paying.

"Aw, Daddy Brooks is taking care of his girls," Harper teases.

"Shut the fuck up," I say as I put my card down on the table.

Everyone laughs, but her comment makes me wonder if other people might consider it strange that I'm having dinner with Harper and two of my younger employees. It's not like this was planned, but I can see how it might look from an outsider.

After a quick glance around the diner, it doesn't seem like anyone is paying us any mind, so I squash those thoughts. What I do is no one's business anyway. Unfortunately, in a small town, everyone thinks they're entitled to everyone else's business.

We all walk out of the diner, milkshakes in hand.

"Thank you for dinner, Brooks," Aspen says.

"Yeah, thanks, Bossman," Jasmine adds.

"No problem. Y'all get home safe."

Harper and I stand on the sidewalk and watch the two girls to make sure they get in their car before we get back in my truck.

"Have you had any luck with Zach?" Harper asks once we're on the road back to the ranch.

I sigh. "No. Not sure why I'm paying for the kid's cell phone bill if he doesn't even text me back on it."

"You know Lacey is poisoning his mind."

"Yeah, I know." I've known for awhile but I was hoping I was wrong. "At this point, she's got him so far on her side, I'm not sure there's anything I can do to win him back over."

"Have you asked Aspen to talk to him?"

I shrug. "Kind of. She said she would ask him to come by the ranch." But I could tell by the way she avoided eye contact with me that she knew he wouldn't.

"I'm sorry, Brooks. I wish there was something I could do to help."

"It's all good. I'm still hoping he'll come around."

She gives me a sad smile because we both know it's unlikely at this point.

CHAPTER 8

Aspen

"YOU'RE SURE this is a good idea?" I ask Harper. I crack my knuckles again out of nervousness. She's walking me to the stables for my first riding lesson with Beck. I've got my boots and belt buckle on per Jazz's instructions. I've even braided my curls back and added a Moonlight Ranch baseball hat. I look the part. But my stomach is in knots.

What if I fall off?

What if the horses don't like me?

What if I can't do it, and then everyone is disappointed in me, and I get fired?

Ok, even I can admit that last one is a bit extreme, but I'm still worried.

"Yes, it's a good idea. You're going to have a blast. Trust me. And Beck is a really good teacher."

"That's what I've heard," I say quietly.

"Then believe it. Come on. If a five-year-old can do this, you can do it."

Well, when she puts it that way… "Yeah, I guess so."

As we get closer to the stables, Harper yells, "Beck, your next victim is here!"

Oh, great. That's reassuring.

Beck doesn't come to the lodge often, but every time he has, he's been very friendly. Today, his face lights up with a smile when he sees me. He's in his standard jeans, cut-off T-shirt, and a worn-in baseball hat. I swear there's something in the water here at the ranch that makes men extra attractive.

"Hey, Aspen. You ready?" he asks me, taking in my pretend cowgirl outfit.

"Uh. . ."

"She is," Harper answers for me as she shoves me forward a little.

"That was rude," I mumble, and the two of them chuckle. "Yes, I'm ready."

"I'll see you in a bit! Have fun." Harper waves before she turns and heads back to the lodge.

"You look a little nervous," Beck states the obvious.

"Well, yeah. These horses are pretty big, and the more I've thought about it, the more I've realized how scary that is."

He laughs and motions for me to follow behind him. "I get it. Horses can be dangerous. They are animals after all. That's why I'll go over safety with you before you even touch a horse. But trust me, if my five-year-old daughter can ride a horse, you can too."

"So I've been told."

"And remember, the horses can tell when you're

nervous, so you need to try to relax a little before you get up there."

I swallow against my dry throat and nod. That's not very reassuring.

Beck gives me a tour of the stable. He shows me where they keep the saddles, the saddle blankets, and the bridles. Then he takes me to the horses. He says each of their names as we pass them, but I know there's no way I'm going to remember them.

"And this is Sparkly Tutu a.k.a Sparkles."

I raise an eyebrow. "That's an interesting name for a horse."

He laughs. "Yeah, Brooks let my daughter, Jade, name her when we got her. She was three at the time, so Sparkly Tutu was obviously the only option."

"Obviously."

"But Sparkles is very tame. I've been using her with my beginners for the past year. She's easy and will give you a smooth ride."

"Alright. I'll take your word for it."

He shows me how to hold my hand up to Sparkles so she can smell me. She nudges my hand, allowing me to pet her.

"Good girl," Beck says as he opens her stall, taking the equipment we grabbed earlier in with him. He gets her all tacked up and ready for me. He goes over a few other safety points as he walks us out to the fenced-in circle just outside the stable. Sparkles trots along next to us, and her calm demeanor definitely reduces my nervousness.

"Alright, I'm gonna hand you this, and you're just gonna lead her around the circle a few times."

I nod and take the bridle in my sweaty hands. Sparkles seems to already know the drill because she starts walking. I do my best to stay a few feet ahead of her, and she seems pretty content to follow me.

After three laps around, Beck stops us. "Ready to mount?"

"Uh, sure." He gives me a look. "No, yes, I'm ready. Definitely."

"That's better."

He brings over a little step stool and puts it down next to Sparkles. "Alright, up you go."

He shows me where to put my hand and how to hoist myself up into the saddle. It's a little rocky getting up there, but I manage.

Beck leads me around the circle, letting me get used to how it feels to be on a horse, and honestly, it's not too bad. I relax into the saddle quicker than I thought I would. After a few circles, he hands me the reins and lets me trot on my own.

I'm feeling pretty good when I suddenly hear clapping and look up to realize Brooks is leaning against the fence. He smiles as he watches me.

"Look at you!" he calls out. "Looks like you've been ridin' for years."

I laugh. "I wouldn't go that far."

Beck tells me how to get Sparkles to stop. I slide off her and hand the reins back to Beck.

"Havin' fun?" Brooks asks.

I wipe my sweaty palms on my jeans as I walk toward him. "Yeah, actually. I was a little nervous, but it was easier than I thought it would be."

He nods. "You're gonna be out on the trails in no time."

"Schedule another time with me," Beck instructs. "And we'll work on going a little faster than a trot. Then Brooks here can take you out on the trails."

"I'll do that. Thanks, Beck." Although I'm not sure that Brooks would want to spend his free time on a trail ride with his assistant slash son's girlfriend. He's too nice to say no right now, though.

"I just came out here to see how you were gettin' on, but if you're done, we can walk back to the lodge together."

I look over at Beck to confirm if we're done. "Yep, all done here. I gotta go grab Jade from her mama's house real quick."

I nod and thank him again for the lesson before I start the walk back to the lodge with Brooks.

Brooks nudges me with his shoulder. "So be honest, what'd you think?"

"Honestly, I loved it. I see the appeal. I mean, Sparkles was definitely in control, but I felt powerful."

I look over to see him smiling at me. "That's what it's all about. I swear, being on a horse and out in the fields is one of my favorite things. Especially at sunrise or sunset. It's a feelin' you can't describe."

"That sounds pretty awesome, actually," I say, trying to picture it. The ranch is very picturesque. When Zach first told me he was from north Georgia, I didn't picture a place with mountains and lakes and trees for miles. This is one of those places you just have to see to believe.

"It is. The boots and the belt look good, by the way."

"Oh. Thanks." I'm not sure why heat creeps up my neck from his compliment. "Yeah, I guess Jazz was right. It does feel good to look the part."

He chuckles. "Don't tell her that, she'll get an even bigger head."

"Don't worry, I won't," I say, smiling. "She's awesome, though. I really like her. I didn't have many friends back in Atlanta, so it's nice to have someone besides Zach to hang out with since he's been so busy."

"I'm glad she's making you comfortable. We're all here for you if you ever need anything. We're a family at the ranch."

I nod. "Yeah, I'm starting to see that. I'm glad to be a part of it."

And I mean it. Coming to work every day doesn't even feel like work. I don't dread it. Granted, I know I'm still new, but this place is different. It truly does feel like a family. Maybe I'm naive to feel that way, but it is what it is. I'm going to enjoy my time here.

"Thanks again for letting me take the lesson," I tell him as we stop by the door of the lodge.

"No need to thank me. Make sure you schedule your next lesson. We'll be out on the trails in no time."

I smile as he walks into his office, and then I realize that he said *we'll*. As in we. Like him and me? I know it doesn't mean anything, but for some reason, the thought of being on the trails alone with Brooks makes my stomach do a little excited flip.

Which makes me feel absolutely terrible.

What kind of girlfriend gets excited to hang out alone with her boyfriend's dad? Gross.

CHAPTER 9

Aspen

THE FOURTH of July celebration arrives in the blink of an eye. With a new job and getting used to my new town, I almost didn't even realize it's already July.

Brooks has asked me to attend the town festival with him while everyone else holds down the fort at the ranch. We coordinated for him to pick me up from my apartment on the way downtown, since it was on the way. Zach made sure to be in the shower and completely unavailable when Brooks knocked on our door. I could tell Brooks was disappointed. I wish I could understand why Zach has decided to completely ignore Brooks. His reasoning doesn't add up to me.

We get in his truck, and he asks, "Is he planning on avoiding me forever?"

I wince. "He hasn't mentioned a specific plan to me."

After a beat of silence, he asks, "Should I give up?"

I swallow hard, knowing I'm in no way qualified to give advice on this. "I don't know," I answer truthfully. "He doesn't really talk about it. Every time I've tried to bring it up or ask him to come visit the ranch, he tells me that family is complicated, but I wouldn't understand since my family is so messed up."

"Jesus. That's harsh."

"Yeah," I admit. "I don't think he means anything by it." Even though Zach surely knows how much it hurts my feelings every time he makes comments like that. He knows I would do anything to have a family that loves me. At least his dad is trying. My parents, the two people who are supposed to love me no matter what, left me.

"Whether or not he means anything by it, he shouldn't be saying shit like that to someone he cares about. We've taught him better than that. Or at least I thought we did."

"I appreciate you saying that, but it's alright. Really." I try to brush it off like it's no big deal, but Brooks isn't buying it.

"Don't let him treat you like that, Aspen, alright? I know he's my son, but he's lucky to have you. Don't let him act like he's not. Don't let him treat you like you're not important."

I bite the corner of my mouth to keep from smiling too big. It's been… awhile since I've had someone on my side. It's nice to know that someone sees me.

"Thanks, Brooks." I'm not sure what else to say. It's pathetic how happy a simple compliment makes me.

He drives us to Main Street, and after circling a few times looking for parking, he gives up and parks in the grass on the side of the road a little ways away.

"So, what's my job today?" I ask as we start heading to the festival.

"Represent the ranch. Meet people. Eli—sorry, Mayor Cunningham—just likes to see that we're involved. Introduce yourself to people." He must see me grimace because he adds, "Don't worry. It's not too bad. This town loves new people. It means new gossip for them. They'll eat you up."

"Is that a good thing?" I ask, not sure if I want the town to *eat me up.*

He chuckles at my confusion. "Yeah. It's a good thing."

"Alright." I run my hands down my white Moonlight Ranch shirt to make sure I look presentable before we're fully immersed in the festival.

Brooks waves and smiles at a few people, and I try to look friendly although I'm not sure how well it works. I imagine I probably look uncomfortable and am sporting a weird smile.

They weren't kidding when they said everyone comes to these festivals. The downtown area is packed not only with people but also with booths, food, and games. It looks like a blast. I can't help but smile when I watch a little kid throw a water balloon at his dad in one of the game booths.

I would've loved this when I was a kid.

"Ah, there you are," Mayor Cunningham says as he walks toward us. He's exchanged the suit for a more casual look of linen shorts and a navy blue collared shirt that says Blue Haven in the corner.

"So, what do you think?" he asks proudly as he surveys all his hard work.

"It looks amazing," I tell him. "Honestly, it looks like so much fun."

We walk as he tells us about each booth we pass. Eventually, he stops in front of a lemonade stand and buys the three of us a lemonade without even asking. I'm grateful for it, though, because I've only been here about ten minutes and I'm already hot.

"Well, I've got to go get ready for the pie-eating contest. You two have fun!" he says as he strolls toward the gazebo in the middle of town.

As soon as he's gone, other people start coming up to Brooks. Some wave and say hello as they pass, but others stop and have a conversation. He always makes sure to introduce me to everyone who stops to talk, like he wants to make sure everyone knows who I am. It makes me feel more important than I probably am, but I like it.

The people of Blue Haven are so polite. My cheeks hurt from smiling after the first hour of being at the festival.

After one couple leaves us, Brooks puts his hand on my lower back and leans down to say, "You're doing great."

I smile back, but I feel like I should be saying that to him. He's the one having to talk to all these people. It's clear that he's a respected member of this community. From the way Zach always talked about him, I guess I assumed that he wasn't great to be around, but I've certainly formed the opposite opinion.

"Thank you," I say barely above a whisper. His hand drops from my back, and I instantly miss it. Then I feel like shit for even thinking that.

That reminds me… Zach. I stand up on my tiptoes to try to scan the crowd for him, but I don't see him yet.

I lower back down right as a pair of hands wrap around my waist, and I jump, turning quickly to see Zach.

"Hey, babe. How's it going?" he asks as he leans down and kisses me. Things between us have been pretty good the past few weeks. We've finally gotten into a routine. He's tired most nights when he gets home, but he's been making an effort to be present with me over dinner. It's nice. It's starting to feel like it did back in Atlanta when we were almost in our own little bubble. It's like we've finally moved past the stress from the move and are settling in.

"Good! This place is so great."

He pulls me close. "Told ya." Then he looks at Brooks. "Hey, Dad."

"Oh, so I do exist to you, huh?"

Zach scratches the back of his head. "Yeah, sorry I haven't responded. Been busy with the police academy and everything."

"Hmm." Brooks knows it's a bullshit excuse. "Well, glad to see you could make it out today."

"Wouldn't miss this. Looks like it's gotten even bigger since the last time I was here."

"Yeah, you know Cunningham. Wants everything bigger," Brooks says. I can see in his eyes that he wants to talk to his son about more than just this stupid festival, but he knows now isn't the time. I hate that Zach treats him like this, but I also know it's not my place to say anything.

Zach turns to me. "I know you're working, babe. I just wanted to come say hey. I'll catch up with you later."

He kisses me again on the lips, and this time, I can feel Brooks's eyes on us, and I suddenly feel like I've done something wrong.

Zach walks off without another word to his dad, and I'm left alone with Brooks again. I expect him to ask me something about Zach's behavior, but he doesn't. With a resigned sigh, he asks, "Ready to go watch this pie-eating contest?"

"I have never been more ready for anything in my life."

He laughs and leads us toward the tables by the gazebo.

The day, while busy, is so fun. After the pie-eating contest, Brooks and I throw candy during the parade. We sample several food trucks. I even won a Blue Haven hat from a ring toss game I played. Overall, it was one of the funnest days I've had in a while.

When my duties for the day are over, the sun is just starting to set. The fireworks show will start soon.

Brooks offered to take me home, but I told him I would be meeting up with Zach so we could watch the fireworks together.

I wander through the crowds of people, looking for my boyfriend. I tried calling him and texting him, but I didn't get an answer. I know he's got to be here somewhere, though.

I wave at people that I met today as I pass. It's so nice to feel like I fit in somewhere. I'm truly starting to believe that I made a good decision moving here with Zach.

Still not seeing him anywhere, I step behind one of the booths to try to find a quiet spot to call him again. I pull my phone out of my pocket and bring it to my ear, but as I look straight ahead, I freeze.

I finally see him.

Zach is standing behind a tree.

With his tongue down another woman's throat.

"Aspen, glad I caught you. You forgot your hat." I hear Brooks's voice, but I don't register what he's saying.

"Aspen? You ok?" he tries again, putting his hand on my shoulder.

"Is that…?" My voice is shaky, and I'm hoping my eyes are playing tricks on me.

"What?" Brooks follows my line of sight. "Goddammit."

"Is it?" I ask again, a little more frantic. "Tell me I'm seeing things."

"Come on. Stop looking." Brooks turns my body and tries to lead me away, but I stay stuck in place.

"No. No! I need to go over there!" My heart is in the pit of my stomach.

"Not here, Aspen. You don't want to make a scene here."

"I do want to make a scene!"

"Aspen, trust me. Not right now."

How could he do this to me? After everything we've gone through. All the promises he made me. I uprooted my life and moved here for *him*, and not even a month later, he's cheating on me?

I look back over my shoulder to see Zach still hasn't

pulled himself away from whatever woman he's decided he wants to throw away our relationship for.

Brooks puts his calloused hand on my cheek and turns my head away from the scene of the crime to look directly at his face. "Stop looking at it, darlin'."

"What am I supposed to do?" I ask faintly. Brooks sighs, drops his hand from my face, and puts his arm around my shoulder, forcing me to move with him as we walk to his truck.

"First step is getting you out of here."

I nod because I can't think of anything else to do besides go rip Zach's fucking face off.

When we get to his truck, he doesn't wait for me climb in; he picks me up and puts me in the seat. Then he straps me in as if I'm not capable, and honestly, I'm not sure if I am capable at the moment. I feel like I'm in shock. How could Zach do this to me?

Brooks gets in the truck and drives us away. I don't know where we're going, and I don't really care.

My anger grows the further away we drive. I should've confronted Zach. Now he gets to enjoy the rest of his night thinking he's getting away with this. "Why did you make me leave? Because you didn't want me to confront your son?" I snap suddenly, surfacing from being lost in my thoughts.

Brooks calmly responds. "No, he deserves whatever plans you're coming up with in your pretty head over there. That was an asshole thing for him to do. I'm just as disappointed in him. I got you out of there because you're new here. This is a small town, and gossip spreads quickly. If one person had seen you going at him, that's what you would've been known for forever. You're better than that. You're better than him."

Yeah, I guess that makes sense, but he's forgetting that the only reason I came to this god-forsaken town was for Zach. If we're not together anymore, which, after this, we will most certainly not be, then where does that leave me? Surely not in Blue Haven.

"Where are you taking me?" I ask, once I realize we've passed my apartment.

"The ranch. My house. You'll stay there tonight, and then tomorrow I'll take you back to your place to do what you need to do."

His house? I'm staying in Brooks's house tonight? I've been here for almost a month and haven't been in his house yet. Why would I? He's my boss, not my friend. It's weird to spend the night at your boss's house, right?

I guess exceptions can be made when his son breaks your heart.

Brooks follows the road from the lodge to his house, leaving his truck parked out front. I attempt to get out of the truck myself, but he's there in an instant, helping me down. I mumble a quick thanks and then follow him to his house.

The inside of his house is way nicer than I was expecting. While it does give bachelor vibes with the leather couches and minimal wall decor, it still feels very homey. There's a giant stone fireplace in the living room, a beautiful rug between the couches to warm up the room, and pillows and throw blankets pepper the couches. Overall, it's very inviting. It's very Brooks. It even smells like his spicy scent in here. The same scent I've noticed in his office.

"I'll show you to your room, but make yourself at home, alright?"

I nod and follow him down the hall. He shows me to the guest room and the bathroom.

"Is there anything you need?" he asks. I can tell he's worried about me, which is nice. I would've expected him to take Zach's side, but he didn't. I was angry at first, but I'm glad he got me out of there. I need time to think about what I'm going to say to Zach.

"You got anything to drink?"

CHAPTER 10

Brooks

"WINE OR WHISKEY?" I ask Aspen. She's sitting on a barstool in the kitchen, watching me rummage through my cabinets. It's been awhile since anyone has been here, and I'm not used to entertaining.

"Wine."

I grab a bottle of wine and two glasses from the cabinet and set them in front of her on the counter. I uncork the wine and fill our glasses.

"You wanna sit on the back porch?" I ask. "It's a nice night."

"Sure." She grabs her glass and follows me out. We settle into the Adirondack chairs I have out back.

She sips her wine while I think about what an asshole my son is. He had a great woman. She's hardworking, fun to be around, and has a great personality. Not to mention how beautiful she is. And he threw it all away for his old high school girlfriend, who has made her way through almost all of his old friends at this point. It doesn't make sense, and I can't figure out what he was thinking.

"Are you alright?" I ask carefully. She hasn't cried at all, and I'm worried that if I say the wrong thing, the floodgates will open. I'm a great listener, but I never know what to do when a woman starts crying.

"Not really," she states calmly. "But I guess at this point, I'm used to people in my life ditching me."

Shit. "Aspen..."

"It's alright. It's not your fault, so please don't apologize for him."

It might not be my fault, but it's definitely making my conscience feel heavy. "He is my son. I feel like I should've taught him better."

"Hard to do when he doesn't answer your calls."

I huff a laugh. Yeah, I guess she's got me there.

She takes a sip of her wine. "You know he talked to me about marriage?"

No, I hadn't known that. I'm obviously the last person Zach wants to talk to about that. "Really?"

"Yeah." She chuckles. "He had a whole plan. We would move here, he would get settled in with the police force, and then we'd get married. Have kids. Live the perfect life like I always wanted. I fell for it, too, like an idiot. I moved to a place where I knew no one except for him. I believed that we were in this together. I wanted so badly to be loved by someone that I trusted someone I shouldn't have. I feel so pathetic."

"Whoa. You're not the pathetic one here. He's the one who had something great and threw it all away." I have to believe that Zach did want those things with her. Marriage, kids, the whole nine yards. I don't think he would've said it and asked her to move her entire life here if he wasn't serious. Which is why I can't figure out why he made the choice to cheat.

"He obviously has a different opinion." She drains her wine glass and holds it out to me for a refill, which I do without question. Hell, she can have the bottle if it'll make her feel better tonight. I know I've been there a time or two.

"You know we've hardly had sex at all since we moved here? I thought he was just stressed, but now I see he was probably getting it from someone else."

I wince.

"Sorry, I know I shouldn't be talking about this with you. I just feel so stupid that I moved my entire life for him."

"Nah, it's ok. I hate that he did this to you."

She sighs. "Me too. I really liked it here, too. Now I'm going to have to find somewhere else to start over *again*. Alone."

Whoa. What? "Why can't you stay here?"

She looks over at me with glossy eyes. "Come on, Brooks. I can't stay here. Blue Haven is Zach's home. Not mine."

"It could be your home. You've got a job. You've made friends."

"But now I have no place to live. I don't know if you know this, but it's slim pickings around here."

Before I can think better of it, I say, "You can stay in my

cabin. The one next door. Until you find something better. I just need to give it a good clean."

"I can't ask that of you, Brooks. You've already done so much for me."

"You're not asking. I'm offering. It's selfish of me, really. I don't want to have to train another assistant. I need you here." It's selfish, alright. It'd probably be better for her to go if she wants to move on with her life, but I want her here. I like Aspen. In a strictly platonic, work kind of way…

She chuckles. "Thank you. I'll think about it. I've got a lot of thinking to do tonight."

"Please consider it. Seriously. It's the least I can do."

"I will, thank you." She drains the rest of her wine glass. "Well, I'm going to go cry myself to sleep. Thanks again for getting me out of there."

"You're welcome. Do you need anything for bed? There should be a spare toothbrush or two under the sink in the bathroom." I hate the thought of her crying herself to sleep, but I know this is probably what she needs to do right now.

"Um, do you maybe have a shirt I could borrow?"

"Yeah, of course."

I follow her into the house. She stops in front of the room she's sleeping in while I continue to my bedroom to grab one of my shirts. It's probably inappropriate to let my son's girlfriend wear my shirt to bed, but I don't really have anything else. This option is better than having her sleep naked in my house. I quickly shake that thought from my head.

I hand her the T-shirt and tell her good night. She gives me a sad smile before she closes the bedroom door.

How could Zach do something so stupid? He had a great girl. Someone it sounds like he was planning a future with, and then he goes and throws it all away.

As if he can feel me thinking about him, my phone lights up with a text from him.

> Zach: Have you seen Aspen? I can't find her and she isn't answering her phone.

Rather than texting him back, I go back outside and hit the call button. For once, he actually answers.

"Hey, Dad. Is Aspen with you?"

"Yeah, she's with me." I know she probably doesn't want him to know, but I know the feeling of not knowing where someone is. They can talk about their future tomorrow, but at least he'll know she's safe. I have to believe he still cares about her.

"Ok, where are y'all? I'll come meet you." It's loud behind him, so I imagine he's still downtown.

"We're at my house."

"What? Why?"

"Because Aspen was looking for you and then found you with your mouth glued to Melinda's."

He sucks in a breath. "Fuck," he mumbles.

"What were you thinking, Zach?"

I hear the frustration in his voice when he answers, "I don't know. It wasn't… it was a mistake. Melinda has been trying to get in my head ever since I've been back."

"And you're that weak? The two of you broke up for a reason. And isn't she with Cory now?" I ask. Not only did he ruin his relationship with Aspen, but he went behind one of his best friend's backs.

"Yes. I know. It wasn't my best moment, alright? I need to talk to Aspen. Can I come get her?"

Oh, now he wants to come to my house? As much as I'd love to have my son here, I know Aspen needs her space right now. They could both use a night to think about what it is they want.

"Not tonight. She needs some space. I'll bring her back to your place in the morning."

He sighs, not liking that answer. "Alright. Will you just… will you just tell her I love her?"

"No, I won't do that. I'm not sure that you do love her after tonight."

"Fine. Whatever. Just bring her back in the morning. "

He hangs up quickly, and I'm left wondering if I made the right decision. Maybe a better father would be on his son's side. Maybe I should knock on her door and let her know what Zach said. But cheating is not something I tolerate. I'll be damned if my own son doesn't learn the consequences of his actions.

I clean up our wine glasses and make my way down the hall to my room. I pause in front of Aspen's room for a moment. I hope she's ok in there. The look on her face when she saw Zach kissing Melinda is one I won't forget anytime soon. It's like I could see her heart breaking, and there was nothing I could do about it.

I shake the thought from my head and continue to my room, shutting the door behind me.

I'm up before the sun as usual, but this morning feels different. I'm painfully aware that someone else is in my house. I'm not sure exactly what I'm supposed to do. Do I get up and make us breakfast? Do I stay in my room until I hear her come out?

I finally decide to get up and shower. I get dressed quickly and then fire off a text to Harper letting her know that I'll be in later today and Aspen needs the day off. I tell her I'll explain everything later. She immediately likes the message. Knowing Harper, she's probably already at the lodge. That woman is more of a workaholic than I am.

No sounds are coming from Aspen's room as I pass, so I head to the kitchen and start a pot of coffee. I peruse my pantry and fridge, trying to figure out if I should make anything for breakfast. Does Aspen like pancakes, or is she an eggs and bacon kind of girl?

Pancakes might be too much, so I pull out a carton of eggs and a pack of bacon and get started. By the time I'm done scrambling the eggs and frying up some bacon, I hear Aspen's door open.

"Morning," she says as she comes into the kitchen, still wearing my shirt from last night. Her curls are wild this morning, and her eyes are red and a little puffy, but she's just as beautiful as ever.

"Hey. Did you sleep all right?" I ask, scooping some eggs onto a plate, trying not to stare at her bare legs.

"Not bad, considering. That mattress is really comfortable." She slides onto a barstool at the counter. "Is that for me?"

"Yep. Hope you're hungry." I set the plate down in front of her.

"I am. Thank you."

"Coffee?" I ask.

"Sure."

"Cream and sugar?"

"Yes, please. The sweeter the better."

I grab a cup from the cabinet and fix it for her.

As I put it in front of her, she says, "These are really good eggs."

"Thanks. The eggs are from a local farm, so I think that makes them taste even better."

I grab a plate for myself and sit down on the stool next to her.

"So, um, did you talk to Zach yet?" I ask.

She shakes her head. "No. He texted me and called me a bunch, but I didn't answer. I want to end things in person."

"You're going to break up with him?" I figured she would, but I did hear the regret in Zach's voice last night. I can't help but feel bad for my son. He's clearly confused right now. I've been there before. But I'm glad that Aspen realizes that she deserves better.

"Of course, I am. I'll never be able to trust him again. Trust is important to me."

I nod. "Well, I'm sorry it came to this, but I understand. Did you think any more about my offer?"

"Yeah, I did actually. If you're still ok with it, I'd like to stay in the cabin. Just for a little bit until I can get myself on my feet again. I like it here in Blue Haven, and I'd like to stay for now."

"Then it's yours. I'll get it cleaned for you for tonight."

"Thanks, Brooks. I really appreciate it. I can pay rent."

"Absolutely not," I say quickly. No way in hell am I taking her money.

She chuckles. "Well, if you change your mind, let me know. I'll try to be out of your way quickly."

"Stay as long as you need." It'll be nice having someone so close. As much as I like the solitude, it does get lonely out here sometimes.

We finish our breakfast, and I do the dishes before she stands and sighs.

"I guess I need to get this over with."

I nod. "Ready when you are." I put on my boots and grab my keys while she changes out of my shirt.

It feels wrong driving her to break up with my son, but I know it's the right thing to do.

CHAPTER 11

Aspen

I STARE out the windshield at the apartment I've only lived in for a month. I don't want to get out of the truck. I don't want to have to break up with Zach. I don't want to walk away from the life I was building.

But I have to.

I can't stay with someone who doesn't respect me.

"Thanks for the ride," I tell Brooks.

"Yep. Of course. Do you want me to… wait?" he asks. Brooks has been so sweet to me over the last twelve hours. From getting me away from the scene of the crime to giving me a place to stay and making me breakfast this morning. I feel spoiled in a way I probably shouldn't.

"No, I'll be ok. Thank you."

He nods. "Alright then. Good luck. Call me if you need anything."

"Thanks."

I slide out of his truck and slowly force myself up the

stairs to the apartment. When I open the door, Zach sits up on the couch. I'm guessing he slept there since there's a pillow from our bed and a rumpled blanket around him.

"Aspen," he whispers.

"Zach." My voice comes out firm and serious. Thank god. I do not want to cry in front of him. Not after the way he treated me.

We both stand across the room from each other, and it's like I'm looking at a stranger. I don't understand how we could spend two years together, but now it's gone. Everything is over. All our plans are out the window. How could he say he loves me and then do what he did?

"Whose shirt is that?" he asks.

I look down and realize that I'm still wearing Brooks's shirt. I didn't have anything else to wear, so I just threw my shorts on underneath. My shirt from yesterday was all sweaty from being at the festival. It dawns on me that Brooks didn't even mention me giving it back.

"Really? That's the first thing you're going to say to me?"

He shakes his head. "No, sorry. It just threw me off for a second."

"Yeah, it seems like a lot of things have thrown you off recently."

He sighs and walks toward me. "Babe, I am so sorry."

He tries to hug me, but I take a step back and hold my hand out to stop him. "Don't touch me."

"Aspen." He has the audacity to look hurt.

"No. Don't Aspen me. You cheated on me!"

"It didn't mean anything, I swear."

"Is that supposed to make it ok? I'm just supposed to be fine and move on from the fact that you cheated?" I ask.

"I made a mistake, Aspen. It was so stupid. I don't want her; I want to be with you. I love you." I'll give him one thing: he does look genuinely upset. Part of me feels like I need to make him feel better, but then I remember what he did to me and that worry is instantly gone. I gave him two years of my life, and he threw it away like it meant nothing.

"It was stupid," I agree. "But you will never have me again."

His eyes go wide. "What? Aspen, no. Please give me another chance. I can't lose you."

"You lost me the second you put your mouth on another woman. You made the decision for both of us."

"I told you it was a mistake. Please forgive me. Give me another chance," he begs. He drops down to his knees in front of me and wraps his arms around my legs.

"I can't forgive you." Seeing him on his knees like this makes me feel even more disgusted. I'm sure he thinks begging will show me how sorry he is, but it just feels fake and way too dramatic. He's not a child, but he's acting like one.

"You can," he pleads. "Please."

I pause and look down at him. His eyes are glossy, like he might cry any minute. "Did you sleep with her?"

"What?" he asks, surprised by my question.

"I saw you kiss her, but did it go any further than that? Be honest."

His shoulders slump, and his arms loosen around me as he admits, "Once."

I nod. That's all I need to hear. There's no reconciliation happening now. Not that I was planning on it anyway, but that admission sealed the deal.

"I'd like for you to leave while I pack my things," I tell him and take a step back out of his grasp.

"Aspen, please. You can't leave me."

"I can, and I am."

"Where are you even going to go?" he asks.

"None of your business, but I've got somewhere to stay for the time being. So, I'm going to pack my things, and then I'm going to leave. Don't make this harder than it needs to be."

"I will make it harder because I can't lose you, Aspen. I love you."

"No, you don't!" I yell, losing my patience. "If you loved me, you wouldn't have done what you did. This is all your fault! Don't try to make me feel bad for taking care of myself now."

He stands up. "You're right. This is my fault, and I'm going to fix it. I'll give you space, but just know I'm not giving up on us. I'm going to keep fighting for you. You'll see."

I sigh and walk past him to the closet to get my suitcase. "I'd rather you didn't."

He grabs his keys off the counter. "Too bad. I'll prove to you that you and I are meant to be."

I shake my head. "Please leave."

He looks at me for so long. I'm afraid that he sees the

pain in my eyes, but I refuse to cry in front of him. I did my crying last night. Now, I'm moving on.

"I love you, Aspen."

I don't say it back as I walk toward the bedroom to pack. I hear the front door close as Zach leaves.

I can't believe I just unpacked all of this stuff and now I'm packing it back up. I can't believe I followed a man to a place where I knew no one. I can't believe the man I thought loved me betrayed me so easily.

My mind reels with anger as I shove as much as I can into my suitcase.

———

I pull up outside of Brooks's little cabin. I texted him on my way over, so he's waiting for me by the door. As I get out of the car, I realize I'm still wearing the shirt he gave me to sleep in last night. I was so focused on packing my things and getting out of that apartment that I didn't think about changing.

Thankfully, he doesn't mention it as he helps me get my bags out of the trunk.

"Everything go ok?" he asks.

"As ok as it can when you're ending a relationship," I tell him.

He nods. "Right. Well, I'm glad you're here. Let's get you settled in."

He takes me to the cabin. He was right, it is small. Just all one big room. The kitchen area is against one wall. The bed is across the room. There's a dresser, a small couch, a small table, and a TV. Just the basics, but it's everything I need right now.

"Well, this is it," Brooks says as he puts my bags down. "Bathroom is right there." He points to the door near the dresser.

"This is perfect. I can't thank you enough, Brooks."

"No need to thank me. If you ever need anything, I'm just next door. Oh, and this place doesn't have a washer and dryer, so you'll have to come to my house when you need to do laundry. Just let me know when you need it, and I'll make sure to leave the door unlocked for you."

"Got it."

"Alright, well, I'll let you get settled. Let me know if you need anything, ok? Seriously. Don't be shy."

I smile at him in an attempt to ease the worry in his eyes. I can tell Brooks has a big heart. He feels terrible about what Zach did and is trying his best to make it up to me the only way he can. I really do appreciate it. "I will. Thank you. And thanks for letting me have the day off today."

He nods and leaves me alone in the cabin to get settled. Even though this place is small, it's really nice. It's obvious Brooks spent a lot of time and effort making this place a home. It's kind of cool to stay in a place he built himself.

While I can understand why Zach didn't like being here when he was a kid because of the lack of privacy, it's perfect for one person.

It doesn't take me long to get my clothes unpacked. I left a lot of my things at the apartment. I focused on clothes and toiletries, leaving all of my furniture and kitchen supplies behind. I don't want them anymore anyway. They're all going to have bad memories associated with them now. This is a fresh start for me.

After I'm unpacked, I head into town to get some groceries. When I get back, Jazz is waiting at the front door of my cabin.

"I am so mad at that motherfucker," she practically yells when I step out of the car. I don't even have to guess who she's talking about. News travels fast in small towns.

"Yeah, that makes two of us."

She helps me grab my groceries and follows me into the cabin, ranting about what an idiot Zach is. I'm not going to lie, it makes me feel better to have someone to share this anger with.

"Why didn't you call me?" she asks once she's finished her ranting.

I shrug. " It all happened so fast, and I didn't want to bother you."

She puts her hands on her hips and stares me down, unsatisfied with my answer. "Aspen. We're friends. You call your friends when bad things happen."

I smile. I'd hoped we'd become friends, but I didn't want to assume. "Noted for the next time I get my heart broken."

"Good. It was nice of Daddy Brooks to let you stay here. This place is nice." She looks around the cabin, taking it all in.

"Oh god, don't call him Daddy Brooks!" I laugh.

"Why not? He could be my daddy any day."

"Stop!"

She laughs. "Come on. You know he's hot." She stops

walking and looks at me. "Oh my god. It would be perfect revenge to sleep with Zach's dad!"

I gasp. "Absolutely not!"

"Why not?"

"Well, besides the fact that it would be weird, he's also my boss. Plus, do you really think he would want to hook up with a twenty-four-year-old with no life goals?"

"I think he would be very interested in hooking up with a hot twenty-four-year-old who is living only a few feet away from him right now."

I laugh. "You're insane."

"Not the first time I've heard that. But for real, I think you should consider it. Make a move. Let him know you're interested."

"I'm not interested!"

"There is not a woman in Blue Haven that isn't interested in Brooks Calloway."

"Well, I'm not interested in sleeping with my ex-boyfriend's dad. That feels illegal or something."

She shakes her head. "Nah, not illegal. It's called an upgrade rebound."

"I can't do that." I can't rebound with Zach's dad... can I? No. No way. That'd be too weird. "And I'm not ready for that."

She sighs. "Fine. Just remember that you're always allowed to change your mind."

"I know."

She helps me unload the groceries. It's not much, but it's enough that I probably won't have to go back to the store for a few weeks.

"Oh, good," she says, pulling two items out of a bag. "You got the essentials: Wine and ice cream. It's gonna be a good night!"

I was planning on spending the night by myself wallowing in self-pity, but it actually sounds a thousand times better to do it with my new friend.

CHAPTER 12
Brooks

"HEY, HOW'S ASPEN?" Harper floats into my office and takes a seat across from me. It's been two days since Aspen moved into the cabin next to mine, and honestly, I haven't seen much of her. She's been at work, but she's mostly kept to herself.

"She seems alright." I've been trying to give her space. I imagine it's a little uncomfortable for her that she's still tied to her ex-boyfriend's dad. "Why? Have you heard something?"

"No. Just wanted to check on her. She seemed ok yesterday, but I was wondering if you've heard any breakup songs blasting from the cabin or anything."

I chuckle. "Not that I've noticed."

"That's good. Have you checked on Zach?"

"Actually, he's texted me every day since Aspen moved out. I don't think he knows that she's staying here, though. He's just asked me if I've seen her and if she's alright. I think he plans on getting her back."

Harper winces. "Is that a good idea?"

"Probably not, but I've interfered enough. I'm not going to stop him from doing what he feels like he needs to do. Honestly, I'm just glad he's talking to me at this point, even if it is just checking on someone else."

"It's so annoying that Lacey turned him against you," she says. We've talked about this so many times. It frustrates the hell out of all of us, but I can't change the past. The damage is done.

"Well, I was a shitty boyfriend, I guess."

"You were sixteen! It's ridiculous that she's still holding a grudge, twenty years later. She's moved on. Just because you didn't want to be with her doesn't mean you're a shitty dad."

I put my hands up in defense. "You don't need to tell me."

"I know, sorry. It always just makes me so mad."

Harper has such a big heart. Sometimes I hate that she spends so much of her time on the ranch and not out making a family of her own. But she insists she loves it here, so who am I to tell her otherwise? "I appreciate it. I hope that Zach and I can work things out eventually. I think he's still got some growing up to do. Maybe this fiasco will help him realize there are two sides to every story."

"Yeah, maybe." She doesn't believe that one bit, and I'm not sure I do either, but I've got to hold out hope. "I still can't believe he did that to Aspen. She's so great. He really fumbled."

"I know. I agree. I'm glad I was able to convince her to stay with us. She mentioned leaving Blue Haven."

Harper lets out a big exhale. "Yeah, that would've sucked. She's a great part of the team. Beck said she's doing great with her riding, too."

"Oh yeah? That's good. I've been meaning to take her out on the trails. Maybe now will be a good time. It'll get her mind off things."

"Yeah, you should do that." She stands from her chair. "Alright, I've gotta go make a schedule. Let me know if you need anything."

I mock-salute her. "Will do, boss."

She rolls her eyes before she leaves my office. She's right, though. I should probably check in on Aspen this afternoon. Maybe I'll make dinner and offer her some to make sure she's eating. I start mentally coming up with what I'm going to make and what I need to grab from the store later.

———

I can't tell you what I was expecting to see outside of Aspen's cabin when I got home from the store, but I can tell you what I was *not* expecting. And that is Aspen sitting out front in a tiny bikini with a can of something in her hand.

She waves in my direction when she sees me. It'd be rude to not go say hello, wouldn't it?

I walk the short distance to her cabin. When I get closer, I notice that her bikini is even smaller than it looked from my truck. Her breasts are barely contained in the small triangles. Is this the universe's way of testing me? By throwing a beautiful woman in my face, who I absolutely should not be looking at?

"Hey, how's it goin'?" I ask her, trying my best to look anywhere other than her body. While I can't deny my attraction to her, I'm painfully aware of our age difference and our circumstances.

"Good. Just trying to soak up some afternoon sun. The sun is better on this side of the house."

I nod. "All good. How's the cabin working out? You need anything?"

She smiles up at me, squinting slightly from the sun. "It's perfect, Brooks. I can't thank you enough for letting me stay here."

"It's nothing. It's nice to see it being lived in again," I tell her, checking out my craftsmanship on the cabin. I've looked at it a thousand times, but now seems like a good time since I'm avoiding looking directly in front of me. "So, have you talked to Zach at all?"

"Nope," she says proudly, popping the P. "He's texted me a few times, but I'm done with him. I'm sure that's not what you want to hear, but I refuse to let someone do that to me, no matter how much it hurts."

"No, I'm glad you're doing what you need to do for you. Zach made a huge mistake. He needs to understand the consequences."

Her smile gets even wider. I must've said the right thing. "Thanks, Brooks. Jazz has been checking in on me, too. I think her 'give no fucks' attitude is rubbing off on me."

I laugh because I can totally see Jazz being that way.

"Well, good. I'm glad you guys have become friends." I lift up my grocery bag. "I gotta get this in the house. Let me know if you need anything."

She nods, and I walk away feeling pretty proud of myself that I didn't let my eyes linger too long on her body. Her very, very nice body. I sigh and shake my head. I'm going to hell for even thinking that.

CHAPTER 13

Aspen

I'VE SHOWERED and changed into a T-shirt and shorts when there's a knock on the door. I'm not expecting anyone, and no one knows I live here except Jazz, Brooks, and probably Harper, so I know it has to be one of those three.

I open the door to see Brooks. He's missing his cowboy hat tonight and has changed from his normal jeans into a pair of sweatpants. He looks relaxed and… gorgeous.

Mine and Jazz's conversation from the other day floats into my head. What would it be like to hook up with Brooks Calloway?

No.

I can't think about that. I wouldn't do that. I've just had one too many canned wines tonight. Plus, the man wouldn't even look at me when I was tanning earlier. He certainly doesn't want me like that.

"Hey," I say as casually as I can, hoping my thoughts aren't painted all over my face.

"Hey." His eyes fall to my shirt, and I realize I'm wearing his shirt again—the one he gave me when I stayed at his house. How embarrassing. He probably thinks I'm obsessed with him or something. "Have you eaten?"

I shake my head. I should've probably at least had a snack to soak up all the alcohol in my system, but I haven't gotten around to it. "No, not yet."

"Well, I made dinner and realized I made way too much. Would you like some?"

That's so nice of him to think of me. "Oh, sure. That sounds great."

"Do you want to come to the house? Or I can bring you some. Whatever is best for you?"

"I'll come over. Save you a trip. Let me get some shoes on."

I quickly slip my sandals on and meet him back at the door. We walk slowly over to his house. The summer sun hasn't quite set completely yet tonight, and it's giving a beautiful glow across the mountains.

"It's so nice here," I say quietly. "So peaceful."

"It's one of the things I love most about this place."

I never imagined myself in a small town. I always thought I was made for city life, which is why I moved to Atlanta as soon as I could. But now that I'm here, I think I could really get used to this.

I follow Brooks into his house, and it smells absolutely amazing. He walks into the kitchen, where I see there's a giant pan of lasagna, a big bowl of salad, and a pan of garlic bread sitting out on the counter.

"Wow. That's a lot of food."

"I told you, I made too much," he says, grabbing two plates from the cabinet.

"Did you accidentally make too much, or did you make this knowing you were going to ask me over?"

He freezes and looks at me from over his shoulder. "Would you be mad if I said I knew I was going to ask you over?"

I laugh, and he instantly relaxes. "No, but I hope you know you don't have to feed me."

"I know that, but I want to make sure you're ok and that you're comfortable here."

"Because you don't want to lose the best assistant you've ever had?" I tease.

He chuckles as he picks up the spatula and cuts into the cheesy lasagna. "Exactly."

He fills a plate up before he hands it to me, then does the same for himself and takes a seat next to me.

The lasagna is easily in the top ten best foods I've ever eaten. It's been so long since I've had a home-cooked meal. Zach and I weren't great at cooking, so most of the food we ate at home was frozen.

"This is so good," I say with a moan. "I'm not going to lie, I didn't take you as a chef."

He chuckles, and I realize how close we're sitting as his knee gently grazes the side of my leg.

"I don't know if I would call myself a chef, but I've been on my own long enough to have figured some stuff out."

"Like making killer lasagna?"

He smiles and glances over at me. It must be the wine in

my system because the look in his dark eyes makes my stomach flip. Yeah, has to be the wine.

I look away quickly. "Why are you on your own if you don't mind me asking?"

"Just haven't met the right person, I guess. I've always been so busy with the ranch that dating was on the back burner."

I take another bite. "You don't think when you're old and gray you won't want to have a partner to sit out here and watch the sunset with you?"

"I'm already old," he says with a laugh.

I playfully shove his very muscular shoulder, and he laughs. "You are not old."

"I feel old some days. But no, you're right. I absolutely do want that. Harper has been getting on me about it for years. I do want to share my life with someone. Just need to find the right person. I don't want it to feel forced."

"Well, what about Harper?" I ask, my curiosity getting the better of me.

"Nah. Harper is like a sister to me. We could never..."

I shrug. "Y'all just seem close."

"We are close. She's my best friend. But as much as I love her, I can't see us ever being anything besides that. She doesn't want that either."

"That's cool. I was just being nosey."

"What about you? Are you swearing off men now? I wouldn't blame you."

I laugh. "I haven't sworn off anything. I honestly haven't thought about dating since everything happened, but I always imagined I'd end up married with a few kids one day."

"You should. Whoever you end up with will be one lucky man."

I feel a blush creep up my neck. "That's a sweet thing for you to say."

"It's true. I want to make sure that what Zach did doesn't hurt your confidence. His actions were all on him and had nothing to do with you. You're beautiful, smart, and fun to be around. He messed up, and I think he knows that."

Before I can stop myself, I ask, "You… you think I'm beautiful?" It's the only thing my brain latched on to.

Brooks chuckles. "Yeah. You're beautiful, darlin'. Anyone with eyes can see that."

Darlin'.

I swallow down the gasp that threatens to escape. My body feels like it's on fire, and I cannot figure out why I feel this way. I mean, I just got out of a long-term relationship. I'm not looking for anything. But maybe my confidence is a little shaken right now. It's nice to hear that an attractive man thinks I'm beautiful. "Thanks, Brooks."

He nods and quickly changes the subject. "So, Harper said you did another riding lesson with Beck."

I focus back on my food and try to get myself to calm down. There is absolutely no way this man wants me as anything besides his neighbor and assistant. I need to make sure I'm not reading too much into his words. They can give me a little confidence boost, but I can't let myself have any delusions that anything would happen with Brooks.

"Yeah, I did. It felt a lot better this time."

"Good. You think you're ready for some trail rides? I could take you out. Show you around some of the easier ones."

"Yeah, that sounds great." Although I'm not sure it's a good idea for me to be alone with Brooks on a trail when my head's having all these crazy thoughts. I blame Jazz for all of this.

"Good. I'll figure out a good time and let you know."

We finish eating, and I make sure to tell him over and over again how good it all was.

"Easily one of the best things I've put in my mouth in the last year," I blurt after he's taken my plate to wash it.

He pauses and looks at me with a smirk before I realize what I said and how dirty it may have sounded.

"Oh my god, I mean—not like that. That's embarrassing. I think the cheap wine I had this afternoon is going to my head. That stuff is strong." I'm rambling, but at least Brooks seems amused by me instead of completely freaked out.

"I see you're still wearing my shirt," he says as he rinses off another dish.

I shrink into myself a little bit, embarrassment heating my cheeks. "Oh. Yeah. Sorry. It's just really comfortable. I'll wash it and give it back to you in my next laundry load."

"It's alright. You can keep it."

"No, really. It's fine. It's losing its appeal anyway."

"How's that?" he asks, sounding a little confused.

Me and my big stupid mouth. "Well, it doesn't smell like you anymore." Oh, god. What is wrong with me tonight? I need to stop talking.

His hand stops moving under the water, and his whole body goes rigid. "And it's important to you that it smells like me?"

"I guess it's just kind of comforting," I say quietly. It's the truth. Putting on his big shirt with his scent enveloping me makes me feel like I'm getting a hug from someone. It's been awhile since I've been held. I guess it's my imagination's way of telling me that someone cares about me. It's pathetic, really. And now I've just made myself look like an idiot in front of Brooks.

"Keep it." He starts moving again. "It looks better on you anyway."

I smile at that, but let the conversation drop before I say something else stupid. Brooks packs a Tupperware full of lasagna for me to take back to my place, and then he walks me out and watches me while I make the short trek to my cabin.

I climb into bed and watch TV for the rest of the night, trying not to think about what Brooks is doing in his big house all by himself.

In the morning, once I'm up and ready for work, I open my door to find a bag sitting on the little mat in front of the door. I look around, but there's no one in sight. Carefully, I bend down and pick up the bag, taking it inside. I open it up to find two oversized T-shirts. My heart races thinking about who left these for me.

I pull one shirt out of the bag and bring it to my nose, taking a large inhale. It smells just like Brooks. He's given me two new shirts that smell like him.

I don't know whether to feel incredibly embarrassed or really, really happy.

CHAPTER 14

Aspen

BROOKS and I don't mention anything about the shirts he left for me. We don't even mention our dinner together. As soon as I step into his office with his morning coffee, it's business as usual. I emailed him a few things I needed him to respond to, and he asks me to check in on one of our guests to make sure they are satisfied after a raccoon snuck into their cabin yesterday afternoon.

After our morning roundup, I head to the front desk to work for the rest of the day. I knock out some paperwork and finalize a few bookings for the fall. I'm finishing that up when Harper stops by the desk to check on me.

"Need any help with anything?" she asks.

I smile at her. "Nope. I'm all good."

Her blonde hair is pulled back in a clip today, and her Moonlight Ranch shirt fits her body so well it's easy to tell she's in shape. I know Brooks said they weren't interested in each other, but it's hard not to recognize what a beautiful couple they would make. It almost makes me feel a little jealous of her, knowing that she would be a better girlfriend for Brooks than I would be. Not that I could or would ever date him, but still. After last night, my head is all over the place.

"We're really glad you're here, Aspen. I hope you know how much of an asset you are to the Moonlight family."

Gah, she's so nice, too. "Thanks, Harper. That means a lot."

She nods and walks past me, probably to Brooks's office. I hope they aren't talking about me. The last thing I want is them both laughing at me behind my back because of the stupid shit I said last night. I can only hope they're not the kind of friends who tell each other everything.

Despite my internal embarrassment, the day runs pretty smoothly. I realize I actually enjoy meeting and talking with new guests as they check in and out. When I worked in Atlanta, everyone was always in a rush, and there was never time to chat with anyone. Things move so much more slowly here. I never realized how badly I needed that. I always thought being busy and on the go go go was what I wanted, but I'm starting to love this slower way of life.

I've just finished up some checkout paperwork when Jazz saunters up to the desk with a huge smile on her face.

"If it isn't my new best friend," she says, coming behind the counter and hoisting herself up onto the desk.

"Hey! How're the cabins looking?"

"Good now. You wouldn't believe how gross some of these people are. Sometimes I feel like I have to wear multiple pairs of gloves and a hazmat suit just to walk inside."

I cringe. "Gross."

"Yeah, tell me about it. At least bossman pays me the good money though, you know?"

I laugh. "Yeah, I guess that's good."

"So, how's your new little love shack?"

"It is *not* a love shack. But it's nice. I'm all settled in. Actually…" I look around to make sure we're alone. "Brooks invited me over for dinner last night."

Her eyes go wide. "You went, didn't you? I will kill you if you didn't."

"Of course, I went. He's a pretty good cook, too."

"Oh my god, you're just making me fall more and more in love with him."

"Do you want me to put in a good word for you?" I tease.

She waves me off. "Nah, my ship has sailed with him. It's your turn, baby."

I shake my head. "I told you, I don't need a turn."

She gives me a pointed look. "And I told you that you do."

"I just got out of a two-year relationship. With his son. Remember?"

"I'm not asking you to marry him, Asp. Just have some fun. I bet he's way better in the sack than little Calloway was."

The sad part is… I think she's probably right. Things were lacking in mine and Zach's sex life. I never felt fully satisfied, but I loved him, so I let it go. Now, I'm wishing I hadn't. I let too much go to the point that he felt he could sleep around and I would forgive him.

"Yeah, well…"

She gasps and grabs my arms. "We should go out! This weekend. Let's go out and try to find you a rebound since you're so against you-know-who."

I wish I could tell her that I'm not against you-know-who, per se. But having a hookup with my boss would not be a good idea. That's just basic common sense.

I'm really not sure I'm ready for a rebound either, but going out might be nice, and who knows. Maybe I'll meet the love of my life while we're out. I'm truly starting to believe that this town is where I belong. There's gotta be a reason for that, right? It's certainly not for Zach Calloway like I initially thought.

"Ok, yeah. That might be fun. Not the rebound part, but the going out. Getting back out there."

She smiles and claps her hands. "Good! It's a date then. Saturday night? I'll come get ready at your place, and we'll go together."

"Perfect."

She starts going through her clothing options, and from the sounds of it, she has a lot more clothes than I do. I haven't had much time to go out recently, so I haven't needed anything for it. Jazz is mid-sentence about what she might pair with a black mini-skirt when she stops suddenly and narrows her eyes. A look of absolute disgust crosses her face.

"What's wrong?" I ask.

"Ew. Asshole alert. Incoming."

"What does that mean?"

I turn to see Zach walking toward the desk with flowers and a big smile on his face.

"What the hell?" I mumble under my breath. Jazz and I both stare at him as he walks over.

"Hi, Aspen. Jasmine."

"Hi, Asshole," Jazz says, and I have to bite my cheek to keep from laughing.

"Charming as always, Jazz." Then he turns to me. "You look beautiful today, Aspen."

I ignore his compliment. "What are you doing here, Zach? I'm working."

He hands me the bouquet. This man has never, in the entire two years of our relationship, brought me flowers, and he chooses now? "I brought these for you."

I grab them and put them down on the counter without even looking at them. He looks from my crossed arms to my unimpressed face, and I can see him start to get a little nervous. I'm not sure what he thought this would accomplish.

"Can we talk for a second? I won't keep you long."

I sigh and look to Jazz. "Can you watch the desk for a sec?"

"Yes, but I'm watching you. Don't try anything stupid, little Calloway."

Zach rolls his eyes and follows behind me. I don't take him to a private room because I don't want to be alone with him. Instead, we stand off to the side of the lobby, clearly visible by Jazz... just in case. I know I don't know her all that well, but I one hundred percent trust that she would have my back if I needed it.

"What's up?" I ask, ready to get this over with.

"I wanted to see how you are. You haven't returned my texts or calls."

"That's because I don't want to talk to you, Zach. I thought that was obvious."

"Aspen, please. I'm so sorry for what I did. It was such a stupid mistake. I miss you so much."

"I don't want your apologies, Zach. You can't take back what you did, and I will never forgive you."

He sighs, and his shoulders slump in defeat. "I know. I'm an idiot. I don't deserve you, but I'm not going to stop trying to prove my love to you, Aspen."

"I'm telling you there is no point in trying."

"I don't believe that. I know you haven't forgotten what we had, and I know I certainly haven't. I made a mistake. We have a future together, I know it, babe. I want you to be my wife, the mother of my children, my partner."

"It's not gonna happen." Honestly, it makes me sick just thinking about it. I could never commit to someone who betrayed me the way that Zach did. I'm embarrassed that I even considered marrying him at one point.

He smirks at me. The same confident smirk that used to give me butterflies but now just makes me feel gross. "I'm not giving up, Aspen. I'll wait however long it takes. So, where are you staying?"

"That's none of your business." It's bad enough he's showing up at my job. The last thing I need is him showing up unannounced at my cabin.

"You're really not going to tell me?"

I shake my head. "I'm really not."

He slowly nods his head. "Alright. I see how this is gonna go. You're gonna play hard to get. That's alright. I can handle it."

"Everything ok over here?"

I'm startled by the sound of Brooks's voice. He looks from me to Zach, concern clear in his eyes.

"Hey, Dad. Yep. All good. Just talking to my girl."

"I am not your girl," I snap.

"She's playing hard to get," Zach says, like I'm a child making a joke.

I sigh and wonder if he's always been this annoying and I just chose to ignore it. "No, I'm not. I don't want you to win me back, Zach. We're done."

I turn and walk away from them, grabbing the flowers as I pass the desk. With their eyes on my back, I shove them in the trash and keep heading down the hall to the offices. As I walk away, I hear Jazz say, "Hell yeah!" which brings a smile to my face.

I sit down in one of the empty offices and hold my head in my hands. After a few minutes, I hear footsteps and hope to god it's not Zach. I'm really not trying to play hard to get. I want him to leave me alone. He can go be with whatever girl he wants now. He's free. I don't care anymore.

"You alright?" Thankfully, it's only Brooks.

"Yeah, just annoyed that he showed up here unannounced. This is my job. That's just embarrassing."

"I think he was just worried. He said he hadn't heard from you."

"That's because I don't want to talk to him!" I snap, and

then immediately feel bad for raising my voice at Brooks. "Sorry, I didn't mean—"

He raises his hand to stop me. "Don't even worry about it. I get it. I told him to leave."

My shoulders deflate. "I'm sorry, Brooks. I know you wanted him to come back to the ranch, and when he finally did, you had to tell him to leave. I feel terrible."

He kneels down beside me so that he can meet my eyes. "Hey, I want my son to come back to the ranch because he wants to, not for whatever game he's playing right now. The ranch is your home now, too. I want you to be comfortable here even while you're working. If his being here while you're working makes you uncomfortable, then he needs to leave. He's the one who messed up. Not you."

I stare at him in awe. He's willing to make his own son leave in order to make me comfortable? "Brooks... I can't thank you enough for everything you've done for me."

"We're a family here at Moonlight Ranch. Don't ever forget that."

I give him a wobbly smile while I try not to cry. He seems to notice that I'm trying to stay strong, so he stands and takes the attention off my face. "Do you wanna head home for the night?"

I shake my head. "No, I've got a little bit left to do."

I follow him out of the office, and he gives me a quick nod before he heads in the other direction. I head back to the desk where Jazz is in the middle of checking someone in, so I stand behind her and wait for her to finish. Once the family has received their map and key, they head off to find their cabin.

"You good?" Jazz asks.

"Yeah, sorry about that."

"Don't be apologizing for that. That was completely inappropriate of Zach, but it was awesome to watch you shove those flowers in the trash can. You should've seen his face when you did it." She laughs, and I wonder if I took it too far. The flowers were nice, but I don't want anything from him. I don't want him to think there's any chance of us getting back together. Because there's not. It's over. The sooner he realizes it, the sooner we can all move on.

CHAPTER 15

Brooks

I STARE at the text I just got from Zach and wonder what the hell he's thinking.

> Zach: Can you please talk to her? She won't listen to me.

> Me: You think she'll listen to me?

> Zach: Yes! She told me before that she likes you. You're my best chance.

> Me: I can't make any promises

> Zach: I know. I'll take anything at this point

I sigh and slide my phone back into my jeans pocket. As a father, of course, I want to help my son. I'll always do whatever I can to make him happy. But I think Aspen deserves better than what he has given her. I can't plead his case and promise that he won't make the same mistake twice when I don't know for sure if that's true. If he truly cared about her like he claims, he wouldn't have strayed in the first place. But how do I tell him that without pushing him even further away from me?

I walk toward the front desk, where I can hear Aspen talking to one of our guests. She's got a big smile on her face as she hands them a map and points in the direction of the cabins. The family has two small kids, so she makes sure to tell them about the water slides by the pool and the ice cream shop down on Main Street. They thank her and head off.

"Hey." I make myself known once the family is gone.

She turns to smile at me. "Hey, didn't see you there."

"Just got here. How's your day?"

"It's good. We've had a lot of check-ins today. It's gonna be a busy weekend."

"That's what I like to hear." Weekends are usually pretty busy for us. A ranch is the perfect weekend getaway for most families.

"What are you up to?" she asks, leaning back against the desk.

"Not much. Just wanted to ask if you had any plans tonight."

"Not unless you consider eating mac and cheese and binge-watching reality TV shows plans. Why? Do you need me to do something?"

"No. Wanted to see if you'd be up for a trail ride tonight."

Her face lights up. "I'd love that."

"Cool. Meet me at the stables at six. I'll have the horses saddled up."

"Yes, sir."

I turn to leave, but then remember something. "And Aspen?"

"Yeah?"

"Don't forget your boots." It's always good to wear boots when you're riding, but more importantly, she looks damn good in them.

"Got it!"

———

Aspen arrives at the stables right on time, which doesn't surprise me one bit. She's never once been late to work. Everything Harper or I have asked her to do, she's done quickly. She's organized and on top of her work. I can only assume that that kind of dedication and work ethic crosses over into her personal life as well.

"Hey, you ready?" I ask her once she's close enough. She's changed out of her work clothes and into some tight jeans and a black tank top, which are accompanied by the boots.

"Ready!"

I hand her the reins for Sparkles and watch her mount. She looks like she's been riding for years with how comfortable she looks in the saddle.

"Gettin' good at that," I say as I mount my own horse.

"Beck has been a great teacher."

"Good. I knew he'd help ya out. Alright, let's go."

She follows me out of the stable, and I slow down a bit so we can ride side by side. A slight breeze catches us, and I hear Aspen take a deep inhale. "It's so nice out here. Makes me wonder why I spent so many years surrounded by buildings and cars and people who don't give a shit about anyone but themselves."

I laugh. "Yeah, this place will do that to you."

"Did you ever think about leaving?" she asks.

That's an easy one to answer. "Nah. This place is my home. Couldn't imagine being anywhere else. Even if the guest ranch failed and we never made another dollar, I don't think I could leave."

"I'm jealous. It must be nice feeling so tied to one place." There's a twinge of sadness in her voice. I hate that she grew up without a strong family presence. I don't know what I would've done without my parents when I was a teenager.

"I'm sure you'll feel tied down somewhere one day," I offer the only encouragement I can, even while secretly hoping she starts to feel tied down to Blue Haven. I'm not really sure why, but I feel like she belongs here.

"Yeah…"

The lull in conversation gives me a chance to bring up the one topic I really wish I could avoid. "So… are you ok after everything with Zach yesterday?"

"Yeah. Thank you for stepping in. I'm sorry that this is coming between you and Zach."

I huff a laugh. If anything, I've talked to him more since their breakup than I have since he moved back. "We were already broken, Aspen. I'm not sure anything can save us at this point."

"Why are you guys broken?" she asks carefully as if she's worried I'll get angry. "Zach wouldn't ever really talk about it."

"It's kind of a complicated answer. I mean, I'm sure I wasn't the best father, but I did the best that I could. Zach and I were basically growing up together. It was hard on all of us. But I think a lot of it stems from his mother. She wanted to get married and have the perfect family life, and I didn't want that with her. She got mad when I ended things, and she's held a grudge ever since. I'm lucky she even let me see Zach when he was younger. I think she only agreed to it so she could get the child support.

I just couldn't give her what she wanted. Not at eighteen years old. She still thinks I chose the ranch over her. And hell, maybe I did. But I still stand by my decision. I wouldn't have been a good husband for her."

"Well, I think it's admirable that you recognized that at such a young age. She's the immature one for still holding on to a grudge after twenty years."

"Yeah, well…"

"I couldn't tell Zach this, but I never got good vibes from her. Honestly, I'm surprised you were ever with her. You two are so… different."

"We're in a small town. There's not a whole lot of options, honestly. Back then, she was willing to let me, well, you know. No teenage boy can turn that down."

She tilts her head back as she laughs. Her curls fall down her back, and the setting sun makes her skin look like it's glowing. I can't help but admire her beauty even when I know I should look away.

An overwhelming sense of guilt washes over me. I should not be looking at her like that. She's practically the same age as my son and completely off limits.

"Right. That makes sense," she says, turning to smile at me. "Do you think you'll ever have any more kids?"

"Wow, you're asking the tough questions tonight." I'm not even sure how the conversation turned to me so quickly. I guess we're done discussing Zach.

"Sorry if that's too personal. You don't have to answer. I'm just being nosey."

"It's alright. Harper's the only one who grills me like this, so I guess I wasn't expecting it, is all. But yeah, I'd love to have another kid. Maybe two. But only if I find the right person. I'm not making the same mistake again."

We ride a little more until we come to an overlook where we can see the sun on the horizon. I come up here a lot when I want to think or be alone. It's so peaceful. Sunrise and sunset are my favorite times of the day. Watching those happen really grounds me and helps me to remember what's important.

Aspen climbs off Sparkles and ties the reins to a nearby tree. I do the same and join her in front of the horses. She sits on the ground and stares out at the mountains in the distance. I plop down next to her, leaving a little bit of space between us. The last thing I want to do is make her uncomfortable.

We sit there in silence, watching the sun slowly go down

behind the mountains. I can tell she's enjoying this place just as much as I do.

"Thank you for bringing me out here, Brooks."

"Anytime, darlin'."

She drops her head on my shoulder, and for a moment, I'm not sure what to do. But then I realize she probably just needs someone to comfort her and I just happen to be here. She's gone through a lot over the last few months and has had no one. She must feel so alone. So in an effort to show her that she is welcome here, I slide my arm around her waist. She scoots closer and settles into me even more. I try my absolute best to not read too much into this.

This is just me comforting a friend. That's all.

If someone were to walk up on us right now, this would not look good. But I know it doesn't mean anything for Aspen. It doesn't mean anything to me either. Although I can't help but realize how much I enjoy her company. Whenever we've spent any time together, it's always easy between us.

But that's not what this is.

No. It can't be. Even if it does feel nice to have her this close to me. Even if I wish I could hold her and tell her everything is going to be ok.

Eventually, she straightens, and I reluctantly let my hand drop.

"We should probably head back," I tell her.

She nods. "Yeah."

But neither one of us moves. We sit there looking at each other as if we're in some sort of bubble. My eyes fall to her lips just as she parts them. Do I want to kiss her? My son's ex-girlfriend?

Dammit, I think I do. What is wrong with me?

I blink and pull myself out of the trance her lips put me under. I quickly stand and extend a hand to help her up. She takes it and stands up, not taking her eyes off me the entire time. It's unnerving, and I wonder if she feels what I was feeling, but I'm not brave enough to ask.

I untie my horse while Aspen does the same, and we get started back on the trail.

Her voice breaks the silence. "Hey, can I ask you something?"

Oh no. I brace myself for whatever she's about to say. "Sure."

"Does riding horses ever get easier on your butt?"

A laugh explodes out of me.

"Don't laugh! My butt has been so sore after every ride."

"Sorry, you're right. I shouldn't laugh. Yeah, it gets easier. It helps if you take a warm bath or give it a little massage. You'll get used to it once you start doin' it more."

"Ok, good to know."

We make it back to the stables. Since Beck is gone for the day, Aspen helps me get the horses back in their stalls, and then I drive us back to our cabins.

"Thanks for the ride," she says once I park in front of my house. "Both of them."

"No problem."

She starts heading toward her cabin. "I guess I'm gonna go massage my butt. I'll see you in the morning."

I'm pretty proud of myself for being able to hold in the

urge to offer my services with her butt massage. Instead of making a fool out of myself, I nod and give her a small wave while I wait to make sure she gets inside her cabin.

Once I'm inside my own house, I let my guilt consume me. My son asked me to talk to Aspen on his behalf, and instead, I've done nothing but form a crush on her. Maybe I am a shitty father. Maybe he's right to keep his distance from me. Maybe I am the problem.

CHAPTER 16

Aspen

"YES! THIS IS PERFECT!" Jazz squeals with excitement as I do a twirl in the outfit she selected for me tonight.

"Are you sure about this?" I ask, looking down at the short jean shorts and the cropped fringe tank top she loaned to me.

"A hundred percent. You're gonna be the hottest thing that has ever walked into Roadside."

I turn and look at myself in the mirror. I do look kinda hot, and most importantly, I feel good. Tonight is all about fun for me, though. I'm not looking for any random hookups or anything like that. I'm just going out with my new friend and enjoying my new town. That's all. If someone wants to flirt with me… well, we'll cross that bridge when we get to it.

"Alright, let's go!"

I follow her out of my cabin and turn to lock the door when I hear tires crunching on gravel. Brooks hops out of his truck and walks toward us.

"Where're you ladies headed tonight?" he asks. His eyes slowly travel down my body, taking in my outfit. He doesn't try to hide that he's checking me out, and it makes my stomach flutter. I like his eyes on me, though I'll never admit that to anyone.

"Roadside, Boss," Jazz answers.

"Ah." He nods. "Should be a fun crowd tonight. Be careful. And if you need a ride, call me. Doesn't matter what time, alright?"

He looks me dead in the eyes and waits for me to agree. "Alright, thank you."

He nods again. "Good. Have fun, you two."

He turns and walks into his house while Jazz and I pile into my car.

"Oh my god, that was so freaking hot!"

"What was?" I ask as I head down the drive.

"Are you kidding me? The way he looked at you! I don't know how your panties didn't melt off right then."

"How did he look at me?" I ask, wanting to make sure I didn't make up what I saw in my head.

"Like he wanted to devour you. Lick, suck, fuck. All of the above."

My cheeks heat at her words. Just thinking of Brooks doing any of that gets me all sorts of hot, but it'll never happen. Ever. I'm too young for him, and even if I weren't, he has Zach to worry about. I doubt his son would appreciate him messing with his ex.

"No, he didn't," I tell her.

"Girl, he did. I saw it with my own two eyes, and I have 20/20 vision." A laugh bursts out of me. "So, we're gonna go to the bar, have a few drinky-drinks, and flirt with a few boys. Then you're gonna call Brooks to come pick us up and let him take you home if you get my drift."

"Not gonna happen, Jazz. I already told you. There will be no hooking up between Brooks and me."

"Girl, I have read this book. Forced proximity. Forbidden. Age gap. It's lining up perfectly. The sooner you admit it, the sooner you can have fun."

"I don't know what you're talking about," I say, but the death grip on my steering wheel says otherwise. If I knew it didn't have the potential to ruin everything, I would possibly consider *something* with Brooks. But I can't.

"Denial isn't just a river in Egypt, babe. Now you owe me a drink for all this frustration," she says just as I find an empty parking spot by the bar.

"Yes, ma'am."

We link arms as we walk to the bar. It's packed tonight. Packed and loud. It feels like everyone is yelling to talk over the loud music booming from the speakers. I follow Jazz to the bar, and she gets the bartender's attention.

"The usual, Jazz?" he asks her with a little smirk.

"Yes, and my friend will have a…?" She looks at me.

"Gin and tonic, please."

He nods and winks at Jazz. "Coming right up, ladies."

"Thanks, Owen."

He gets to work on making our drinks, and I look at Jazz. "So… Owen?"

She rolls her eyes and waves me off. "We hook up occasionally. Nothing serious."

"He's cute! Why not something more serious?"

She shrugs. "I'm not looking for serious."

I laugh and shake my head at her, but before I can ask any follow-up questions, Owen is back, sliding our drinks across the bar.

"Start a tab for us, babe!" Jazz calls out to him as she grabs her glass and walks off to find a table.

She sees a group of her friends and leads us over there.

"Guys, this is my new friend, Aspen. Aspen, this is everyone!" Jazz announces.

There must be at least ten people standing around this table, and they all smile and wave at me.

"She's here to have a good time tonight. Can we give her that?"

"Hell yeah!" someone calls out.

"Hell yeah," Jazz repeats and clinks our glasses together. We both take a big sip of our drink, and then I'm whisked into conversation with everyone here. A lot of these people Jazz has known her whole life. Unfortunately, while I haven't met them yet, most of them have heard of me through the grapevine. It seems it was news that Zach Calloway was back in town with a new girl, and then it was news again when Zach was no longer seen around town with said new girl.

"You dodged a bullet if you ask me," a girl named Misty says. "I like Zach, but he was always immature. And Melinda? Let's just say she made it easy for the boys, if you know what I mean."

"The two of them were so on and off in high school. One minute they were all lovey dovey, and the next she'd have her tongue down another guy's throat," Isla adds. "And he usually would string another girl along until Melinda came crawling back."

"I didn't know all this. I guess I saw a different version of him."

"It's not on you. He showed you what he wanted you to see. Now you know his true colors. At least you got out before it was too late," Hope says.

"Thanks, guys. It's just crazy how you think you know someone until you see a whole other side and your world comes crumbling down."

"Well, we're gonna help you build it back up!" Misty says.

"Yeah, no more sad talk about that loser tonight. Let's dance!" Jazz grabs my hand, and five of us head out to the dance floor. The music is turned up so loud tonight that it almost rivals being in a club in Atlanta.

I have no idea how many songs we dance to, but at one point, I see Isla's eyebrows raise as she turns and smiles at Hope. Then Hope smiles. I wonder what's going on when I feel someone touch my arm. I look over and see a man standing next to me.

"Hey, what's your name?" he asks.

I glance at my new friends to get their approval before I tell him. All four of them nod in encouragement, so I take it to mean they know this man and he must be ok.

"I'm Aspen. You?" I yell over the music.

"I'm Dawson. Can I get you another drink?"

Dawson is cute. He has a nice smile and looks about my age. He's tall, and his blond hair is curling out from under his hat.

"Um, yeah, sure. That'd be great." I smile at my friends, and they shoo me away to go with him. I follow Dawson to the bar, where he puts a hand on my lower back and leans down to ask me what I'd like to drink. It feels strange telling a new man what my drink of choice is.

Zach knew almost everything about me. I never thought I'd have to start over, but here we are.

Dawson hands me my drink after Owen makes it and then ushers me over to sit down on one of the two barstools that just opened up.

"Are you new in town? I don't think I've seen you before."

I nod and sip on my drink. "Yeah. I've been here since the beginning of June. Just haven't gone out much. Have you lived here your whole life like everyone else?"

He chuckles. "I moved here when I was fifteen, so I haven't technically lived here my whole life. But sometimes it feels like I have. You move here for work or something?"

"Uh, well, no, not technically. I moved here with my ex, but that didn't work out."

"Your ex, huh? Any chance that was Zach Calloway?"

I nearly choke on my gin and tonic. "Wow, news does travel fast in small towns."

"Yeah, it does. Zach's an idiot, though. His loss is everyone else's gain."

"Well, thank you, I think. I appreciate that."

"So, you decided to stay in town?"

I nod, "Yeah, for now. I started a job at Moonlight Ranch and really like it. I didn't really have anywhere else to go, so I figured I might as well stay for a bit. See how it works out."

"Well, I'm glad you did."

Dawson goes on to tell me that he works with his dad at the tractor mechanic shop, which I didn't even know was a thing. He played football in high school and went to a two-year tech school right after, but he always knew he wanted to work with his dad. He seems like a nice guy. Which is why when he buys me another drink and asks me if I want to dance, I agree.

I let him put his hand on my hips as we sway to the music. It's not as awkward as I expected it to be. He keeps the conversation going so that I'm not worried about where to look or where my hands should be. We just talk (as best as we can over the music) and move a little bit. My new friends eventually make their way over to us, but Dawson doesn't seem upset about it.

"Having fun?" Jazz asks into my ear.

"Yeah, I am."

"Could he be the rebound?"

The music is loud enough that I'm sure Dawson didn't hear her, but I'm still embarrassed by the question. I shrug. "Maybe." Although I really don't want to force anything when I don't feel ready.

"Good."

Jazz disappears briefly and comes back with a round of shots. I'm not a shots girl, but I do it anyway because she looks so excited about it.

"I've got to head out," Dawson tells me a little bit later.

"I've got work in the morning. But I'd like to see you again. Would it be alright if I got your number?"

"Yeah, that'd be great."

It feels strange giving another man my number. In the back of my head, it feels like I'm doing something wrong even though I know I'm not. He puts my number in his phone and then sends me a text so I have his.

When he's gone, we all head back to the table. I'm definitely feeling the effects of the alcohol right now. I'm warm all over, giggly, and a little lightheaded. But I've had so much fun tonight that I don't want it to end. Unfortunately, it has to.

"I'm going to Owen's tonight," Jazz tells me. I'm happy for my friend. Even if she doesn't think it's anything serious with Owen, I saw the way he looked at her, and I know she's going to have a fun night.

"Oooo, Owen," I tease in a sing-song voice.

"Shut up." She laughs. "You need to text you-know-who to come get you."

I groan. It seemed like a good idea when we got here—have a few drinks, then have Brooks come get me. But now that I'm drunk and a little horny, I think being around Brooks is a terrible idea.

Unfortunately, I don't really have a choice. There are only two Ubers in this town, and they both have a long wait.

"Yeah. I guess I have to."

CHAPTER 17
Brooks

IT'S after midnight when my phone finally pings with a new message.

> Aspen: Hey bossman. You stillll up??

> Me: Yep. Need a ride?

> Aspen: If you don't mind.

> Me: Stay put. I'll be there in 10.

> Aspen: Thanks

I hop off my couch and head straight to my truck. I wouldn't say I've been waiting for this text all night, but I'm definitely usually asleep by now if that says anything.

Aspen looked good when she left her cabin. Too good for any of the boys in this town. I know that because I've watched most of 'em do the most idiotic things you could think of over and over again. Another curse of living in a small town: no one forgets anything. Can't think of a single one of them that would be good enough for her.

I pull up in front of Roadside in no time. Aspen is standing out front with Jasmine, the both of them laughing. Watching Aspen laugh is becoming one of my new favorite activities. Her entire face lights up every single time. It's almost as if she's letting herself be happy for the first time ever. Like she's surprised that she's laughing. It's cute.

"You ladies need a ride?" I yell once I've rolled the window down on my truck.

"Just me. Jazz here has plans," Aspen explains with a giggle and a hiccup. Looks like I'll be handling drunk Aspen tonight. This should be fun.

"Yep. A certain bartender is taking me home tonight. Lucky him," Jazz says as she gives Aspen a hug.

"Well, you be careful, Jasmine. And call if you need anything."

"Got it, bossman. You just worry about getting my girl here home safe. She had all the boys at the bar buying her drinks."

Jasmine helps Aspen into my truck, and I clench my jaw thinking about all those boys trying to get Aspen's attention. I wonder if she liked any of them. It's not my business, but something inside me really wants to know.

"That's not true," Aspen says with a slight slur. "It was one boy buying me a few drinks. You bought the rest!"

Jasmine laughs. "That's true. Alright, you two have a good night." She winks before she shuts the door. I'm not sure exactly what that wink was supposed to mean, but I'm choosing to ignore it.

"So, first night out and already got people buying you drinks?" I ask as I pull back onto the main road. I want to know who it was so I can tell her how he's not good enough for her. That's what I should do for Zach's sake. He wouldn't want his friends messing around with Aspen. Not when he's still trying to convince her to give him another chance.

"It was one person. And he was nice. Not pushy at all. We had a few drinks and danced a little."

My grip tightens on the steering wheel as I picture someone putting their hands on her. "Hmm. That sounds fun. Who was it?"

The question comes out before I can stop myself. I just need to know.

"His name was Dawson. I didn't catch his last name."

"Tall? Blond hair?"

She sighs. "Yeah. You know him?"

"Yeah. He's a nice kid." Unfortunately, he is actually nice, and I can't think of a single thing to say to make her not like him.

"Well, that's good. Maybe nice will be a good change for me."

My knuckles are practically white from how tightly I'm gripping the wheel. What the hell is wrong with me? "You gonna see him again?"

She shrugs. "He got my number, so I guess we'll see."

"Right. That's good. I'm happy for you." That's a lie, but I can't figure out why I'm actually not happy for her. She deserves better than Zach. He didn't treat her right. Dawson comes from a good family. I have no doubt he'd be nothing but respectful to Aspen. But it still doesn't sit right with me. It's almost as if. . . I'm jealous. But no. No, that can't be it.

Her phone pings from where she's holding it in her lap. She looks at it and immediately groans and leans her head back against the seat. "Oh my god!"

"Everything alright?"

"No offense, but your son is the most annoying man I've ever met in my life. Why can't he just leave me alone? Hasn't he done enough?"

"Did he text you?" I ask, trying to get some context before I answer her, although I'm not sure she's actually looking for an answer from me.

"Yes. You wanna hear this shit? 'Are you trying to hook up with one of my friends?' Like that's any of his business."

She starts typing on her phone. I know she's probably not sober enough for this conversation, but I'm also not going to stop her. She finishes typing, and her phone chimes almost immediately after.

"Ok, I told him it's none of his business, and he said, 'It is my business, but if you need to hook up with someone to get back at me, I understand. I'll still keep waiting for you.' He understands? What the hell?"

She starts typing again, but this time it's accompanied by an evil cackle, and I feel like I should be concerned now. "Hey, what are you saying back?"

"I'm saying 'good. I'll send you a pic of me riding someone else's dick since you're so understanding.'"

Great. Now, I'm picturing her with him. What the fuck

is wrong with me? Both Calloway men cannot be immature assholes to this woman. "Aspen, did you send that?"

"Hell yeah, I did."

"Jesus Christ," I mutter.

Her phone pings again. "Oh my god. He's laying it on thick tonight. 'I deserve that, Aspen. I deserve all the bad things you want to do to me. But that won't stop me from loving you.' Why won't he take no for an answer?"

"I don't know. I guess he doesn't want to lose you." I feel bad for Zach. He does seem to be trying. If he didn't love her, I would've thought he would've given up by now. Unfortunately, his trying seems to be too little too late for Aspen.

"He's already lost me. I'm not changing my mind."

She starts typing something, and curiosity gets the better of me. "What'd you say back?"

"I told him to lose my number." Then she turns her phone off. Guess she's done with the conversation.

I park the truck in front of my house and turn off the engine. I lean back in my seat and turn my head toward Aspen. She does the same to me.

"You ok?"

She sighs. "Yeah. I'm never getting back with him. I just wish he would understand that and let me move on."

"I'm sorry. I can talk to him again if you want me to," I offer, even though he hasn't listened to me yet.

"No, no. I don't want to put you in the middle of this."

I think I'm already in the middle of this, but I don't say that to her. "Well, I'm here if you need anything."

She gives me a soft smile. "You know what I would love?"

"What?" I ask carefully, worried about what she's about to say. I hope she doesn't ask me for something I can't give her, because the way she's looking at me right now with sleepy eyes and a shy smile, I might just try to give it to her anyway.

"I would love a bath."

I chuckle. That I can do. "You wanna use my tub?"

"Can I? I promise I won't take too long."

"Come on, darlin'. You take as long as you need."

I open my door and climb out of the truck. Aspen attempts to get out but ends up practically falling out of the open door. Luckily, I'm right there to catch her. "Easy does it."

She laughs and hiccups, so I sling my arm around her waist and help her to the house. I open the door and help her inside.

"Mmmm, your house always smells so good," she tells me after I've shut the door and started us down the hall to my bathroom and the big clawfoot tub.

"Oh yeah? What's it smell like?" I guess I never notice the smell of my own home, but I'm glad to know it's not bad.

"It smells like you mixed with something sweet."

"Me?"

"Yeah. All spicy and manly." She giggles.

"Well, I'm glad you like it." If I'm not mistaken, she might be drunkenly flirting with me. While I know that what she's saying probably doesn't mean anything, it still makes me feel something I shouldn't. Not for her.

I lead her through my room and into my bathroom.

"Wow, this is beautiful," she says as she releases herself from my grip and spins around, taking in the whole bathroom. I went all out when I did the renovations for this house. I wanted it to be perfect in case one day I did decide to bring a woman into my life permanently. I wasn't looking for a bachelor pad. I wanted a home, and that's exactly what I got.

The bathroom has his and hers sinks and a giant shower with a seat and a rain shower head. A clawfoot tub that's big enough to fit me and potentially another person in it is off to the side of the shower, and that's where I head to turn the water on. I dump a ton of bubbles into the running water and watch it start to fill up.

"Oh god," I hear her say from behind me.

I stand and turn around to face her. "What's wrong? Are you ok?"

"I'm fine. I'm fine. I just realized…"

"What?" I ask, trying to figure out what I missed.

"It's just, you're wearing sweatpants," she whines and points to my gray sweatpants.

"And that's a problem for you?"

"Well, yeah. Kinda." She says this like I should know why my sweatpants are a problem. I think she's forgetting it was well after midnight when she called me to come get her. I don't typically lounge around in my jeans.

"Care to enlighten me on why?" I ask.

"Because they look hot as fuck."

"What?" I manage to choke out.

"Yeah, look. I can practically see your…"

I look down and see that she's gesturing to my dick. I turn to face the mirror and realize that you can, in fact, see the outline of my package. "I never noticed that before."

"Yeah, well…"

"Would you be more comfortable if I changed?" I ask.

"I'd be more comfortable if you… never mind. No. Don't change."

I raise my eyebrows at her, curious about what she stopped herself from saying.

"Alright, well, the bath is almost ready. I'll leave you to it. Do you need anything?"

"Um, can I have some water?"

I nod and excuse myself. I need to get out of there before I say or do something we'd both regret. She's drunk. She doesn't know what she's saying. But I'm completely sober and way older than her. I should know better.

I distract myself by going to the kitchen and getting her some ice water and ibuprofen. I give myself a minute in the kitchen to get my head on straight. It feels like I have a crush, which is something I haven't experienced in like twenty years. It's a foreign feeling, and I absolutely cannot be feeling like this for my son's ex-girlfriend. I'm supposed to be helping her out. Giving her a job and a place to stay because of my idiot son. Not wondering what her lips would feel like.

After my brain and my body calm the fuck down, I force myself to head back to the bathroom and give Aspen her water. Looking back, I probably shouldn't have offered up my bathtub when I've been having inappropriate thoughts about her recently. It's almost as if I want to torture myself.

The bathroom door is cracked open just a little bit, so I knock to make sure she's not naked.

"Aspen? I've got your water. Can I come in?"

"Yeah. I'm covered."

I walk into the bathroom, and the first thing I see is a small pile of her clothes on the floor. It's impossible to miss the black lace thong sitting right on top. Dammit. Maybe I should've changed out of these sweatpants. It's going to be hard to hide what's currently stirring to life in my pants.

I look up and realize that when she said she was covered, she meant just barely and only by bubbles in the bathtub.

"Ah, shit. Sorry. I didn't realize you were already in the tub."

She smiles at me, and I wonder if she wanted me to find her like this. "It's ok. I don't mind."

She reaches her soapy hand out for the glass of water. I also hand her the pills.

"Here. Take these. They'll help you in the morning."

"Thank you." She pops them in her mouth and takes a big sip of water. I do not watch her throat bob as she swallows them. No. I definitely don't do that.

I need to get out of here immediately.

"Alright, I'll leave you to it. You can use that towel right there. Just yell if you need anything."

I turn to leave, but before I make it to the door, she stops me. "Brooks?"

"Hmm?"

"Can we forget about this conversation in the morning? My sober mind will understand that it's not appropriate to be checking out my boss and be humiliated."

She looks at me with her big eyes and rosy cheeks, her skin glistening from the water.

I chuckle at her question and also at my out-of-control thoughts. "Afraid not, darlin'. It's not every day I've got a beautiful woman telling me I look 'hot as fuck.'"

She groans. "Fine. But I still get to keep my job, right?"

"Don't worry. I won't say a word to HR."

"Do we have HR?"

"Sure don't. Enjoy your bath, Aspen."

She giggles as I shut the door, leaving her alone. I head back to my living room and try not to think about the naked woman in my bathtub. Unfortunately, I fail miserably.

CHAPTER 18

Aspen

MY ALARM JOLTS ME AWAKE. It takes me a minute to remember why I feel like absolute horse shit, but the night before quickly comes rushing back to me. So many drinks. Dancing. A bath. Brooks.

Oh my god.

I'm really regretting all those drinks right about now. I mean, who goes out drinking until after midnight when they have to work the next morning? Me, I guess. Don't even get me started on how embarrassing I probably was last night.

I roll out of bed and realize I'm in one of Brooks's shirts. This is a new one. He must've given it to me last night after I got out of his tub.

I may have been completely wasted, but there's no way I could forget how good he looked last night. Cowboy Brooks is one thing, but relaxed, casual Brooks might be my favorite.

There's a knock on my door, which forces me to get out

of bed faster than I wanted to and makes my head spin. I yank open the door and find Brooks standing there with a bright smile.

"Good mornin'."

"Is it?" I croak.

He chuckles. I can't imagine how terrible I must look right now. But I forget all about that when his eyes move down my body and stay focused a moment too long on my bare legs.

"I, uh, wanted to see if you needed the morning off."

"Absolutely not," I tell him. "I'm an adult and will have to live with the consequences of my actions."

"Figured you'd say that, so I brought you coffee and a breakfast burrito." He hands me a brown bag and a coffee in a to-go mug.

"Did you make this?" I ask, trying not to freak out about the fact that he took the time to make me breakfast and bring it over to me. Do not swoon for this man, Aspen. Do. Not. Swoon.

He shrugs. "Yeah. Figured you'd be hungry and need something to soak up all that alcohol."

I wince. "Yeah. Sorry about… all that."

"Don't be sorry. You needed a night out."

"I did. It was a lot of fun."

"Good. I'm glad. Well, I'll leave you to it. You can take the UTV on the side of the house to get to the lodge this morning. We'll go get your car this afternoon." He hands me a set of keys. "See you in a bit."

"Yeah. Thanks for breakfast and for last night."

"Anytime."

He tips his hat in my direction. I never thought that simple move would be so attractive, but the flip of my stomach says otherwise. He turns to walk to his truck, and I take a moment to admire him. His white T-shirt stretches across his broad shoulders, which must be from all the manual labor he does on the ranch. And his jeans fit just right over his ass.

I forget that I'm staring until he looks at me from over his shoulder and smirks.

Caught.

Dammit.

I quickly shut the door in an effort to hide my embarrassment, but I doubt it worked. Why the hell am I so horny, and why is my ex's dad suddenly the object of all my desires? I almost touched myself in his bathtub last night. Thankfully, I had enough sense to stop. I would've had to pack up and move if he'd have caught me doing that.

I quickly get dressed and throw my curls into a bun on top of my head. Then I dig into the breakfast burrito. Everything Brooks has made me has been fantastic, and this is no exception. Is there anything the man isn't good at?

I wish he weren't so perfect. It'd make it easier to get over this little infatuation.

———

The morning goes by quickly, probably because I'm attempting to distract myself from the constant headache that won't go away. Before I know it, I've gone through all of the notes from the night team, answered emails, and prepped check-ins for this afternoon. Pretty productive considering how I feel.

I'm so in the zone that I startle when a plastic bag is set down in front of me.

I look up to see Brooks smiling at me. My heart skips a beat. Dammit.

"Brought you a sandwich."

"Seems you've got a bad habit of feeding me, Mr. Calloway."

"I wouldn't say it's bad at all."

Why does he have to say stuff like that? I can't even try to wipe the goofy smile off my face. He's certainly not making this any easier for me.

"Ah, Aspen. Good to see you again." I turn to see Mayor Cunningham walking toward the desk.

I straighten my shoulders a little bit. "Hi, Mayor Cunningham. How are you?"

"Doing well. You still enjoying your time in Blue Haven?" he asks.

I nod. "Very much."

"Aspen," Brooks says. "This man is following me. Call security."

Mayor Cunningham rolls his eyes. "I am not following you."

"Cameras would say otherwise. Sandwich shop, gas station, now here."

"We have a scheduled meeting," Cunningham says, defending himself.

"Likely excuse," Brooks mumbles as he starts walking to his office.

I laugh and reassure the mayor. "Don't worry, we don't actually have security."

"He's so dramatic sometimes."

He stalks off to follow Brooks down the hall. I take out my phone and shoot him a quick text.

Me: Thanks for the sandwich

Brooks: Anytime

"What's got you smiling like that?"

I jump and look up to see Jazz walking toward me.

"Nothing," I say quickly, putting my phone in my pocket. "Just excited for lunch."

"How come you look so good today? I feel like shit," she whines.

"No idea. Just good luck, I guess. How was the rest of your evening?" I ask, trying to change the subject.

"Oh, you know," she says with a smile. "A little of this and a little of that."

"So what you're saying is Owen served it up well."

"I would never say that because it's way too cheesy but basically."

I laugh. "Good, I'm glad."

"And… how was yours?"

"Fine. Definitely not as exciting as yours."

Her shoulders slump in disappointment. "Seriously? He just… took you home?"

"Yes. I don't exactly know what you think is going to happen between me and my ex's father. He is not interested, and he is my boss, remember? It would be so inappropriate."

"I know, but damn. I was really hoping for something. A little slip-up, maybe."

As much as I want to give her all the details of my night, I know it's not a good idea. It would just give her hope that something might actually happen. We flirted. I checked him out. He checked me out. That's it. There's an invisible line that neither one of us is willing to cross. And I'm fine with that.

"Well, I'm sorry to disappoint you. But hey, at least Dawson got my number. So maybe that will be something." I don't really want it to be something, but I feel like it will make Jazz feel better if she knows I'm not sitting around moping.

"Yeah. Dawson's a good guy, too. I'm surprised he hasn't already blown up your phone."

"You'll be the first one to know as soon as he does."

"Good! Alright, I gotta get back to cleaning. I'll come see you later."

"Ok, have fun."

She starts to walk away, but then she stops when she sees the sandwich bag Brooks left for me.

"Where'd you get that?"

"Oh, uh, Brooks brought it for me." Her eyes go wide, and I quickly add, "It doesn't mean anything."

"He brought you lunch!" she whisper-shouts.

"So? He knew I was gonna be hungover."

"He likes you!"

"No, he probably feels bad for me," I try to explain.

"Men do not bring lunch to women that they don't like. It's a fact. He thought of you!"

"Don't you have rooms to clean?" I ask. I don't want her to get any sort of skewed view of what is going on between Brooks and me. But I also don't want to get my own hopes up. I can't ignore the butterflies I get every time he's near me. I'm so very obviously attracted to the man. As much as I don't want to admit it, I like that he does little things to show me he's thinking about me, like the coffee this morning, the lasagna dinner, and taking me on a trail ride. It does feel like… something. And I'm trying very hard to convince myself that it's all in my head.

Jazz turns to walk away but not before singing, "Aspen and Brooks sitting in a tree K-I-S-S-I-N-G."

My entire face turns red, and I'm glad no one else is here to see it.

I grab my sandwich and sit down at the desk to eat it really quick.

By the time I'm almost finished, Mayor Cunningham and Brooks walk out of the hallway.

"Pleasure doing business with you, Brooks."

"Glad it's a pleasure for one of us," Brooks says back. I secretly love it when he acts all feisty.

"Have a great afternoon, Aspen." Mayor Cunningham waves to me as he leaves.

"How's the sandwich?" Brooks asks once it's just the two of us. "I wasn't sure what you wanted on it, so I kept it basic."

"It's perfect. Thank you. How'd your meeting with Mayor Cunningham go?"

"Oh, you know. Same old, same old. Wants to talk 'donations' for the Halloween Festival."

"Halloween?" I can't even think about Halloween when it's August and still a hundred degrees outside during the day.

"It'll be here soon enough. And he's gotta put down a deposit on a few things."

"You can't say no, can you?"

"I wouldn't say no even if I could. If I didn't fund it, then it probably wouldn't happen. And people have a lot of big memories connected to the town festivals and events around here. I remember taking Zach to as many as I could when he was little. I want the kids these days to be able to experience that fun too."

"That's really sweet of you, Brooks."

His cheeks turn pink as if he's embarrassed about being sentimental. He shouldn't be. I think it's cute.

"Yeah, well, don't tell anyone."

"Your secret is safe with me."

"You busy later? Thought we could go ridin' again after work."

My stupid, hopeful heart starts to beat a little faster. "Yeah, I'd love that."

"Cool. After we get your car this afternoon, we'll go to the stables."

"Thanks, boss."

He taps the desk once and winks at me before he leaves. Am I making this up in my head, or is he actually flirting with me? I have no idea. What I do know is that I get to go riding again with my super hot boss, which I am very excited about.

CHAPTER 19

Aspen

"SO, GUESS WHO HAS A DATE TONIGHT?" I ask, with a smirk on my face.

"No way, really?" Jazz says. "Dawson called?"

"Yep. We talked for a little bit last night, and he asked if I was busy tonight." The past few nights, I've been doing trail rides with Brooks. We've gone every single night since he asked me to go after my night out on the town. It's been a lot of fun, and I'm getting a lot more comfortable on a horse. Beck even said I'm starting to look like a pro, but I think he was just humoring me.

Unfortunately for me, it's only intensified my attraction for Brooks. We talk about everything while we ride from the ranch, to my life before this, to books we like. Last night we discussed our favorite movies. I was shocked to find out how much he loves *The Last Samurai*.

Talking with him is dangerous, though, because I'm starting to get even more attached. And I can't do that with him. I'll only end up hurting myself. So when Dawson asked me to go out, I thought why not? I owe it to myself. And who knows, maybe Dawson is the one. Or at least maybe it'll help me move past this little crush I have on my boss.

"So, where are you going? Do you need to borrow an outfit?"

"He said we'll go to Melvin's Tavern. I went there once with Zach and Brooks. I think I can put together an outfit with what I've got."

"Well, I want pictures of this outfit before you go so I can approve. And I want texts after the date telling me everything. Unless you end up in his bed, then the text can wait until the morning."

I laugh. "I'm not gonna sleep with him on the first date."

She shrugs. "Wouldn't blame you if you did. It's been awhile for you. You need to get some."

It has been awhile, and I'm starting to feel the effects of that. Literally everything Brooks does these days turns me on. Watching him put a saddle on a horse: hot. Lifting a big bag of feed: hot. Hammering something to fix a fence: hot.

I need to get my mind off of Brooks and on to someone more appropriate.

"Yeah, well, I'm not planning on anything happening, but I guess I wouldn't say no if we were connecting."

"That's my girl. Alright, I've got one more cabin to clean before I'm outta here for the day. Don't forget to text me. I mean it!"

"Sir, yes, sir!"

She laughs and heads toward the exit. I work on a few

more things I need to do before the night shift closer gets here. We had a ton of check-ins for the weekend. School recently started back in our area, so people are loving the weekend getaways at the ranch. I'm not complaining, though. I love getting to meet new people, and I've already met a few families who have been back a few times since I started working here. I also can't believe I survived my first summer season at the ranch. It makes me wonder if I'll still be here next summer.

I'm finishing up an email when I hear footsteps behind me.

"Hey."

I turn to see Brooks casually leaning against the desk. He's got a backward baseball hat on today instead of his usual cowboy hat, and he looks a little dirtier, which leads me to believe he's been outside working somewhere. That would explain why I haven't seen him much today.

"Hey. You been rolling around with the horses?" I ask.

He chuckles and smiles. He has a great smile. "Somethin' like that. You wanna go riding later?"

My heart sinks. I want to say yes. There is literally nothing else I'd rather do than go riding with him. But I can't. I have to stay strong. I have to get over this crush, and the only way I can think to do that is to try to date someone else.

"I can't tonight."

His smile fades a little. "Oh, you got plans?"

"I do actually. I'm going on a date." I wince a little bit as I say the last word and hope he doesn't pick up on it. I am excited about this date. I am.

His eyebrows shoot up in surprise. "Oh, cool. You going with Dawson?"

"Yeah, he called me last night."

"One day's notice? That's… anyways, where's he taking you?"

"Melvin's."

"Nicest spot in town. You deserve nothing less. Well, good. Hope you have fun." He's smiling, but there's a weird tension between us now. I hate it. We've gotten so comfortable with each other over the last week, I'd really hate for this to ruin it.

"Thanks. Maybe we can go riding tomorrow?"

"Yeah, I'll be around."

He taps the desk twice, his signature sign that he's leaving, before he turns and walks away. It takes a lot of effort from me to not yell and tell him I'll cancel all my plans for him, but I manage to keep myself composed.

I try to focus back on work, but my head is all over the place now, so as soon as Stacia, the night shift front desk attendant, gets in, I clock out.

I head back to my cabin and turn my music up really loud while I try to get in the headspace for this date. I know I shouldn't need to hype myself up for a date, but I truly believe that I need to redirect my focus on someone else. This date *will* be good for me.

I get some of the frizz out of my hair and spruce up my makeup before deciding to wear a white sundress that I haven't had anywhere to wear to yet.

Dawson texts me to double-check that I still plan on meeting him at the restaurant. He wanted to come pick me up, but I told him I'd meet him there. It's not that I don't trust him, it's just this area on the ranch—my cabin and Brooks's house—feels like a secret spot. I don't want anyone to know about it. It's silly, really, but I text Dawson back, confirming that I'll meet him at the restaurant.

I glance towards Brooks's house as I lock my door. His truck isn't there. I wonder if he went riding without me. I shake the thought from my head. I can't be thinking about that tonight. Tonight is not about Brooks; it's about Dawson. And most importantly, me.

Dawson looks just as handsome as I remember when I see him waiting outside of Melvin's Tavern. I was worried that all the alcohol from our initial meeting had made him look cuter than he actually is, but that's not true. He's dressed in nice jeans and a red button-down shirt with the sleeves rolled up. He's hatless tonight, which I've noticed is unusual for guys in Blue Haven. Men like their hats around here. His hair is a little messy, but it gives him a rugged look that I kind of like.

"You look beautiful," he says when I reach him.

"You don't look so bad yourself."

"You hungry?"

"Starved."

He smiles and ushers me inside the restaurant, and the only thing I can think is, 'I wonder what Brooks is doing.'

CHAPTER 20
Brooks

ASPEN'S CAR is gone by the time I get back to my house. I guess that means she's on her *date*. That's good. I'm glad she's doing that. What I don't understand is why it irritates me so damn much. She should be out dating, especially after what Zach did to her.

But I don't like it. The thought of her laughing and smiling with another man, kissing another man, makes my head start to pound.

Which is how I find myself quickly showering and putting on a clean pair of jeans and a T-shirt before I get back in my truck and drive to town.

It's when I park in front of Melvin's Tavern that I realize that this must be what people say is jealousy. I've formed some sort of attachment to Aspen. It's not hard to see why. She's fun to be around, hardworking, and has a drive that's not easily ignored. I like hanging out with her, and I've subconsciously started to want to do more than just hang out, even though I know I can't.

This date is messing with my head.

Before I left my house, I called in a 'to-go' order at Melvin's. I don't want to crash her date. I only want to see how it's going. Make sure she's ok. I head inside to the hostess and give her my name for the pick-up order. When she goes to grab it, I start my perusal of the restaurant. I spot Aspen first. She's facing toward the door. She has more makeup on than she normally wears at the ranch, and her curls are down and not as wild as usual. I like it when they're a little wild, like she's been riding and the wind has blown through her hair.

The moment my eyes find her, she looks in my direction.

It's like the world stops when her eyes meet mine, and I know deep in my soul that this is not a one-sided attraction. I know she feels it too.

Her body goes stiff, but she keeps a smile plastered to her face, trying to play it off like nothing has happened.

The hostess comes back and hands me my bag of food.

"Thank you, ma'am. I'm gonna go say hi to a friend real quick," I tell her before I start walking in Aspen's direction.

I don't know what I'm doing. I didn't think this part through. I just had to see her, but now I can't walk away.

It's not like I can walk up to her and announce that I like her and she should leave this date right now. No. That wouldn't be fair. But before I can think of what I'm doing, I'm at their table.

"Hey, guys. Fancy seeing you two here," I say, sounding like a psychopath. Aspen tilts her head in confusion. She knows she told me where she'd be tonight.

"Hey, Mr. Calloway." Dawson stands and shakes my

hand. Like I said, good kid. "Haven't seen you in a minute. Staying busy?"

"Oh yeah. The Ranch has been packed this summer."

"Good. That's great to hear." Dawson sits back down with a smile on his face. Poor kid has no idea I'm here to sabotage his date.

"What are you doing here, Brooks?" Aspen asks me as calmly as she can.

I hold up the bag. "Came for some dinner."

"At Melvin's?"

"Yep. Looks like it."

"Tonight of all nights, you wanted Melvin's?"

I look her directly in her pretty blue eyes and repeat, "Yep."

Her brows furrow, causing a little crease between them. She knows I'm full of shit.

"Melvin's is good," Dawson interjects, likely picking up on a weird tension between us.

"It is," I agree. "So, how's your evening going?"

"It's great," Dawson answers, but he's not the one I was asking. "We're getting to know each other." He reaches his hand out to Aspen, and she takes it and nods in agreement.

I look at her, and she gives me a wide-eyed stare before she says, "Yes, tonight is going great. Dawson is a great guy."

I know he's a great guy. I told her as much on the way home from the bar that night. The problem is he's not me, and I want to be the one sitting across from her.

"Aspen's pretty great, too. Can't believe I got lucky

enough to be the first one in town to ask her out. And she said yes."

He smiles at her, and it feels like a punch to my stomach.

"She's the best," I agree with him. Dawson is the perfect guy for her. Not me. I could never be with Aspen the way he could. With our age difference and Zach? It would never work between us. But that doesn't stop me from hoping. "Alright, I'd better get home before my food gets cold. You two have a good night."

"Thanks, Mr. Calloway."

Aspen doesn't say anything as I nod quickly and walk away. I have no doubt she's wondering what the hell I'm doing. I've given her no reason to think I have feelings for her, and honestly, I didn't want to admit to myself that I did. But now that I've acknowledged it, I can't get her out of my head.

I leave Melvin's feeling stupid and deflated. What was I hoping would happen? That she'd leave her date and come home with me? If anything, I've just made everything worse. Now she knows I'm into her, and I can't do anything about it.

———

After I eat my cold burger, I change into sweatpants and decide to sit on my front porch. I genuinely enjoy being outside, but tonight I'm specifically waiting for Aspen. I want to make sure she makes it home ok. Or at least that's what I tell myself.

Maybe I just like to torture myself. I'm starting to think that's a real possibility.

Her car eventually pulls up the gravel drive. It's not late at all, which tells me that the date didn't go very far.

She turns the car off, tosses her purse by the door, and stomps over in my direction.

"What the hell was that, Brooks?" she asks. Fuck, she's cute when she's mad.

"How was your date?" I respond calmly.

"It was great," she spits out. "We had dinner. Then ice cream while we walked around town. Now answer my question."

"Do you like him?" I ask.

"He's a very nice guy. Now again, why were you at Melvin's?"

"I told you I was hungry."

"I've seen you cook. You make enough food to have leftovers for weeks, and in the couple months I've lived here, I've never seen you go to Melvin's for takeout." It seems she might know me a little too well. Better than I thought, anyway. Honestly, it gives me hope that maybe she feels the same about me as I do for her.

I shrug one shoulder. "Felt like Melvin's tonight."

"On the one night you knew I was going to be there on a date?"

"Coincidence."

Her shoulders slump. "Brooks, I'm going to ask you one more time. Why were you at Melvin's tonight?"

She's mad and has every right to be, but for some reason, I can't get myself to admit why I was there. I mean, what am I supposed to say, *"Sorry I came to crash your date because I just realized I might have feelings for you and I got jealous."* Yeah, no. I can't see that going over well.

We stare at each other. She's breathing heavy after all that yelling, and even though I know she's pissed at me, she still looks so beautiful.

She got dressed up for him. Of course she did. Because she wants to date him. He's a better option for her than I am.

After I don't say anything, she huffs and turns around, stomping back to her house, all the while mumbling something about how unbelievable I am.

Watching her walk away from me triggers something in my brain, and I'm up and following her in seconds.

I catch up to her as she gets to the front door. I grab her arm and spin her toward me, pushing her back up against the door.

I don't say anything. I don't need to. Because the second she looks up at me with her big blue eyes, I'm a goner. I bring my free hand to the nape of her neck and lean down to kiss her.

I don't bother going slow. This woman has been consuming my every thought since she walked onto my ranch. No, this kiss is not slow. It's everything. All the frustration, all the jealousy come out in this kiss. She doesn't try to resist me. She molds herself to me, opening her mouth and letting me in.

She whimpers as my tongue slides around hers. After her initial shock wears off, her hands wrap around me, tugging at the back of my shirt like she needs to be closer. I rock my hips against her, and she moans.

I kiss her until it feels like I need more. I need everything. I pull back to tell her to open the door and let me in, but when I see her swollen lips and hooded eyes, the realization of what I've just done comes hurtling back at me.

I kissed my son's ex-girlfriend. The same girl he's still in love with. I kissed my much younger employee.

What have I done?

I drop my hands and take a step back.

She looks at me, her brows furrowed in confusion when she realizes I'm not taking this further.

Her hands release my shirt and drop to her sides.

"Brooks?" Her voice is barely above a whisper.

"I-I can't. I'm sorry."

I turn away quickly before I change my mind. I don't look back. I can't. I know if I see her again, I won't be able to walk away. And that's exactly what I need to do right now.

CHAPTER 21

Aspen

NOTHING.

Not a single word or explanation.

In fact, Brooks Calloway is acting like he didn't completely take my breath away with that kiss last night.

I had planned to talk to him this morning when I dropped his coffee off, but he wasn't there. When he finally showed up in his worn-in jeans and dirt-covered cowboy boots, he smiled at me, tipped his hat, said good morning, and walked straight to his office. I started to follow him back, but I saw Harper following him, so I stayed put. The last thing I want is for people to find out I crossed a line with my boss.

By the time lunch rolls around, there's still nothing from Brooks. No text, no email, no note. It's almost as if I dreamed that kiss, but I know I didn't. I'd never be able to dream something that good.

Jazz comes stomping up toward the desk with an

eyebrow raised. "Ma'am. I did not receive a post-date text from you. I'm very upset about this."

Shoot. I did forget to text her because I was so consumed with Brooks and that kiss. "I'm so sorry. The night just got away from me."

Her scowl turns to a smile really fast. "That good, huh? I knew he'd be good in bed!"

My eyes widen. "What, no. We didn't sleep together. We had dinner and ice cream, and he was a perfect gentleman."

"Well, that's disappointing," she says. "Did he at least kiss you at the end of the night?"

He did kiss me, actually. It wasn't anything like the kiss I had with Brooks. It was a quick peck on the lips before I got into my car. I feel terrible because I was so preoccupied with thinking about Brooks that I don't think I gave Dawson a fair chance.

"He did."

"And?"

"It was nice," I say noncommittally.

"Aw, damn. I had high hopes for him, but nice? Nah, that's not gonna work."

I laugh. "No. Nice is good. We had a great time, and he's already texted me today to say he'd like to see me again."

"Ok, well, that's something, I guess. Are you going to see him again?"

I've been thinking about this question all day. I was hoping to ask Brooks what that kiss meant, but if he's avoiding me, I can't do that. I refuse to be seen as a mistake, and that's how Brooks is making me feel right now.

"Yeah, I think so," I admit, even though it feels wrong. Deep down, I know I'm hoping it will make Brooks jealous.

"Why don't you seem excited?" she asks, and I instantly feel bad that I'm not. Dawson is such a nice guy. He's sweet, funny, and we had a good time together. He should be perfect for me. But all I can think about is Brooks.

"What? I am excited. Works just been stressful today. Got a lot going on."

I'm not sure if she believes me, but she lets it go. "Yeah. We got a lot of people here this weekend."

"Excuse me." A man is standing behind Jazz with a vase full of flowers. "Do you know where I can find an Aspen Fallon?"

"Oh, um, that's me." I just know my face instantly turns red.

"Ok, then. Here you go." The man hands me the vase.

"Who are these from?" Jazz asks.

I shrug, and the man says, "Dunno. There's a card in there, though. Have a good day."

Once he's gone, I set the vase on the desk and rummage through the flowers to find the card.

"Do you think it's from Dawson?" Jazz asks excitedly.

I suppose it could be, but I'm really not sure. I open the small envelope and pull out the card. My shoulders immediately slump, and instead of being excited, I'm now irritated.

"Fucking Zach."

"Oh my god!" Jazz groans. "Why can't that man take a hint?"

"I have no clue."

At that moment, Harper and Brooks reemerge from the back hallway.

"Aw, did someone get flowers?" Harper asks.

"Yep. Ms. Hot Stuff right here has boys chasing her all over town," Jazz says.

"That's not true," I quickly add. "These are from Zach. He still hasn't gotten the message…"

Harper gives me a sympathetic look, and when I glance at Brooks, I can tell he's doing his best to look at anything but me.

"I don't want them, though. Can we put them in a cabin for one of the guests?"

"I don't see why not," Harper says. "But are you sure you don't want them? They're really pretty. Accepting the flowers doesn't mean you're accepting his apology."

I shake my head. "No, I don't want them."

"Alright. Well, Jazz just pick a cabin and put them on one of the tables."

Jazz picks up the vase. "You got it, boss." She heads off toward the cabin while Harper heads to the front door. Brooks stays frozen by the desk. His eyes finally meet mine, and my heart rate starts to pick up. How can one look affect me like this?

He opens his mouth as if he's finally going to say something, but then his phone rings. He looks at the screen and quickly answers it as he walks off.

I exhale the breath I was holding, and my shoulders fall. I guess we won't be talking today.

———

I'm standing in the middle of my cabin after work, just staring at the walls. I've really come to love this place. It's small and exactly what I need. But it was never meant to be permanent, and if Brooks is going to keep actively avoiding me, then it's probably time I try to find another place to live.

I sit down on the couch and start searching for apartments nearby. As expected, not much comes up, but there are a few rooms for rent.

I'm looking through one of the listings when there's a knock on my door. I'm very surprised when I open it to see Brooks standing there.

His hands are in his pockets, and he looks like he might be a little nervous. "Hey, uh, I made Philly cheesesteaks. You want one?"

"Um, what?" That's really the first thing he's going to say to me?

"I made food. Are you hungry?"

"Brooks, you cannot be serious."

"What do you mean? We've eaten together loads of times."

"Yeah, but that was before you kissed the life out of me and then acted like I didn't exist all day," I say. Did he think I was truly just going to overlook that?

"Look, ok, I know. Come over and eat with me, and we'll talk."

I cross my arms across my chest. "Maybe I already made dinner."

"No, you didn't," he says confidently.

"How do you know? It could be getting cold right now."

"I know you well enough by now, Aspen. You don't like to cook. Best case, you made yourself a sandwich, which I can assure you, mine is better. So come eat, and we'll talk."

Dammit. He's got me there, and I am hungry.

"Fine."

I follow him over to his house. He's got our food already plated up at the counter as if he knew I'd say yes. I hate being predictable.

I take a seat on my normal barstool because I've been here enough times by now that I have a usual seat.

I take a bite of the sandwich. I know he's not going to talk unless he knows I'm eating. Then I ask, "So, wanna tell me why you were avoiding me all day?"

"I-I didn't mean to avoid you, Aspen. Really. I was just freaked out. Put yourself in my shoes. I kissed my son's girlfriend."

"Ex-girlfriend," I clarify.

"Yes, but a woman he obviously still cares about. How do you think he would react if he found out I'm developing feelings for you?"

My brain freezes. Whoa. Feelings and kissing are two different things. I know how I've been feeling, but hearing that he might be feeling the same thing changes things. It wasn't just a kiss for either of us.

"I don't imagine he would like that," I admit slowly. "But he made his bed. He's the one who pushed me away. I don't think he should have any sort of say about what we do."

"In any other situation, I would agree with you, but he's my son. My blood, Aspen. I've finally got him to talk to me again. This would only make everything worse again."

He's choosing Zach over me. I understand it, but it doesn't mean it doesn't suck. When I first came to Blue Haven, I would've been over the moon to know that Brooks and Zach are talking more. But with the circumstances as they are, I selfishly wish that Zach were still holding onto whatever grudge he had before.

"I'm sorry I kissed you, Aspen." Ouch. Not what I was hoping to hear. "It was irresponsible and selfish of me. I let my emotions take control, and I-I was jealous seeing you with someone else."

He was jealous. I like the way that feels more than I should, but I hate that he feels like our kiss was a mistake. "Ok."

"Ok?" he repeats.

I shrug, trying my hardest to be calm and collected about all this, even though I feel completely crushed on the inside. "Yeah, ok. I mean, it's not what I was hoping you'd say, but it is what it is. I've started looking at potential rooms for rent, so I should be out of your hair shortly."

"What? No. Aspen, you don't have to leave."

"It feels like I should."

"No. Don't feel like that. I want you to stay. The cabin is yours. For however long. Forever if you want it. It's nice having someone there."

"You sure it won't complicate things?" I ask.

"No. I won't let it."

"Alright. Well, thank you."

I finish the rest of my food as quickly as I can. As much as I normally love being around Brooks, tonight has been a lot for me, and I'd like to be by myself to process this. After he kissed me, I thought… Well, I certainly didn't think he was going to regret it. So this almost feels like another breakup to me.

"Thank you for dinner. I should go." I stand to go wash my plate, but he stops me by grabbing my wrist. We both look to where his fingers are wrapped as if touching me is going to make us both combust.

He pulls his hand back. "I've got the plate. Don't worry about it."

"Alright. See you tomorrow?"

He gives me a small smile. "See you tomorrow."

Once I'm back in my cabin with the door locked, I finally let all of my pent-up emotions out. I can't believe I'm crying over another Calloway man. What has my life become?

CHAPTER 22
Brooks

IT FEELS like a brick is on my chest when I wake up. Last night was hard. I hate that I did what I did to Aspen. She doesn't deserve any of this. I took advantage of a situation, and I feel terrible about it.

I'm grateful she handled it as well as she did, but I still feel like the biggest jackass. Maybe I should have told her to find a new place to live. That probably would've been the smartest thing. But the thought of her not being in the cabin didn't sit right with me. Maybe it's my loneliness talking, but I like knowing she's there. I like being able to cook for her and take her food. I like knowing that if she needs anything, I'm only a few steps away.

Even if that means I have to see her dating someone else.

I force myself out of bed and into the shower. Afterward, I get dressed, eat breakfast, and pretend this is just a regular day. Like before I kissed her and screwed everything up. I'll see her at the Lodge. Maybe I'll get her lunch.

Hell, maybe I'll even ask her if she wants to go riding again tonight. If I pretend everything is normal, then maybe we can both move past this like adults.

Except I remember the way her lips felt on mine. The way she grabbed me and pulled me in closer.

No.

Stop it.

I have to get the thought out of my mind.

Grabbing my keys and my hat, I make my way to the front door and freeze when I see Zach getting out of his car in my driveway. He looks confused as he looks from my house to Aspen's car in front of the cabin.

It must've slipped my mind to tell him that I offered her a place to stay. Or maybe I thought I would be safe since he hasn't set foot over here in years.

"Mornin', Zach," I say, like it's the most normal thing in the world for him to be here this early.

"Is that Aspen's car?" he asks in lieu of a greeting.

"Yeah. Yeah, it is."

"Why is it there?"

"She's, uh, been living in the cabin."

"For how long?"

Before I can answer, the door to the cabin opens, and Aspen comes out. Every time I see her, it takes my breath away a little. She's in jeans and a Moonlight Ranch T-shirt, and her curls are down today. My favorite.

She stops when she sees us. "Oh, good morning."

"How long have you been living here?" Zach asks her.

"Since I moved out of our apartment."

"Are you kidding me?" He looks back at me. "Dad, I

asked you so many times if you knew where she was living."

"Hey!" Aspen yells, walking closer to him. "I asked him not to say anything. Where I live is no longer your business."

"But this is weird! You're living next to my dad?"

"I'm living at my place of employment. Your dad was kind enough to offer me a spot after his son embarrassed me in front of the whole town. And it's not like we're living in the same house. We hardly see each other. You're being dramatic," she tells him. We certainly see each other more than she's alluding to, but I'm keeping my damn mouth shut. Zach doesn't need to know that. He certainly doesn't need to know that I wish I could kiss her again right now.

Zach takes a deep breath. "Yeah, ok. Sorry. I was just... surprised." He takes a step toward her, and she holds out a hand to stop him. "Did you get the flowers I sent?"

"Zach, I don't want your flowers. Stop it. I'm begging you to leave me alone at this point."

Zach's shoulders slump, and I think I might be witnessing him realize that he lost her for good.

"Ok. Ok. I'm sorry, Aspen. I was hoping after some time apart, you'd see that I was serious about us. But I'll leave you alone if that's what you really want."

"Thank you," she says sternly. She glances at me but doesn't say anything else before getting in her car and leaving.

"Sorry I didn't tell you. It's just she asked me not to..." I try to explain.

"It's fine. I'm glad you gave her a safe place to stay." He watches as her car gets further down the gravel drive.

"Do you wanna go grab some coffee? My treat."

He sighs. "Sure."

He follows behind me as we drive to the little coffee shop on Main Street. I should be at work right now, but spending time with Zach is more important. Especially if he's willing to actually talk to me.

We order our drinks and find a small empty table near the window.

"So, how is everything going? Are you almost done with the police academy?" I ask him once I realize he's not going to be the one to break the awkward silence.

"It's good. I've still got about three months. Some days are pretty tough..."

"Yeah, I imagine it's not a cake walk."

"But it's good. I feel like this is what I'm supposed to be doing. I'm just itching to get out in the field."

"That's great, Zach. I'm glad you found something you love."

"Yeah, look. I'm sorry I didn't want to work the ranch like you wanted me to..."

"No, don't even worry about that. All I've ever wanted is for you to be happy. Would it have been nice to pass it down to my son one day? Of course. But I would never want to do that if it wasn't what you wanted. Ranch life is not for everyone, and I understand that."

He nods and sighs. "Seems like Aspen is liking ranch life, which surprises me. I didn't think she would like it as much as she does. She looked good today, though. Happy."

I nod and try to think of an appropriate thing to say without making it sound like I'm interested in her. I settle on, "She is fitting in well. She's a hard worker."

"I know that. I just… I miss her, and I'm afraid I've lost her forever," he admits.

After a pause, I tell him, "I think she's moving on, Zach. You hurt her pretty badly. Don't you think it might be best to just let her be happy?"

He rubs his hands down his face as he takes in my words. "I know. God, I know. I hate myself for cheating on her. Hell, I don't even know why I did it. Sex with Aspen was fantastic." My hand freezes on my coffee, and I try to remain calm, but I really don't want to be thinking about Aspen having sex with anyone, especially not my son. "She would be willing to try whatever I wanted. Sex with Melinda is so… boring."

"Why'd you do it then?"

"I don't fucking know. Because she wanted me, I guess? When we moved here, Aspen was really stressed. She was nagging me a ton, putting all this responsibility on me. And then Mom was trying to monopolize all my time. I could tell Aspen didn't want to hang out with her. I was worried about the academy. It just felt like everything was crashing down on me.

"Then Melinda showed up and basically opened her legs wide for me, no questions asked. It was easy. She was easy. But I don't want to be with her. I want to be with Aspen."

"Well, son, I think you might need to plan for what might happen if you don't get Aspen back. I saw her go on a date the other night…" I don't need to add that I was insanely jealous and tracked her down.

"Yeah, I know. Fucking Dawson. I love her, though. I guess I thought she'd see that and come back to me."

I nod. "I know how hard it is to lose someone you love, but sometimes the way to show them how much you love them is to let them go."

"Did you ever love Mom?" he asks, suddenly. I'll admit, I wasn't expecting that.

"I did. Of course, I did. But we didn't want the same things. The ranch was always my plan, and she didn't want that. I knew that if I had stayed with her, neither one of us would've been happy. She would've ended up resenting me."

"I guess I can understand that." For the first time in years, I think this might be a turning point for us. "So, you think I should let Aspen go?"

I swallow, knowing that the answer is going to hurt him but also knowing that I feel like complete shit for having feelings for the woman he's still in love with. "I think that's what she wants."

"Yeah…"

He sits in silence for a minute, taking that in before he quickly drinks the rest of his coffee. "I should probably go, but thanks for the coffee. And thanks for giving Aspen a job and a place to stay. I'm glad she likes it here."

"Yeah, of course."

He leaves while I stay at the table for a few more minutes, just thinking. How did I end up here? How did I start falling for a woman who is way too young for me and the only woman in all of Blue Haven that I literally cannot have?

I can be friends with her. I can be her employer. But I cannot let it go any further than that. I'm a grown ass man and should be able to control myself.

I clean off our table before I head back to the ranch. Aspen is already at the desk. She's smiling at someone when I walk up. Her eyes glance in my direction as I pass, and I give her a slight nod.

Yeah, I can do this. I can stay away from her.

I hope.

CHAPTER 23

Aspen

"I'VE GOT to run into town for some things. Need anything?" Brooks asks me one day after work when he sees me outside my cabin. It's almost as if he read my mind because I do actually need to go to town.

"Actually, yeah, can I ride along with you?"

Without any hesitation, he says, "Of course."

Things with Brooks have slowly gotten back to normal. I know he'd rather I forget about the kiss, but there's no way I could ever do that. The best I can do is to pretend I've forgotten for his sake. Unfortunately for me, my crush on him has done nothing but grow since that night.

But pretending everything is fine has worked out so far. We've even started up our nightly rides again. Things are starting to feel normal again.

I get in his truck, and he drives us to town.

"Where do you need to go?" he asks as he finds a spot in the center of town.

"The pharmacy. It should be quick. Do you want me to meet you somewhere?"

"I'll just come with you," he offers.

My hand freezes on the door handle. Oh, crap. I didn't think this part through. I'd really rather him not be with me while I pick up my birth control refill, but I can't ask him to leave me alone. I should've just driven myself.

"Ok," I say slowly, but he's already walking toward the pharmacy. The man walks with such confidence, I can't help but stare. I've noticed other women like to stare at him, too. I wonder why he doesn't go on any dates. From what Jazz tells me, there are plenty of single women around town who make it very obvious that they would love a chance to try to win over Brooks Calloway. He's a smart man. I refuse to believe that he doesn't know about his charm. So, I wonder why he keeps them all at arm's length? I'd ask him, but after everything that's happened, it would feel like I was too invested. It's best if I keep my thoughts to myself.

Once I catch up to him and we're inside the pharmacy, Brooks points to the other side of the store, telling me he'll be over there, which is a relief. The last thing I want this town to start talking about is how I picked up birth control with my ex-boyfriend's dad.

I get to the counter where an older lady stands waiting to help me.

"Hi. I'm here to pick up a prescription for Aspen Fallon."

She smiles and types my name into her computer before turning to find my medicine from the shelves. It takes her forever to find it, and by the time I see her coming back, I'm checking over my shoulder to see if Brooks is making his way over here yet. Thankfully, I don't see him.

The woman scans my bag, and as I'm paying, loudly asks, "Now do you know how to use this, dear?"

"Yep, I got it."

"It's important to take this at the same time every day. I've seen too many girls your age not take it right and end up pregnant."

"I know. I have a reminder set on my phone, but thank you." I take the clear bag from her outstretched hand and move away from the desk as quickly as I can, trying to unzip my purse so I can shove it in there. But before I can get it in, I run into something. Not something. Someone.

I drop the bag and look up at Brooks, whose hands are on my arms to steady me.

"Whoa. Where are you runnin' off to, darlin'?"

Oh god. Why does he have to call me darlin'? He hasn't said it in weeks, but hearing the nickname again makes me want to melt right here and now. Judging by the little smirk he gives me, I think he knows exactly how much I enjoy it.

"Oh, not running. Just didn't want you to have to wait too long."

He bends down to pick up the bag before I have a chance to stop him and pauses, clearing his throat, when he registers what it is. "Here you go."

"Thanks," I say, quickly taking it and shoving it in my purse.

"It's good you're being safe." I know my face is beet red right now.

"It's to regulate my periods." Why did I say that? Please stop talking, Aspen.

He nods. "That's good too."

"Yep." There's an awkward pause while we both attempt to figure out how to change the subject. "Did you get what you needed here?"

"Yeah, I'm good. Gotta hit up the grocery store next."

"Let's go then," I say, gesturing to the door. He follows me out and down the sidewalk to the store.

We each pick up a basket and split up to get what we need. I grab some ramen, macaroni and cheese, and bread for sandwiches. All easy stuff. Ever since I left Zach, I haven't really wanted to cook anything. Not that I did much cooking while we were together, but I definitely did more than I am now. I just can't be bothered.

"Aspen."

"Hmm?" I turn to see Brooks scowling as he looks in my basket.

"I know I pay you enough to eat decent food."

"You do."

"So why are you buying all that crap?"

I shrug. "I don't really like cooking. I'd rather just have quick options to grab."

"No, you're not eating this." He starts putting my stuff back on the shelves.

"Hey!"

"When you're hungry, you come to my house, and I'll feed you," he says as if it's the most obvious thing in the world.

"I can't ask you to cook for me every night."

"You're not asking. I'm telling you. I will be cooking for you as long as you live in my cabin."

"Brooks—"

"Don't fight me on this, Aspen. You know I have plenty of food. My mama never taught me to cook for just one anyway."

I sigh. I have seen how much food he makes, but still, he shouldn't have to cook for me after he also gave me a free place to live. "I don't think that's a good idea."

"You don't have to eat with me if that's your hesitation. I can package it up for you and bring it over if that makes you more comfortable."

I love that he's concerned for me. "I'm not uncomfortable around you, Brooks. It's just the opposite, actually."

We stand in the middle of aisle five staring at each other. I watch his Adam's apple bob as he swallows, and I realize that maybe our situation is just as hard on him as it is for me. "We can be friends, can't we, Aspen?"

"Friends," I repeat in a raspy voice. "Yeah, we can be friends."

"Good. Then we'll have dinner together. As friends."

I nod slowly. "Alright. I'll let you cook me dinner if it'll make you happy."

He smiles, and I swear he's trying to kill me. Happy Brooks is adorable. And I know grown men shouldn't be adorable, but he's always so serious. Or in work mode. So when he smiles, I feel like he's letting some of his true self shine through.

"It makes me very happy," he says as he moves his attention from me and focuses on grabbing a few more items from the shelves. I follow him around with an empty basket. I feel kinda silly that he's going to be cooking for me, but I'm also excited because that means I get to spend more time with him. I am so down bad for this man.

After the grocery store, we make one more quick stop at the post office next door so Brooks can drop off a few letters, and then we're on our way back to the ranch.

———

Brooks parks his truck in front of his house and then grabs the groceries from the backseat.

"Should I bring you dinner tonight, or do you want to eat at my house?" he asks, and I suddenly feel awkward because I had forgotten earlier that I already have dinner plans for tonight.

"Oh, I don't need dinner tonight."

He stops what he's doing to look at me. "You going out?"

"Yes."

"With Dawson?"

I nod. "Yes."

"Ok."

He finishes grabbing his things, but before he gets to his front door, I stop him.

"Tell me not to go," I blurt out. If he told me right here and now not to go out with Dawson, I'd cancel with no hesitation. It's probably a sign that I shouldn't be going out with him, but if Brooks really doesn't want to see where we could go, then I have to at least try to move on with my life.

"Dawson is a good guy," he says.

"He is," I agreed. *But he's not you,* is what I wish I could say.

"You should go, Aspen. Have fun."

I nod and swallow back my tears. At least I tried. "Alright."

He nods, and I turn to walk away. I don't look back at him, but I don't hear his front door open, so I know he's watching me. And when I leave for my date, he's sitting on his front porch.

When I get home after a night of food, drinks, and dancing with Dawson, Brooks is still sitting there. Almost as if he was waiting for me to get home. I suppose I should be grateful he didn't show up at the restaurant again this time.

I don't walk over to him, and he doesn't call out to me.

I simply pretend he's not there, which I'm sure is what he wants. But once I'm inside my cabin, I let out a long exhale. I'm never going to get over him if I have to see him like this every damn day.

CHAPTER 24

Brooks

"WHAT ARE YOU GUYS DOING?" I ask from the doorway.

Jasmine and Harper are both standing on a table in our small break room with some sort of banner in their hands.

"Oh, it's Aspen's birthday today, so we're hanging decorations," Jasmine explains.

"Hmm. I don't remember either of you hanging decorations for my birthday." I know it's Aspen's birthday today. I saw it on her new hire paperwork and set a reminder in my phone. And if that wasn't enough, Zach texted me yesterday to ask if he could bring her balloons while she's working. I told him no because it would be a distraction. I hope that will keep him away. I have a feeling his presence would ruin her day.

"Well, maybe you're not as important as Aspen," Jasmine teases.

Harper laughs. "We're trying to make her feel like she's part of our family here."

"Aaaand she hasn't mentioned her birthday to me at all, so I thought it would be fun to surprise her," Jasmine adds. I'm glad Aspen and Jasmine have become such good friends. She needs that.

"We got decorations and some cupcakes. And I got her a gift card to the boutique in town," Harper says.

"I got her some new books from the bookstore. She goes through them so damn fast."

"Oh, so I'm gonna look like the asshole who didn't get her anything?" I say, moving to the coffee maker to pour a cup. I already got her something, actually, but I'm not giving it to her in front of everyone. I'll stop by her cabin later and give it to her with the cake I made. Yes, I made her a cake. I couldn't very well go into town and order some-thing. There's no doubt that it would get out that I bought a cake for someone, which I've never done.

"Don't worry," Harper says while rolling her eyes in my direction. "I wrote that the gift card is from both of us."

I chuckle. That is something Harper would do. She takes care of everyone. I hope one day she can find someone who can take care of her for a change. "Always looking out for me."

"Someone's got to."

"Where is Aspen, by the way? Isn't she usually here by now?" I know she is, but I'm trying to play it off like I don't know her entire schedule. Between the gifts, the cake, and always wondering where she is and what she's doing, I'm starting to feel a little crazy. She's always in my head, and I can't decide if I want her there or not.

"We sent her to the coffee shop to get us coffees. We told

her we wanted fancy coffees, not that black crap you drink." Jasmine's head nods in the direction of my cup.

"You're having her run your errands on her birthday?" I ask.

"Well, how else were we gonna get her out of here long enough to decorate?" Jasmine asks as she rolls her eyes. "Now, either help us with these decorations or see yourself out."

I have every right to tell her this is my ranch and I can be wherever I want, but after knowing Jasmine for so many years, I just laugh and put my cup down to help them finish decorating.

We manage to get all their girly decorations up and the cupcakes out on the table by the time Aspen is back, and the three of us shout "Happy Birthday" when she walks in.

The look of shock on her face is priceless. She jumps a little but manages to steady the coffees in her hand.

"Oh my god," she whispers, and then she starts shaking, which is a strange reaction. Jasmine and Harper notice, too. They walk over to her and grab the coffees, and Jasmine wraps her in a hug as the tears start flowing. "How did you know?"

"I told you we were going to be best friends. Best friends know each other's birthdays and celebrate them!"

Aspen pulls back and looks around at all the decorations. Her eyes land on me for only a moment before she looks away.

She wipes the tears from her cheeks. "I'm sorry. I don't know why I'm crying. It's just that no one has ever done anything like this for me. I'm just overwhelmed, I guess."

"Well, get used to it. You're part of our family now," Harper says, rubbing Aspen's back to help calm her down.

Aspen walks over to the table to look at the cupcakes and the gifts. "This is too much. You guys didn't have to do all this."

"We wanted to," Jasmine tells her sweetly. "Now come on. Cupcakes happen to be my favorite breakfast pastry, and we have presents to open!"

I clear my throat to grab their attention. "I'll let you girls do your thing. Happy Birthday, Aspen."

She smiles at me. "Thanks, Brooks."

I nod before I leave the three of them alone, knowing I'll celebrate her birthday with her later.

———

I leave work a little early to put the final touches on Aspen's cake. I wanted to make sure it was ready by the time she gets home from work. I watch out my window like a stalker waiting to see her drive up, and when I finally see her car, I walk outside as casually as I can.

"Hey, Birthday Girl. Got a sec?" I call out to her.

She smiles and walks toward me. "Hey, where'd you run off to this afternoon? You didn't even get a cupcake."

"I had some work I needed to do in one of the guest cabins, and then I wanted to get back here to finish up your birthday surprise."

Her eyes go wide. "What?"

"You didn't think I wouldn't celebrate your birthday, did you?" I ask.

"You've already done so much. The decorations, the gift card. . ."

I shake my head. "Nah, that was all the girls. I can't take credit for any of that. I had my own thing planned. Come in."

I wave her into the house, and she follows behind me. "This is too much."

"It's not. It's not enough." Nothing will ever be enough for her.

She follows me to the kitchen, where the cake is sitting out on the counter, with a small gift bag next to it.

She looks down at the cake that's covered in chocolate frosting. "Brooks, did you make this?"

When she looks up at me with glossy eyes, I wonder if I've gone too far. I'm trying to not fall in love with my son's ex, and yet here I am, baking her a fucking birthday cake. Sometimes I wonder if I like to torture myself.

"I did, but just know I've never been much of a baker, so I'm not sure how good it's going to be."

"It's the thought that counts, Brooks. This is so special. Thank you so much." I hear the waver in her voice, and I hope she doesn't start crying. This was supposed to be a happy moment to celebrate her. The last thing I want to do is make her cry.

I nudge the bag closer to her. "Here. Open your gift."

She rummages through the tissue paper before pulling out a square box. My heart is beating annoyingly fast as I watch her open it. I don't give gifts to people often. Zach usually just wants money. My parents just want my time. I usually get Harper something on her birthday and Christmas, but it's always pretty generic. Aspen deserves something special.

Now that she's opening it, I'm nervous that she won't like it.

She opens the box and gasps.

"Brooks…" She pulls out the belt buckle I had custom-made for her. It's a smaller one, nothing like the big ones I wear. It's got a horse with a few flowers around it and her name engraved in it. The outside has a border of sapphire gems for her birthstone.

"You're gettin' so good on the horse that I, uh, figured you needed to look the part."

Her voice cracks as she repeats my name. "This is incredible. Thank you. Really. Thank you."

"Of course."

"Can I… Can I hug you?" she asks. The question doesn't help my heart rate. It feels like my chest is about to explode. Unfortunately, I can't seem to deny Aspen anything.

I open my arms wide, and she walks right into them. I wrap myself around her, holding her close. I've been trying to keep her at a distance these last few weeks. It's been tough to say the least. This hug, feeling her against me, means just as much to me as it probably does to her.

"Happy birthday, darlin'."

"Thanks, Brooks."

I hold her for longer than I should, just feeling her in my arms. She fits perfectly against me.

She pulls back and looks up at me. "Can I ask for one more thing for my birthday?"

"Sure."

"Can I have a kiss? Just one. I promise it won't mean anything."

That's a lie, and we both know it. It'll mean something to me. But I can't say no to this woman. I know I shouldn't do this. It only adds more hope and complications to our situation.

"One kiss," I say as though I'm trying to tell myself.

She nods.

I swallow hard as I move my hand up to her cheek and back through her curls until I'm cradling her head in my hand. Then, I pull her close. I hesitate only slightly before my lips land on hers.

I could've gone with a quick peck. It might have been easier to walk away after that. But, no. I can't half-ass anything. If I'm only going to get one kiss, it's gonna be the best damn kiss I can give her.

She makes it easy, melting into me, letting me take whatever I want.

Her lips part, and I press my tongue into her mouth. She meets me stroke for stroke. Kissing her feels like an out-of-body experience. Like this is where I'm meant to be.

She lets out a breathy moan, which sends a shock straight through me, bringing me back to reality. I drop my hand from her head and slowly separate myself from her.

Her eyes take several seconds to reopen, and when they finally fall on me, the lust in them is overwhelming.

I shouldn't have kissed her. I was doing so well staying away, pretending like that first kiss never happened. And now, because of my inability to say no to her, I'm going to have to start all over again.

"I…" I start to say something, but nothing seems appropriate.

She swallows and squares her shoulders. "Thank you. That might be the best gift I've ever gotten."

She turns from me and starts collecting her things on the counter. I know she's trying to make this not awkward between us, and I appreciate it more than she knows.

"Can I take the cake?" she asks.

"Oh, yeah. Let me get the lid."

I grab the plastic lid from the other counter and seal it up for her.

"Are you going out tonight to celebrate?" I ask even though I don't really want to know. It just makes this harder.

"Yeah. I'm meeting Jazz and a few of her friends at Roadside later. Dawson is taking me to dinner first."

"So things are going well with you two?" I ask.

She shrugs noncommittally. "Yeah, I suppose. I mean, he knows I'm not trying to rush into anything. But he's fun to hang out with."

I want to ask what else she's doing with Dawson but stop myself before I make everything worse. I saw her birth control. I'm not an idiot. They're both young and attractive. Of course they're doing other things.

"Good. That's good. Well, happy birthday and have fun."

I walk her to the door and open it for her.

"Brooks?"

"Hmm?"

She turns and looks at me. "Tell me not to go."

Don't go.

Don't go.

Don't go.

I swallow hard and shake my head just slightly, but it's enough to see the disappointment flash across her eyes. "Go have fun, Aspen. Enjoy your birthday."

She nods. I know she doesn't like my answer, but I have to believe she understands it.

She walks off, and I shut the door and lean my head against it. I just sent her off to be with another man.

Fuck, I'm going to be thinking about that kiss for the rest of my life.

CHAPTER 25

Aspen

IT'S BEEN two days since my birthday. Which means it's been two days since the most incredible kiss of my life. I knew it was risky asking for that. I also expected him to say no. Needless to say, when he pulled me close and looked at me like he was going to devour me, I thought I was dreaming.

I could barely think straight all night. Dinner with Dawson was awkward because I think he's catching on that I'm not as interested in him as he is in me. I'm trying, really trying, to like him, but I can't stop thinking about Brooks. Even when we were all at Roadside, I kept watching the door like he'd walk in and sweep me off my feet.

It's stupid.

He told me we can't be anything else. I'm trying to respect that, but it's so hard when I want so much more with him.

Thankfully, I've managed to keep my cool around him. He brings me dinner every night. He knocks on my door and hands me a Tupperware full of whatever he made that night. It's always delicious. I can't even explain how nice it feels to have someone take care of me for a change.

We both keep things more than professional at work. We're hardly ever alone together, which is probably for the best.

But that changes one day while I'm working on his budget for the Blue Haven Halloween Festival. Brooks walks up to where I'm working and closes my laptop. "You wanna go see the newly renovated guest cabin?"

"I would love to!" Not only do I want to see the renovations that Jazz has been going on about, but I'd also do just about anything to spend time with Brooks.

"Let's go."

I slip my laptop into a nearby drawer and follow Brooks out of the lodge and down through the walking paths to the guest cabins. Our hands brush more than once. I wish he would just reach out and take my hand, but I know that's not going to happen.

"Are you renovating all of the cabins?" I ask as he pulls out the key to the one we're seeing.

"Eventually, yes. But we're starting with the ones that needed a little more TLC first."

He opens the door and ushers me inside. I haven't been to the cabins since my initial tour with Brooks all those months ago. I remember them being pretty bare bones, but this one has been modernized.

"Wow," I gasp, looking around. "This looks so nice."

The kitchenette has been upgraded. The walls are still natural wood, but the furniture is new, and there's a colorful rug in the center and beautiful artwork hanging over the couch.

"We're still going to leave a few cabins as they were because we have plenty of guests who come here for the traditional cabin feel and escape. But for some of the new guests with younger families, we wanted to make it an escape but still be comfortable and what they're used to at home and other potential hotels."

"This truly looks fantastic, Brooks. I think this will bring in a lot of younger families. Have you updated the website yet?"

I turn to find him watching me, arms crossed over his chest, smiling at me.

"What?"

He shakes his head. "Nothing. I just like watching you."

I bite my lip to keep from smiling too big.

"We haven't updated the website yet, no. I think Harper was going to work on that next week."

"I can help with that, if she's too busy."

"I'll let her know."

He's standing across the room from me, but I still feel his pull. My stupid heart is fluttering. It takes everything in me not to walk over to him.

"Do you wanna see the upstairs?" he asks.

"Yes," I croak out. Anything to get me out of this trance he puts me in every time we're together.

I turn and force myself up the stairs. I figure it will give me a moment to get myself together, but then I hear footsteps and realize that Brooks is following me. Of course he is.

The upstairs is a loft area with a large bed and a small couch. Both are way nicer quality than what was in here before.

With this being one of the smaller units, Brooks has to slide behind me to get onto the landing. He puts his hand on my lower back to keep me steady, but once we're both up there, he doesn't remove it.

"What do you think?"

I swallow and pretend like I'm not extremely aware of his hand on me. "It's so nice, Brooks. Really. You guys did an awesome job."

"I'm glad you like it."

I look over at him and smile. "You trying to impress me or something?"

"Your opinion matters to me, yes."

My mouth suddenly goes dry. "Why's that?"

His gaze drops from my eyes to my lips. Oh my god, is he going to kiss me?

"Because you're important to me." His voice is low and gravely, and it makes my breath hitch.

I'm important to Brooks Calloway? Until he said it, I never realized how much it would mean for someone to say that to me.

He leans in ever so slightly as his eyes dip to my lips and then… the door of the cabin bursts open.

We jump apart, and I inhale deeply to calm my nerves before peering over the railing to see Jazz coming in.

"Hey!" I shout down at her.

She jumps and looks up. "Jesus Christ! You scared the shit out of me. I didn't think anyone was here."

I laugh and make my way downstairs with Brooks following an appropriate distance behind me.

"Sorry. Brooks was showing me the renovations."

"Ah, right." Jazz looks from me to Brooks and narrows her eyes. I haven't told her about anything that has happened with Brooks. She stopped asking after I started hanging out with Dawson more. But she looks suspicious today, and I can only imagine what her interrogation will be like later.

"It looks really good," I say, trying to ease some of the awkwardness.

"It sure does," Jazz agrees with a smirk on her face.

Brooks gently touches my shoulder. "I'm gonna head back to the lodge. I'll see you later."

I nod, a little disappointed I won't be walking back with him, but it'll be good for us to have some space after that moment we just shared. "Alright. See you in a bit."

He turns to Jazz. "Have a good afternoon, Jasmine."

"You too, bossman."

Once Brooks is a safe distance from the cabin, Jazz blurts out, "What the fuck did I walk in on?"

"Uh, a cabin tour?"

"Don't play dumb with me, Aspen."

"I'm not!" But my voice comes out way too high. She knows I'm lying.

"Are you messing around with Brooks?"

"No! I told you I won't do that." The lie feels sour on my tongue.

"I know what you said, but I also know what I saw."

"And what exactly did you see?"

"The two of you. Alone. You with flushed cheeks."

Oh god. Are my cheeks flushed? I do feel hot. Why does he affect me like this? He said nothing can happen between us. Nothing did happen.

"I—I..."

"Don't lie to me."

"I'm not lying. Nothing happened here today."

"But something has happened previously?" she questions, picking up on my words.

I shrug one shoulder and look away. "Maybe."

She shoves my shoulder. "You dirty skank! Tell me everything!"

"It's nothing really. We've. . . kissed. Twice. That's all."

"Oh my god! I cannot believe this! You kissed Brooks? I am so jealous. How was it? He's a great kisser, isn't he?"

I let out a big breath. "It was so good, Jazz. Like the best kiss I've ever had."

"I knew it! So what's going on then? Are you gonna kiss some more?" She wriggles her eyebrows.

"No. He said we can't, and I agree. It would ruin his relationship with Zach and complicate my position here at Moonlight. It wouldn't be good."

"Oh, come on," she groans. "Those are stupid reasons. Well, I get the whole Zach being his son thing, but Zach isn't a little kid anymore. He's a big boy. He should be able to handle this."

"I know, but I have to respect Brooks's decision, you know?"

Her shoulders slump. "Yeah, but that sucks!"

"Tell me about it."

"So, that's why you haven't done anything with Dawson yet?"

I sigh. "It feels wrong to take it any further when my head is stuck on someone else."

"I get it. Must be so hard having so many guys falling at your feet."

I bark out a laugh. "Oh my god, stop. There has been zero falling."

"Please! Zach is begging for you back. Dawson is being all cute and taking you on dates. And Daddy Brooks is looking at you like he needs you alone in his bedroom stat."

I slump down onto the couch, and Jazz sits next to me. "I don't know how this happened."

"Well, you're hot, babe."

I laugh. "I don't know what to do."

"Why do you need to do anything? We're young. Dawson isn't pushing you for more, is he?" I shake my head. "So keep going on dates with him. Keep kissing Brooks when he's feeling weak. And keep little Calloway far, far away from you. Done!"

"You make it sound so easy."

She shrugs. "We don't need to overcomplicate anything. Just have fun."

"Yeah. I'll try my best."

"And… if anything else happens with Brooks, I'd better be the first to know! I can't believe you didn't tell me!"

"I know, I guess I was just a little embarrassed because he kissed me and then acted like it was a huge mistake."

She scoffs. "Yeah, that's a dick move. But, and not to

make excuses for a man, it sounds like he has a lot of conflicting feelings he's trying to work out."

"I know, I'm trying to be respectful of that, but then he just keeps being so nice to me."

"Damn him and his kindness!"

We both laugh. "This is so messy."

"Life wouldn't be fun if it weren't a little messy," she tells me as she rubs my back to comfort me. "You'll figure it out, though. You don't need to rush."

"Thanks for being such a good friend to me, Jazz."

"One of my many many skills," she teases. "But I've gotta get to work. They want me to finish cleaning up in here before I can head out for the day."

I stand from the couch. "I'll leave you to it then."

I take my time walking back to the lodge. My brain has been running overtime recently, but maybe Jazz is right. I'll just let everything play out and see what happens.

CHAPTER 26

Aspen

I'M off work today and spending my morning eating pancakes with Jazz at the diner in town. I don't typically venture out for breakfast other than the pastries at the coffee shop, but she insisted that I have to try these pancakes. As it turns out, they are pretty good, and they have every flavor of syrup you could ever want.

"So, are we gonna meet up at the fair tonight?" Jazz asks through a mouthful of fluffy pancakes. She went with blueberry syrup on hers.

"Yeah, for sure. I'm meeting Dawson, too, though. Is that ok?"

"Hell yeah. The more the merrier. Owen might make an appearance as well."

I raise my eyebrows. "Wow… a public outing together? Must be getting serious."

"Shut up. You know I don't do serious. But he has tonight off and mentioned that he wanted to go to the fair. I just casually suggested we could meet up. Friends and all that.."

"Yeah… right." I smirk at her, and she rolls her eyes.

I've been told that the fair is a pretty big deal around here. It's one county over but not a long drive. There are rides, games, concerts, and food. I'm pretty excited about it. It sounds like it'll be fun.

"You think Daddy Brooks will be there?" She wriggles her eyebrows at me, and my eyes go wide.

I lean forward. "Keep your voice down." She just laughs. "And I don't know. He hasn't mentioned anything to me about it."

He's been dropping off my dinners and leaving quickly lately, so we haven't spent much one-on-one time together. It feels like he's trying to avoid spending time alone with me. It sucks, but it's probably for the best.

"Well, if you need to sneak off with him, just let me know, and I'll keep Dawson busy."

I wish. "Yeah, not gonna happen."

She laughs, and we continue our breakfast as she tells me what they usually have at the fair. Halfway through her story about the fun house where she got caught making out with a boy in one year, her body goes rigid.

"Ok, don't look now, but be cool," she says in a low voice.

"What?" I start to turn around, but she stops me.

"No. No. Don't look. It's Zach. Maybe he won't see you."

I groan and slump my shoulders a little bit. It feels like forever since I've seen him. Not since I yelled at him in front of Brooks's house. No flower deliveries. No texts or calls. No random pop-ins to my work. It's been nice. I'm not angry at him anymore. I just feel… nothing toward him.

Probably because my attention is focused elsewhere.

At least if Zach does see me now, it's because I just happened to be here. Not because he's seeking me out.

"Who's he with?" I whisper.

"His mom," she says. "They're headed in this direction. He's probably gonna notice you."

"Great," I murmur.

I focus on the last few bites of my pancakes, hoping that he walks right past our table. Unfortunately, I'm not that lucky.

"Aspen? Hey!"

I look up from my plate and try to act totally surprised to see him there. "Oh, hey Zach. Hi, Lacey. Good to see you two."

His mom looks at me and glares as she says, "Hello."

"You two having breakfast?" Zach asks the obvious.

"Yep."

"Are you going to the fair tonight?"

"We are," Jazz answers for me.

"Cool. Maybe I'll see you there then?"

"Yeah, maybe," I answer noncommittally.

He looks at me for a minute as if he's hoping for me to say something else, but I stay quiet.

"Ok, well, enjoy your breakfast. See you later."

I nod. "Bye."

He walks off to find a table with his mom.

"Ok, that wasn't too bad," Jazz says.

"Yeah, but now I've got to be worried about seeing him later," I groan.

"We won't give him a chance to ruin our night. Don't worry, girl."

I laugh, and we finish before quickly exiting the diner.

———

The fair is like nothing I've ever seen before. It's basically a small theme park. There are flashing lights everywhere, and we're hit with the scent of sugar and fried food as soon as we walk through the gates. I can hear country music coming from the speakers next to the stage, but I can't remember who they said was performing tonight.

Dawson grabs my hand, and we start through the place. It's crowded, and several times we have to push our way through groups of people. He buys us fried Oreos and a funnel cake after we eat a corndog and freshly squeezed lemonade.

"You ready to ride some rides?" Dawson asks once we've finished the funnel cake.

I grimace. "We probably should've ridden rides before we ate all that food."

Dawson laughs. "Don't worry. We'll start off slow. Let's do bumper cars!"

Ok, we must have different definitions of slow.

I follow him to the bumper cars, which ends up being really fun. Then we meet up with Jazz and Owen and start riding some of the other rides. I'm very dizzy and a touch nauseous by the time we finish our third ride. I step out of the attraction exit, looking for a bench to sit down on, when I walk directly into someone.

"Oh my gosh, I'm so sorry!" I say as strong hands grab my arms to steady me.

I look up into very familiar eyes.

"Brooks," I whisper. It seems I can't get away from him even if I'm actively trying.

"You alright?"

"Yeah, just lost my footing there," I say. He slowly lowers his hands as Dawson walks up beside me.

"Hey, Mr. Calloway. How're you?"

"Doing good, kid. You?"

"Good. Just out here getting Aspen all dizzy, I guess," he says with a laugh.

Harper is with Brooks. I hadn't noticed her standing there at first because I was so focused on him, but my attention is diverted when Jazz starts asking them to go on the big coaster.

Now, when she says big, it's not *that* big. But it's big enough that it has me questioning the safety of it as part of a traveling fair.

Harper immediately agrees to a ride, so Jazz pulls her along with us.

"Guys, I am not riding that," I tell them, needing a break to settle my stomach. "I'll wait for you at the exit."

"Are you sure?" Dawson asks. "I can hold your hand."

I know he's trying to be cute and flirty, but holding his hand would not save me in the slightest if something malfunctioned. "Yeah, I'm sure. I'm feeling dizzy after that last one, so it's probably best if I chill for a minute."

"I'll stay with her," Brooks offers. "I'll make sure she doesn't run off."

Dawson smiles, probably thinking he's leaving me with a trusted adult. How on Earth would he know that he's leaving me alone with the one man I can't stop thinking about? The one man who is the entire reason why I haven't taken my relationship with Dawson any further.

Jazz shoots me a knowing look, but thankfully doesn't make any of the comments I know she's dying to get out.

"You don't wanna ride?" Dawson asks Brooks.

"Brooks hates these things," Harper interjects. "I can never get him to ride with me."

"Well, you can ride with me then, Harper," Dawson offers, and Brooks and I watch as the four of them go stand in line for the ride.

Brooks and I find an open bench near the exit to sit on and wait. Unfortunately, he keeps an appropriate distance between us on the bench.

"Having a good date?" he asks after a few uncomfortable moments of silence.

"Yeah, it's pretty good. I didn't realize you were going to be here tonight."

"I try to avoid these things if I can, but Harper convinced me to come."

I know that Brooks and Harper are close, and I know he's told me that they're only friends and nothing more, but the thought of them together is always at the back of my mind. She knows him better than anyone, and deep down, I think I'm jealous because I want to be that person. I want to be the one to convince Brooks to go out. I want to know what Brooks likes at each restaurant in town. I want to know all of his embarrassing stories. I want to know everything about him.

That jealousy bubbles up inside me until I find myself asking, "Would you have come tonight if I had asked you?"

Brooks turns his head to meet my eyes. "I think we've established that I can't say no to you."

"You've said no about one thing," I remind him. Us. Taking this further. Being together. The biggest thing of all that he's said no to.

"Yeah, and it's killing me every single day."

His admission sends a chill down my spine, which doesn't go unnoticed.

"Are you cold? Here. Take my jacket." Brooks slides out of his jacket and hands it to me.

I'm not cold, but I'm also not going to turn down a chance to be wrapped in his warmth. Even if it's just a piece of clothing.

"Thanks." I wrap the jacket around me. "So you don't like riding the rides?"

"No. It's not for me. If I'm riding anything, it's gonna be a horse."

I laugh. "Well, you are good at that."

"So are you. We haven't been out in awhile."

"I didn't think you wanted to be alone with me," I admit sheepishly.

"All I want is to be alone with you, darlin', but what I want isn't what's best for either of us. At least if we're out on the trail, I know I won't try anything."

I smirk. "Never had outdoor sex, Brooks? You're missing out."

He chokes out a laugh, and I swear a slight blush appears on his cheeks. "I try to be a gentleman. That typically doesn't include sleeping with women on riding trails."

"Hm. That's a shame."

"Aspen…" he warns.

I shrug. "What? I'm just saying you might need to live a little."

"I live plenty, thank you very much."

That sentence shuts me right up. I haven't seen Brooks with any other women since I've worked on the ranch, but that doesn't mean he hasn't been with any. The thought of him with someone else makes me want to throw up. I wonder if this is how he feels every time he sees me with Dawson. If it is, it makes my heart hurt for him.

"I'm sure you do," I say quietly before I return my focus to our little group making their way through the line. Dawson spots me and gives a little wave. I smile and wave back, but really, I'm contemplating whether I should get up and run. Get out of this town as fast as I can. It feels like everywhere I turn, my heart is breaking or I'm making the wrong decision.

"You ok?" Brooks asks, noticing the change in my demeanor.

"Yep. All good."

I don't think he believes me, but he doesn't press me.

After our friends all ride the coaster, we meet them at the exit.

"How was it?" I ask Dawson.

"Just as good as last year," he says with a laugh. He notices my jacket. "Did you get cold? I'm sorry, I should've left you my jacket."

"Brooks is always there to save the day," Jazz says. I immediately glare at her and feel Brooks's eyes on me. Shit. I shouldn't have told her everything that happened, but I had to talk to someone.

"So, where to next?" I ask, trying to move past this awkward moment.

"Wanna do the Ferris wheel?" Dawson asks me.

No. "Sure."

"We're gonna go get some food," Harper announces, taking Brooks along with her. He doesn't say anything as they leave us, but I wish he would stay. I wish he were the one taking me on the Ferris wheel.

I link my arm with Dawson's as we head toward the Ferris wheel. I really hate these things. Who wants to be stuck in a swinging bucket that high up off the ground? Not me. But I do it anyway because I know it will make Dawson happy, and unfortunately for me, I'm a people pleaser.

When we get to the top, Dawson leans in to kiss me. It's not the first time we've kissed. I was hoping it would get better with time, but I still feel absolutely nothing when his lips touch mine.

And I know it's because I'm kissing the wrong man.

CHAPTER 27

Brooks

SHE KISSED HIM. I saw it with my own two eyes, and it knocked the wind right out of me.

I let it ruin my entire mood until Harper finally gives up and says we can leave. I feel shitty about the way I acted, but I couldn't stay there and watch Aspen kiss someone else all night. Even when I tried to focus on something else, my eyes were always searching for her curly head of hair, wondering what she was doing.

It's pathetic, really.

Even after I got home, I sat inside by the window so I could keep an eye out for when she got home. I could say I just wanted to make sure she got home ok, but really I wanted to make sure she actually came home and didn't stay the night with *him*.

I didn't go to bed until I knew she was home. Which was late.

So now I'm in my office in a shitty mood while I work through a pile of emails I've been avoiding for the past week. I keep getting Aspen's friendly yet pushy emails—*Following up on this* or *Please respond at your earliest convenience.*

I can't respond because all my stupid brain can think of is her.

There's a knock on my office door.

"Come in."

Aspen walks in looking nice and refreshed and not pissed off and tired like I am, which only pisses me off even more.

"Morning, Brooks. Here's your coffee and your jacket from last night. Thank you for letting me borrow it."

Why does she have to be so nice? And so fucking beautiful?

"No problem. You can just put it there." I point to the chair, and she lays it down.

"You got home late last night," I say, sounding like an overbearing father. Can I not just be calm for five seconds?

"I didn't realize I had a curfew," she says with a smirk.

"You don't," I say quickly. "Of course you don't. Just noticed you got home late."

"We all went out for a drink after the fair," she explains.

"Hmm."

"Why? Were you worried I went home with someone else?"

Yes. "Nope. You can do whatever you want."

"That's right. I *can* do whatever I want. Because your son broke my heart and you're well on your way to doing the same."

Wait. What?

"Aspen—"

She holds up her hand. "No. I don't want to hear it again. I know why you won't do anything with me. I understand it. But I cannot sit around pining over another Calloway man."

"I know that."

"I'm trying my best to move on. To get you out of my head. Dawson is nice. He's responsible. He's fun and attentive. He should be the perfect guy for me. I'm trying to focus my attention on someone besides you."

I grit my teeth and try to remain calm. "I understand that, Aspen."

"Really? Because it seems like you're judging me for staying out late with a man who has been nothing but kind to me."

"Fine, Aspen. Do whatever you want. I don't care." I'm not mad at her. I'm mad at myself for caring so much. I'm mad that she's right. I am being unfair. I've said that nothing can happen between us, but every time we're near each other, I want her all over again.

"Fine."

"Fine."

She turns on her heels and storms out of my office. Not even a second later, Harper appears in the doorway looking very confused.

"Everything ok?" she asks slowly.

Shit. I wonder how much of that she heard. "Yeah. All good."

"You sure? Aspen looked pretty upset..." She looks from me to the hallway.

"She's fine. Do you need something?" I snap at her.

"Whoa. Someone's in a bad mood. Is there… something going on between you two?"

Obviously not now. "No," I state firmly.

"Are you sure? Because if there was, you know you could tell me, right?"

Harper has always been kind to me. We've been through so much together over the years, and she's my right-hand woman here at the ranch. If I ever needed to get something off my chest, she would be my go-to.

But I can't find it in me to admit that I have feelings for Aspen. I mean, she's over a decade younger than me, and Zach… God, Zach would never forgive me if he found out what's happened between Aspen and me.

No, I need to keep all of this to myself.

"Yeah, I know, Harper," I say, much calmer than before. "But nothing is going on there."

She sighs. "Alright. I was gonna see if you wanted to grab lunch later at that new place down past Fourth Street, but I don't really wanna go if you're gonna be like this."

"No, let's plan on it. I need to go into town anyway." I stand from my desk. "I'm gonna go ride for a bit. Text me when you're ready to go."

"Ok." She looks at me strangely, but I don't stop to try to figure out why. I need to get out of here, and I do my best thinking on the back of a horse.

———

I spent the rest of the day avoiding Aspen. Childish, yes, but necessary. I don't know what's gotten into me. I've never been this messed up over a woman. Maybe it's because she's the one woman I can't have. Maybe it's because I actually enjoy being around her. Maybe it's because it feels like she's the perfect woman for me but we've been thrown into a shitty circumstance. I don't know.

What I do know is that I want her to be mine. I don't know how to stop wanting her. No matter how hard I try, she's always on my mind.

So that evening when I see her step out of her cabin with an overnight bag on her shoulder, I freak out.

She's trying to forget me like I'm trying to forget her, but I know deep down that I don't want her to forget me. Which means I have to stop her.

She's going to him.

Blood thunders in my ears. I can't let her go.

Fuck it.

I yank my front door open and step out into the slight drizzle that's just started.

"Aspen!" I call out to her.

She stops and looks over at me. "What do you want?" she yells back, her voice laced with annoyance.

"Don't go."

It's what I should've said the first time she told me to tell her not to go. I'm an idiot for waiting so long.

"What?" she asks after several seconds of neither one of us saying anything.

"Don't go," I repeat a little louder.

The rain is starting to come down harder now, but I can see her slowly blink as she processes what I'm saying.

She takes a step toward me, and I do the same to her.

"Are you saying this out of jealousy?" she asks.

"I'm saying this because I'm done pretending that I don't want you. I'm done pretending that there's nothing between us. I can't stop thinking about you."

She runs at me, and I open my arms, ready for her to make the jump. I lift her up, her legs wrapping around me as her mouth crashes down on mine.

It's happening.

It's finally happening, and I'm not going to stop it this time.

I walk us back to my house since we're both soaking wet from the rain. Once we're inside, she drops her bag to the floor, and I gently set her down, but I don't break our kiss.

She's mine now. All mine.

I grab the bottom of her wet shirt and pull it up over her head, dropping it down on the floor.

She does the same to my shirt as we slowly make our way to my bedroom. I unhook her bra and let it fall in the hallway.

We're walking too slow for my liking, so I pick her up again and finish the walk back to my room, placing her down on my bed. I kiss down her neck, all the way down to her nipple. I pull it into my mouth and suck.

She moans loudly, and the sound goes straight to my dick.

"Goddamn, you're perfect," I murmur as I move to her other nipple.

She reaches for my belt buckle, and I let her undo it. Her hand presses against my chest until I climb off of her so she can get my jeans off.

She unbuttons my jeans and pushes them all the way down with my boxers. She watches me carefully as I step out of my jeans and kick them away.

She starts to lower to her knees, but I stop her. "Darlin', you don't ever need to be on your knees for me. I'm the one who should be worshipping you."

In one swift movement, I've got her back up and on the bed, tugging off her wet leggings. She's completely bare in front of me, and it's the most beautiful thing I've ever seen.

I drop to my knees and trail slow kisses up her thighs. I blow gently on her pussy, which makes her wriggle.

"Brooks, please."

"Hmm. You want me to eat your pussy, Aspen?"

"Please!"

I give her center one long lick before I zone in on her clit. My fingers play at her entrance. She's already so wet for me, so I easily slide two fingers inside her. She squeezes them tightly, and I can already imagine how my cock is going to feel inside her.

"Oh my god!" She grabs onto my comforter.

I keep licking and sucking until her legs are shaking around my head.

"Brooks, I'm gonna come!"

I don't stop what I'm doing to tell her I've been dying to have her come on my tongue for months. I keep my momentum steady until she cries out my name again.

When I pull away, I focus on her swollen lips and

flushed cheeks, and all I can think is that she's finally all mine.

I crawl up her body until my cock is perfectly lined up with her entrance. "You're sure about this?" I ask. "There's no turning back after this."

"I've always been sure about this, Brooks."

Yeah, that's right. I'm the one who's been an idiot.

My eyes close as I press inside. She's so fucking tight. It feels too good.

Once I'm fully seated inside her, I open my eyes. She's watching me carefully.

"Are you ok?" I ask.

"Yes, I just need you to move."

"I just need a second."

It's been so long since I've had sex, and she feels too damn good. The last thing I want is to embarrass myself by coming too soon. Once I steady my breathing, I start moving. Slowly at first, but then I get into a rhythm. She lifts one knee closer to her chest, which helps me get a deeper angle.

"Holy fuck, Aspen. Too good. It's too good."

"I know. I know!" she cries.

Her tits bounce with every thrust, and I find myself absolutely entranced with this woman. The way her mouth opens in an O when I hit deep inside her. The way her back arches off the bed. The way her eyes roll back. The way we fit together. Everything about her is perfect.

I feel myself getting closer to the edge. I know I'm going to come any second. It's in this moment that I realize I've fucked up because I forgot a condom.

I pull out of her quickly and finish on her stomach.

As I catch my breath, I stare down at her in pure amaze-ment. It's never been like that before. Sure, I love sex. Who doesn't? But with Aspen, it felt like so much more.

She's ruined me forever. And I think I might be ok with that.

CHAPTER 28

Aspen

AFTER BROOKS CLEANS ME UP, he pulls us both under the covers and wraps his arms around me. I can't believe I'm finally here: in his bed, in his arms. Right where I wanted to be.

"So what made you change your mind?" I ask quietly after a few moments of silence.

"I saw you with your overnight bag and knew you were going to him. I couldn't let that happen," he admits.

I bite the corner of my lip to keep from laughing. "So you were jealous that I was going to Dawson's?"

He sighs, and his breath tickles my neck. "Yeah, darlin'. I was jealous. Does that make you happy?"

"Very," I say with a smile. "But you should know that I wasn't going to Dawson's."

He props himself up on his elbow to look at me. "What?"

"Yeah, I, uh, actually ended things with him earlier today."

"Why?"

"Because it wasn't fair to him. I knew I didn't want anything with him, and I was tired of trying to pretend to feel something."

"So where were you going then?" he asks.

"Jazz and I were gonna have a sleepover at her place."

He laughs and drops his head back to the pillow.

"If I had known that all it would take for you to give in was to schedule a sleepover with my friend, I would've done it sooner."

"Alright, get out," he teases.

"Too late. I'm here now."

"Yes, you are. And I'm never letting you go now."

He brushes a piece of hair off my face and then leans down to kiss me.

When he pulls back, he says, "You should probably text her and tell her you won't be attending that sleepover."

"Oh?"

"Yeah, you're not leaving this house tonight."

I smile up at him before I slide out of bed to find my phone and then quickly climb back in next to him. I have several texts from Jazz asking where I am.

Me: Hey, sorry. I'm not going to be able to make it.

Jazz: Uh, you better have a damn good reason.

Me: *sends selfie of me in Brooks's bed with his arm visible*

Jazz: NO FUCKING WAY

Jazz: Ok, that's a good reason.

Jazz: As you were, my friend. Can't wait for details

Me: <3

"She's been kinda rooting for us this whole time," I explain when I see him reading the texts.

"Really? Didn't know we had a team behind us."

"Surprise, I guess."

He pulls me closer. "We should probably keep this quiet until I figure out a way to tell Zach."

I swallow. I knew this was coming, but I still hate hearing it. I don't want this to be a secret, but I understand Brooks has a responsibility to his son. I never wanted to come between them, and I hope Zach will find it in his heart to accept this.

"Ok. I can do it with you if you think it will help."

"No, it should be me. You're such a sensitive topic for him, so I'm not expecting a good outcome."

"I'm sorry."

He kisses my forehead. "Nothing for you to be sorry about, darlin'. I made this decision. I can handle the consequences."

"I know, I just hate that it has to be like this."

"Listen, if it weren't for Zach, I never would've met you. So, I'm not sorry for the way things played out. It's just unfortunate that he's still hoping for a chance to rekindle his relationship with you."

"You think he still is?" I ask. He's left me alone for awhile now. I was kinda hoping he'd moved on.

"Yeah. But let's not talk about this anymore tonight. Tonight is about us. And I'm taking full advantage of it."

He kisses down my neck, his scruff tickling me as he goes. His kisses cover every inch of my body. I've never felt more worshipped than I do right now. Brooks isn't trying to get a quick fuck. He's trying to make sure I enjoy every moment of this. My body craves his. My skin gets hotter and hotter with each kiss he gives me. Just when I think I can't take anymore, he's pulling me on top of him. I straddle his hips and look down at his impressive erection.

"Let's test out your new riding skills, darlin'."

"Yes, sir."

Then I slide down on him, filling myself with his cock.

———

Brooks wasn't kidding when he said I was his for the night, and he definitely took full advantage. After our second time, we both jumped in the shower. Then he fed me, and we cuddled until we both fell asleep.

That wasn't enough for Brooks, though. Nope. He woke me up at two in the morning by kissing my neck, his hands trailing down my naked body. I let my legs fall open for him, and he made the wake-up call well worth it.

Now, I'm waking up, cuddled up in his bed, but he's nowhere to be seen. The sun is shining through the curtains, so I know it's probably mid-morning by now. I slowly slide out of his bed and find one of his T-shirts to throw on. I quickly brush my teeth with the toothbrush that I brought in my overnight bag and make my way out to the kitchen, where Brooks is cooking up some French toast.

When he hears me, he turns and does a double-take when he sees me in his shirt and only his shirt.

"Damn, baby, do you look good in my shirt."

I walk over to him and wrap my arms around his back. He's shirtless and in those gray sweatpants I love so much.

"Good morning," I say groggily.

"Morning, beautiful. You want some coffee?"

"Yes, please. You're making breakfast?" I unwrap my arms from him and make my way to the barstool while he pours me a cup of coffee.

"Yeah, of course. It's the least I could do after all the exercise I put you through last night."

"I'm pretty sure I've got beard burn on my thighs," I tease.

"Good."

The deep baritone of his voice sends a shiver down my spine. This man has me feeling things I've never felt before. He looks at me like he wants to consume me. And I think I want to be consumed. Especially by Brooks.

He plates up my breakfast while I sip my coffee that he made exactly the way I like. How is the one man I'm not supposed to want the perfect man for me?

He sits next to me while we eat.

"Got any plans today?" he asks me.

"Not really. Since I'm off today, I might try to find Jazz to apologize for ditching her last night." He starts to say something, but I don't let him. "Not that it wasn't totally worth it, but I'd be a shitty friend if I didn't try to make it up to her. She's the only real friend I've ever had, and I don't want to ruin it."

"You didn't have any friends back in Atlanta?"

I shake my head. "No, not really. I think that's why I latched onto Zach so quickly. He gave me attention. He wanted to hang out with me. It felt nice to have someone want me around."

He looks down at his plate when I mention Zach's name. I know it's eating him up inside, and I hate that it's because of me. I really hope they'll be able to work through this.

"What about back in Florida?"

"No. I had acquaintances and things, but no one I really confided in or would have sleepovers with or anything. And no one I still talk to." It feels like a freaking sob story, but honestly, I wouldn't change it. I didn't want to be friends with most of the people at my high school because they were all too judgmental.

"So you're saying I ruined your first friend sleepover?"

I smirk in his direction. "Yeah, but I'm sure whatever Jazz and I were going to do wouldn't have been as fun as what we did."

He chuckles. "Good."

"So what are your plans today?" I ask, trying to get the conversation off of me.

"I've gotta go do a little work in the stables with Beck, but tonight I want you here with me."

I try to hold back my smile, but I'm excited that he wants me to come back again tonight. I was worried we would wake up this morning and he would've changed his mind.

"I think I can be available."

"Oh, you think?" He puts two fingers under my chin and turns my face toward his before he leans in for a soft kiss.

"Yeah, I can be available if there's more of that."

"There will definitely be more of that and some other stuff too."

"Ok. Then I'll come over again tonight."

"Good."

He gives me another kiss before we finish eating. I watch him change into those damn jeans I love so much, and he kisses me goodbye before he heads out for work.

CHAPTER 29
Brooks

I RIDE up to the stables, ready to get to work with Beck. He's just getting back from a ride on one of the horses, so I wait for him to get her back in her stall before we start fixing the fence on the round pen. It's a pretty simple fix and shouldn't take all day. We've got to tear down a section of the fence that has seen better days and replace it with new, sturdier wood.

I used to spend so much time out here when I was younger. Before I took over the ranch, the stables were my second home. I've ridden around this ring so many times and taught hundreds of kids to ride here, too. Even Zach.

He was so excited the first time his mom agreed that I could teach him to ride. It's one of my favorite memories with him. He was a natural. Wasn't even scared of how big the horse was or anything. He just wanted to ride.

After that, we rode together a lot until he decided he wanted nothing to do with the ranch. It still kills me that he pulled away from me so much, but I've tried my hardest to accept his decision.

I'm afraid he's only going to pull away more when he learns about Aspen and me. I know I fucked up, and I know he's going to be pissed, but there's something between us that I can't deny anymore.

It's more than a physical attraction. It feels so right being with her. And last night… fuck. It was amazing. Better than I ever thought it could be. And when I woke up and saw her lying next to me, her hand gently resting on the pillow by my head like she just wanted to be close to me, I felt like everything was perfect. In that moment, in our little bubble, nothing else mattered.

I want her to feel important. I want her to know that I want her. As much as I wish I could've stayed away for the sake of my relationship with my son, she makes me happier than I've been in a long time.

Which becomes embarrassingly obvious when Beck calls me out on it after we've been working for a few hours.

"You seem to be in a good mood today," he says as he hammers a nail into the two-by-four.

"Why do you say that?"

"Uh, you're whistling, man."

Oh, shit. Was I? I hadn't even noticed. "Oh. Guess I just slept good last night."

He laughs. "Whatever you say, man."

"What's so funny?" Harper comes around the stable doors with two bags from the sandwich shop in town. "Thought you two might be hungry."

We drop our hammers and walk over to her. Even

though it's the end of September and there's a slight breeze in the air now, we've still worked up a sweat rebuilding this fence.

"Thanks, Harp," I say, taking one of the bags from her.

"Brooks here has been whistling while he works," Beck tells her in answer to her original question. I was hoping we could all move on from that, but I guess not.

Harper looks at me with furrowed brows. Apparently, I've never whistled while I worked. Note to self to never do it again. "Did you get laid last night or something?"

Beck laughs again. "That's what I was thinking."

"What the fuck? No," I say quickly, hoping they don't pick up on the lie. "Just slept good."

I wonder how badly they would judge me if they found out what I actually did last night. And with who. Would they tell me I'm a terrible father? I already know I am, but to have someone confirm it to my face would hurt more than I care to admit.

"You slept good?" Harper repeats. Yeah, she definitely doesn't believe me.

"Am I not allowed to be in a good mood? What's with the third degree? It's not like I'm always a grumpy asshole."

Harper holds her hands up in surrender. "Alright, alright. Calm down. As your friends, we're just looking out for you. If you're happy about something, we want to be happy with you." She gives me a pointed look, and I know she's on to me. The seed is planted in her mind about Aspen and me, and she thinks she knows what's going on.

I wish I could talk to her about it. Harper has always

been my sounding board when I need it, but this is something I need to handle on my own. At least until I can wrap my own head around it.

"I appreciate it, but really, there's nothing to report right now."

"Alright. Well, I wanted to see if you wanted to go to town tonight. Maybe catch a movie or something," she asks as we all sit down at the picnic table by the stables.

"Can't tonight."

"Why? What're you doing?" At this moment, I'm regretting letting Harper in on every aspect of my life. She knows I hardly ever have any plans after work. Most of the time, I sit in my house on my own. She always tries to get me to go out, which I normally appreciate, but today, it's getting on my nerves. Now I've got to come up with a believable lie.

"I've got a lot of laundry to do." Dammit. I could've come up with something better than that.

"You're gonna sit in your house and do laundry all night?" she asks skeptically. Beck chuckles next to her. This is one of those times I wish I were better at lying.

"Yes. I've been putting it off. So, unless you all want me wandering around the ranch in my underwear, I've got to do it."

"The ladies might like it," Beck quips.

"Alright, Brooks. Have fun with your *laundry* then." She turns to Beck. "What about you, Beck? You busy tonight?"

"Nope. Free as a bird. Jade is with her mom tonight."

"Cool. Text me when you're done here, and we'll meet up."

"Yes, ma'am."

Harper stands from the table and gives me one more disapproving look before heading back toward the lodge.

"Thanks for lunch!" I call out after her.

"I put it on your credit card!" she yells back.

I roll my eyes. Of course she did. Not that I care.

"So, how's Jade doing?" I ask Beck after realizing I haven't gotten an update on her recently. Beck has been a single dad for a few years now. I've seen him struggle in the same ways I used to when Zach was little. I've always tried to do whatever I could to help Beck when he was getting on his feet, including giving him a place to live here on the ranch.

"Man, she's great. I swear she's growing so fast. I'll bring her by the lodge next time I've got her to say hey."

"I'd like that."

He goes on to tell me how Jade is doing in pre-school and what she's interested in. He smiles the entire time he talks about her. It's great to see one of my friends so happy. I'm glad his shot at fatherhood is going so much better than mine did.

We finish our lunch and then get back to work on the fence. After a few more hours of hammering and tightening and making sure everything is lined up, we're done with the section we were replacing.

We clean up our work area, and then I head back home. Aspen's car is gone, so I head inside to take a shower and straighten up a bit. Her scent still lingers in my bedroom, and I realize I miss her. It's been less than ten hours and I miss her. I have it so bad for her. There's no denying that.

Now I've got to figure out a way to tell Zach without losing my son forever.

A little while later, I look out the front window and see Aspen's car. I waste no time walking over there and knocking on her door.

"Hey, what's up?" she says when she answers the door. Her curls are down today, and her cheeks are pink even though I can tell she has very little makeup on. She's fucking gorgeous, and now she's all mine.

"What are you doing?" I ask, leaning against the door frame.

"Oh, I was just hanging out a little bit."

"Why aren't you hanging out at my place?"

She shrugs her shoulders. "I thought you might want some time by yourself. I don't want to overstay my welcome."

"Not possible. And I don't want alone time. I want to spend all my time with you."

She tries to hold back her smile, but it doesn't work. Good. I want her to be happy about spending time with me.

"Now, let's go." I bend down and pick her up, putting her over my shoulder fireman-style. I give her ass a nice little smack.

"Brooks!"

"Everything ok back there?" I ask from over my shoulder.

"I can walk, you know," she calls back.

"Yeah, but this is more fun."

She laughs, but I don't set her down until we're back inside my house.

CHAPTER 30

Aspen

FINGERTIPS TICKLE the side of my face. I inhale deeply and know exactly who it is. I spent all night wrapped up in Brooks's arms. It was blissful, and I'm scared I'm going to get used to it too quickly. He feels like a drug that I can't get enough of.

"Good mornin', darlin'." He runs his nose down mine before giving me a quick kiss on the lips.

I stretch out my legs and slowly crack my eyes open. It's still dark in the bedroom.

"What time is it?" I ask him.

"Early. But I was kinda hopin' you'd be up for a morning ride to watch the sunrise."

This man loves to ride, and I'm starting to enjoy it just as much. If not for the beautiful views, then for the time I get to spend with him. "That sounds amazing."

"Good. Let's get going then."

Brooks jumps out of bed, while it takes me a minute to slowly roll out on my side. We brush our teeth side by side in his bathroom before getting dressed. He lets me borrow one of his shirts, and I tuck it into my jeans from yesterday before I slide into my boots. Boots are slowly becoming part of my daily wardrobe. I have two pairs now. One for riding, one for daily use.

The ranch is quiet at this time of the morning. There's no one out. Not even Beck is at the stables yet.

"Will we get in trouble for taking the horses out?" I ask as Brooks gets the saddle situated on my horse. Sparkles is quiet but clearly excited to go out.

He chuckles. "Aspen, this is my ranch. Who are we gonna get in trouble with?"

"Right. I guess, I mean, won't Beck worry if he gets here and two horses are missing?"

He smiles at me from over his shoulder as he adjusts the stirrup for me. "I doubt it, but I can leave him a note if it'll make you feel better."

"Maybe. Just in case."

"I'll do that as soon as I finish up here. You know, I'm glad you care so much about the ranch and the people here."

I shrug. Without realizing it, this place has started to feel like home. More of a home than I've ever had before. "I like it here."

"I like having you here. We all do."

I look away so he doesn't see me blush. This feels too good to be true, but I'm too desperate to have a place to call my own that I can't see past the here and now. This feeling that I get from him, like he truly cares about me and not just what I can do for him, is addicting. He's the one who wants to take care of me, and I've never had that before. Ever.

I know when the news of our unconventional relationship gets out, things won't feel as smooth. I don't even want to think about how Zach is going to react. Hell, he might personally try to run me out of his hometown.

Until that happens, I'm going to embrace this little bubble Brooks and I have created and get as much enjoyment out of it as I can.

"Alright. All set." He hands me the reins for my horse.

We mount our horses and set off down one of the trails we've done before. It's an easier trail, but it'll give us a great view of the sunrise.

Brooks and I ride in silence, taking in the morning. The world feels calm and serene as it wakes up around us. A few birds chirp, the leaves rustle in the wind, and the sky is turning a beautiful shade of purple as we trot down the trail.

We come up to a small cliff overlooking a lake just as the sun peeks over the horizon. We tie our horses to a tree and sit down on a nearby boulder to watch. We've done this before, but this time, Brooks has his arm around me, and I'm tucked in close to him. He kisses my head and tells me this is one of his favorite things to do on the ranch. I smile and inhale the fresh morning air. What I don't say is that everything about this place and him is becoming my favorite thing. I'm afraid to get too attached, but I also want it so damn bad.

"Thanks for bringing me out here this morning," I tell him once we're back on our horses.

"Sorry about the early morning wake-up."

"Eh, it's not so bad getting up early when you're there." I laugh at myself. "That was cheesy, wasn't it?"

He shakes his head. "Maybe, but I feel the same."

I assume Brooks's plan was for us to be back and have the horses in their stalls before anyone else showed up at the stables. Unfortunately, that's not the case. Beck is standing with his arms crossed, looking between us when we ride up.

"You two are up early," he says slowly, probably trying to figure out what is going on.

"Should say the same for you. What're you doing here so early?" Brooks asks. He sounds so unbothered, but I wonder if he's worried about Beck finding out about us.

"Got to get a head start on some things, and I have an early trail ride for a family before they check out," he explains.

Brooks nods. "We'll get these horses back up for you then."

He offers no explanation about why the two of us are here, and Beck doesn't ask any follow up questions, but I see the confusion in his eyes. I try to think of some sort of explanation, but my mind is blanking.

"You can leave Sparkles tacked up. I'm using her on the trail ride," he says instead of asking the questions he really wants to.

"Ok." I walk Sparkles to the fence and tie her up.

Brooks says something to Beck, and then he motions for me to follow him back to the UTV we rode over here in.

"Aren't you worried Beck is going to tell people he saw

us together?" I ask once we're far enough away from the stables.

"No. Beck isn't like that. He won't say a word to anyone until he hears it straight from me. If he asks me, I'll tell him the truth but let him know we're keeping it to ourselves for now," he assures me.

"And what exactly would you tell him?"

"That I've fallen head over heels for the most amazing woman."

I turn my face slightly so he doesn't see the huge grin on my face. While Brooks has definitely shown me just how interested he is in this thing between us, it's different hearing him say it. It makes it more real, like I'm not making it up in my head.

"You don't think he would judge us? Not only because of Zach but because of our age difference?"

"I think our ages will certainly be the talk of the town for awhile once people find out, but I'm not worried about it. It's none of their damn business if I'm being honest. They can huff and puff all they want, but at the end of the day, my happiness is not dependent on what this town thinks of me." He pauses, and I notice his hands tighten around the steering wheel. "Does our age difference bother you?"

The only time our age difference bothered me was when I realized I was attracted to him. It scared me because it felt wrong, but really, I think I was worried about what other people might say. Brooks is right, though. It doesn't matter what anyone else thinks. We are who we are, and we're not doing anything wrong.

"No, it doesn't," I tell him honestly.

The corner of his mouth tips up in a small smile. "Good."

When we get back to his house, he makes breakfast while I shower and get ready for the day. It all feels so strange and domesticated, yet I've never felt so calm and content in my life. Brooks makes me feel safe. He makes me feel wanted.

I can only hope that this doesn't completely blow up in my face, but I'll enjoy everything he gives me while I can.

CHAPTER 31

Brooks

"YOU NEVER TOLD ME, are you going to the Halloween Festival in town this weekend?" Jasmine asks Aspen. The three of us are loitering at the front desk. Well, Jasmine and I are loitering. Aspen is actually trying to work.

It's been a few weeks since Aspen and I took our relationship to the next level, and as far as I know, Jasmine is the only one who knows. That's partly because I'm too chicken shit to tell my son what I've done, and I really wanted him to be the first one I tell. Unfortunately, I think I need some moral support from my friends before I talk to him. I'm planning on telling Harper and Beck soon. Very soon.

Aspen sighs, and I look up at her. I had assumed she'd be going to the festival because, well, everyone in town goes to the Halloween Festival. If there's one thing Blue Haven loves, it's a festival. And with Eli Cunningham marketing the hell out of these things, they're hard to miss.

I'm convinced he'd drag us all from our own homes if he realizes someone hadn't shown up.

"I don't know…"

"Come on!" Jasmine whines. "It'll be fun. Everyone dresses up. There's candy and games and these really awesome brownies that Mrs. Leanne only makes for Halloween. You have to come."

"It's just the last town gathering I went to didn't end up very well for me."

She glances at me for barely a millisecond, but it's all I need to remember. The last town festival was the Fourth of July, where she caught Zach cheating on her. I've never seen someone look so hurt and so angry at the same time as when I saw her spot him. I hope she never has to experience that again in her life, and I don't plan on that happening because of me.

"Yeah, but that was when you were dating that dill weed," Jasmine says, quickly adding for my benefit, "No offense."

"None taken." I've come to terms with the fact that I've failed my son in more ways than one. The first being teaching him how to properly treat a woman.

"And now you've got the town prize. Do you know how many women would try to fight you for him?" She gestures to me.

Aspen laughs. "Well, it's a good thing no one knows yet. I'll need to brush up on my self-defense skills."

I know it's all in jest, but I hate the thought of her not enjoying time with her friends because of what Zach did to her. "You should go," I tell her. "You'll have fun."

"I'm sure Brooks will be there too so he can scare away any bad things for you." Jasmine wriggles her eyebrows, and Aspen laughs.

"I will be there, but I doubt you'll need me. And if you do, you know I'll be there in a second," I confirm.

Aspen smiles at me as her cheeks turn an adorable shade of pink.

"Aww, that's sickeningly cute," Jasmine teases.

"Ok, fine. I'll go, but I don't have a costume."

Jasmine waves her off. "Please. I have a ton. Come over, and you can borrow one of mine."

"Should I be concerned that you have so many costumes?" Aspen asks.

Jasmine shrugs one shoulder. "Maybe."

Both of them laugh, and I take that as my cue to get back to work. As much as I love taking all of Aspen's attention, I know she needs time with her friends.

"I've got to get going, but I'll see you later?"

"Yes, sir," Aspen says.

Never one to not have the last word, Jasmine adds, "Oooh, kinky."

I lean forward slightly as if I'm going to kiss Aspen, but her eyes go wide. I remember that we're not at home and quickly pull back. I clear my throat and give her a tight nod before turning and heading back to my office to answer some emails. But first, I need to text Harper and Beck and invite them to drinks at Roadside tonight. I've got some shit I need to get off my chest.

———

Roadside has been non-smoking for over a decade, but that doesn't stop the place from smelling like someone has been chain-smoking at the bar all day. Unfortunately, it's been a staple in Blue Haven since before I was even born, so I'm certain we'll never get rid of it, and we're all far too loyal to allow another bar to pop up anywhere in the vicinity of this place.

"So drinks are on you, right? For this little impromptu drink meeting?" Harper asks as she slides onto the stool across the table from me. Beck sits down next to her.

"What if I said no?"

She shrugs. "I'd tell Owen to put them on your tab anyway."

"That's what I thought."

We order drinks when the server stops by our table, and Harper adds an appetizer for the table.

"So, what's going on?" Harper asks. "You've been a little MIA recently."

"Yeah, that's kind of what I wanted to talk to you about." My palms are sweating, which is ridiculous because these are my best friends. I've known them for longer than I can even remember. I'm fairly confident that they won't judge me. Or if they do, it'll be less than everyone else will.

"Well, spit it out, man." Beck gives me an expectant look.

"Ok, ok. I've kinda been seeing someone." They both look at me with blank expressions, so I continue assuming that they've already figured that much out. "And it's Aspen."

Harper throws her hands up. "Oh, there it is! Thank god you finally got that out in the open."

Wait, what? "You knew?"

"Well, you haven't exactly been trying to hide it," she says.

"Yes, I have."

She laughs. "Well, then you're terrible at it."

"Did you think I wouldn't realize what was going on when you took her on a sunrise ride? If that's not romance, I don't know what is. I figured you would tell me when you were ready, so I didn't pry," Beck says.

"Ok, and how did you figure it out?" I ask, focusing on Harper.

"Brooks, you look at her like she's the only thing in the room every time she walks in." I don't know what she's talking about. I don't do that. "You get a goofy smile on your face when she looks at you." Definitely don't do that. "You've been hanging out at the front desk way more than usual." That's not true at all. "And I saw you kiss her behind the lodge last week." Well… damn.

"Why didn't you say anything?"

"Because, like Beck said, I knew you'd come to me when you were ready. But I was seriously dying inside to talk to you about it."

I sit back and let out a breath. "Alright, well, now you know. But you two are the only ones who know besides Jasmine, so keep it between us for now. I'm having a hard time figuring out how to tell Zach."

"I was wondering if he knew yet. I figured he'd be making a big fuss if he did."

"Yeah. I've been meaning to tell him…"

"You just gotta rip that Band-Aid off," Beck says. "You know he's gonna be pissed, but if you're sure about Aspen, then you just gotta do it."

"I know… It's just, it feels like I just kind of got him back. I mean, he's been texting more. We even went to lunch last week. I'm just worried this is going to set us back again."

Harper gives me a sympathetic look. "Yeah, it probably will, Brooks. Zach hasn't been quiet about wanting to get Aspen back, and now he's essentially being blocked by his own father. I don't see any way for you to come out winning from his perspective."

"Yeah, I know. That's the worst part about all this. I don't want to lose him."

"I think you kinda made that decision when you slept with his ex-girlfriend, don't ya think?" Harper slaps Beck's shoulder. "Ow. What? It's true!"

"I know, but you don't have to say it like that. He's our friend," she says.

"Yeah, and as our friend, he deserves for us to be frank with him. He made a decision, and now he's got to deal with the consequences. Is Aspen worth the risk?" Beck asks.

"I've never felt this way about anyone," I admit. We haven't said the L word yet, but I feel it. I know it's there. She's all I think about. When I'm not with her, I wonder what she's doing. I love watching her sleep in my bed. I love cooking breakfast and dinner for her. I love how she smiles at me when she finally gets to see me at the end of the day. I love the way her body fits with mine. I love the way she cares about me and the ranch. She's my dream woman. It's just unfortunate that my son got to her first.

"If you're going to pursue this with Aspen, then you know there's a very good chance you're going to lose Zach. Are you ready for that?"

"I don't fucking know." I pick up my beer and take a huge swig of it. This feels like the hardest decision I'll ever have to make.

"I will say… I don't think I've ever seen you this happy, Brooks. Zach gave up on your relationship a long time ago. He pushed you away, and no matter what you did, he didn't seem to care. I know he's your son, and I can't imagine how difficult this must be for you, but you deserve to be happy too."

Beck nods along to everything Harper says.

"Maybe he'll be ok with it?" Even as I say it, I know it's not true. When we met for lunch last week, he mentioned Aspen at least five times. He wanted to know if I knew if she was dating anyone. If she's been going out. If she's planning on staying in Blue Haven. I felt terrible lying to him, but I just couldn't get the words to come out. I didn't want to hurt him, even though I knew I hurt him the moment I caught feelings for her.

"Brooks…"

I rub my hands down my face. "Yeah, I know. I'm gonna tell him."

"You should probably tell him soon so that he can hear it from you and not someone else. I love Jazz, but she's not one to keep her mouth shut."

I nod because she's not saying anything I don't already

know. I don't want to lose Aspen, so I need to just suck it up and tell Zach. He might be pissed off for awhile, but hopefully he'll understand that we didn't do this to hurt him.

"I am happy for you, though. It's about time you found someone. While Aspen is younger and the circumstances aren't ideal, you two seem good together. She fits in well on the ranch, which is what you need," Harper says.

"I agree. Aspen is really great. It's not hard to see how you fell for her," Beck adds.

"Thanks, guys. It means a lot to me to have your support."

"Were you expecting something else from us?" Harper questions with a cocked eyebrow as she sips her beer.

"I don't know. I guess I expected you to give me a hard time."

"Oh, we're still gonna give you a hard time, but we'll do it with love."

The three of us laugh. "I guess that's all I can ask for."

"Alright, let's get another round of beers." Harper raises her hand to get our server's attention. I sit back and realize how fucking lucky I am to have two best friends who genuinely care about me and a woman who has made me feel like I deserve to be loved without having to change who I am. Now all I need is to figure out a way to not lose my son completely.

CHAPTER 32

Aspen

"HAVE I died and gone to Hell?"

I turn around at the sound of Brooks's voice. He's standing by the kitchen entrance staring me up and down.

"Oh, do you like it?" I ask, posing to show off the Halloween costume Jazz let me borrow. It's a black and silver witch costume, but the dress is extremely short, and the top definitely does not hide anything.

"Oh, darlin'. I more than like it. Please tell me I get to take this off of you later." He walks toward me and runs his fingertip along the top of my breasts.

"Yes, but later. After the festival."

His eyes fly up to meet mine. "This is what you're wearing tonight?"

"Well, yeah. Is there something wrong with this?"

"It just shows… a lot."

"I know, but if you can believe it, this was the best option she had. Everything else felt more like a bathing suit than a costume."

"Jesus." He looks me up and down again. "Well, I'm gonna have to stay away from you tonight then. I can't be walking around with a hard-on all night."

I lean forward and cup his cock and confirm he is, in fact, hard right now. "Don't worry, I'll make sure you're taken care of tonight."

"With the costume on?"

"Whatever you want."

He kisses me hard, not caring that he's smearing my red lipstick. I don't care either. I love it when he kisses me like he can't wait another second.

"Fuck," he moans, pulling away. "I've got to stop, or I'm gonna rip this off you right now and fuck you on this counter."

"If Jazz wasn't on her way to pick me up, I might let you."

He exhales deeply as if he's trying to get himself under control before he takes a step away. "You are trouble."

"But you love it," I tease, and his face changes from tortured to something more serious. The look in his eyes makes my heart flutter. Over the last few weeks, we've been pretty inseparable. I can't even remember the last time I slept in my cabin. Anytime we're not working, we're together. It's been so nice to feel like someone actually wants me around. There have been several moments where I thought he might tell me he loves me, but every time I think it's coming, the moment slips away.

I know we haven't been together very long, but what we have feels more important than any relationship I've ever been in. I know Brooks cares about me, but I know I can't be the only one who feels like I've met my other half.

"That I do," he agrees after a moment. He gives me one more kiss before I hear a car horn, alerting me that Jazz is here to pick me up. I wish Brooks and I could go together, but I know we're not there yet, unfortunately. I'm trying to be patient with him. I know telling Zach is going to be hard for him, but keeping us a secret is getting harder and harder.

"I'll see you there?" I ask him.

"Yeah, I'll be the one drooling over you."

He slaps my ass as I turn to leave.

"Be careful, darlin'."

"You too."

He watches me leave, and I just know his eyes are glued to my ass. I grab my bag and meet Jazz in the driveway. As soon as I open the passenger door, she says, "Yeah. I knew this would be hot."

I laugh. "Brooks certainly enjoyed it."

"I bet he did."

She drives us to town, finding a spot close to the town square where the festival is happening. The sun's getting lower in the sky, creating the perfect backdrop for the night. There are games, bounce houses, a haunted house, and so many booths with fun treats and items. I can smell the sugar from the car.

Jazz pulls a flask out of her bag. "Little pregame." She takes a long sip from the flask before she hands it to me.

"Aren't you driving tonight?"

She gives me a knowing look. "You know Daddy Brooks

is gonna sneak you out of here as soon as he can, and I may or may not have plans to get some myself."

"So Owen's here tonight?"

"He's at the mobile bar they have set up."

I smile, happy that my friend has someone, even though she refuses to say they are anything more than a situationship.

"Well, in that case." I take a big swig of what turns out to be straight tequila. My eyes water from the burn, but I make it through.

Jazz gives me a devious smile before we get out of the car. She links her arm in mine and leads me to the festival, pointing out all of her favorite things and letting me know when she sees something new for this year.

I wave at Mayor Cunningham when we see him by the haunted house. We pass Beck and his daughter, Jade, playing a carnival-type game. She dressed up as a princess, and I assume Beck is meant to be her prince, but the cowboy hat throws it off a bit.

We meet up with Jazz's friends by the mobile bar, and Owen makes us a drink before we start playing games.

I know the moment Brooks shows up at the festival. It's like I can feel him. And when I look over my shoulder while we're in line to play some sort of ring toss, Brooks is already watching me as he greets Mayor Cunningham.

Harper is by his side, dressed as a football player. Brooks isn't dressed up, but he's telling everyone he's a cowboy. I can only imagine he does that every year.

I wish I could be the one by his side, and by the look of longing on his face as he stares at me, he wishes I could be, too. Hopefully, this will give him the extra push he needs to tell Zach what's going on.

I'm so focused on Brooks that I don't notice when someone steps in front of my view. I let out a little shriek, and the person laughs.

"Didn't mean to scare you, Asp."

Even though his face is painted, I still recognize Zach's voice.

"I wasn't paying attention."

"I can tell. You ok?"

I square my shoulders and force a smile onto my face. Zach has been leaving me alone like I asked him to, but I still have a sinking suspicion that he hasn't quite given up yet.

"Yeah. All good."

"You look great," he says, and I can feel his gaze run down my body. While I feel confident in this outfit, in this moment, I wish I were wearing more clothes.

"Oh, thanks. Jazz let me wear one of her costumes."

"Yeah, it definitely looks like a Jazz kind of thing."

Jazz hears him and gives him the finger from behind her back. She doesn't bother turning around to greet him.

"So... how are you?" he asks. It's weird that it feels so awkward to talk to him now. The same person I thought I'd be with forever, who I thought knew me better than anyone else, is now a complete stranger to me.

"I'm good. Really good." I want to add 'because of your dad,' but I manage to hold my tongue. "How about you?"

"Good. I've got one more month before I graduate from the police academy. It's been going really well."

"That's awesome. I'm happy for you."

"Thanks, Aspen." He pauses and then says, "I wish—"

"Zach," I warn, cutting him off.

"No, I know. I know you're done with me, and I still hate myself for fucking this up. But I do wish things were different. I hope we can try to be friends one day."

I shrug my shoulder non-committally because I know his feelings on that may change once he finds out about Brooks and me. "Maybe."

He smiles like I've just given him the world. "I'll take a maybe."

Someone calls his name, and he turns toward his group of friends who are waiting on him. He looks back at me. "I'd better get going. I just wanted to come say hi."

I nod.

"You really do look amazing," he tells me as he starts to walk away.

"Yeah, she knows," Jazz says, linking her arm and pulling me close to her. "Ugh, we are so done with him."

"I know, but I have to be nice. He might be in my life for awhile in a different way, you know?"

She laughs. "Yeah, I know. You'll be his stepmom!"

"Let's not go that far."

She gives me a knowing look. "It's true, though."

"We're going to pretend like it's not."

"Ignorance is bliss, I guess." She holds up her plastic cup, and I tap mine on hers before we both take a sip.

When I look back over my shoulder, Brooks is nowhere to be seen. Jazz quickly gets my attention again when it's our turn to play the game.

We spend all night playing games, eating Halloween-themed treats, and checking out everyone's costumes. Before I realize, the best costume award has been announced, and people start heading out.

Jazz makes heart eyes at Owen while I look around for Brooks. There's a chill in the air now, and I wish I had more than this flimsy cloak to wrap around myself as I stand off to the side of the square watching people leave.

A hand slides around my waist, and for a moment, I panic until I inhale the spicy scent I've gotten so used to.

"You ready?" he whispers in my ear, sending goosebumps down my arm.

"You have no idea."

Someone walks in front of us, and Brooks quickly removes his hand from my waist. I visibly deflate as soon as his hand leaves my body. I hate hiding what we are. It was fine at first, but it's starting to feel like I'm not important enough for him. It could also be the couple of drinks I've had that are making me feel angrier about this.

"Let's go."

I say a quick goodbye to Jazz, who is more than ready to run off with Owen, and follow Brooks to his truck, keeping a safe distance from each other so no one gets the wrong idea. Or I guess it would be the right idea in this scenario.

We spend most of the ride home in silence. The secrecy put a damper on my mood real fast, but I still let him take my hand to help me out of the truck. I still find comfort in his hand on my lower back as we walk inside. And it still feels like I'm home when he shuts the door behind us.

I walk to the kitchen and grab a glass of water.

"You're mad," Brooks says from somewhere behind me.

I sigh and turn to face him. "I hate feeling like a secret. It was fun at first, but I don't want to hide anymore."

He nods. "I know. You've been incredibly patient with me, and it's not fair to you. If I'm being honest, I'm scared to tell him, which is what's taking me so long."

While he hasn't outright said he was scared before tonight, I knew it anyway. Anytime I mention telling Zach about us, he brushes it off and quickly changes the subject. I've let him get away with it because I know he's in a difficult place, but at some point, I have to think of myself, too.

"But I will tell him. This week. I promise."

He takes a few steps toward me and reaches out to tuck a loose strand of hair behind my ear.

"I'm sorry, darlin', for ever making you feel like you were a secret. I want everyone to know, too. This thing between us feels more real than anything I've ever felt before."

"Me too."

The corner of his mouth tips up in a half-smile. "Good."

I take a step closer and wrap my arms around his waist. I know there's nothing we can do about this tonight, so I might as well end the night on a high note. "So, how are you going to make it up to me?"

He cocks a brow. "I think I have an idea."

In the blink of an eye, he's lifting me up and setting me on the kitchen island. He stands between my legs, takes my witch hat off, and tosses it to the ground.

He trails soft kisses across the tops of my breasts. "Do

you know how hard it was to watch everyone check you out tonight?"

I laugh. "I doubt *everyone* was checking me out."

"They were," he responds seriously. "Harper had to pull me away a few times."

Knowing that Brooks was jealous is surprisingly hot. He's always so confident and sure of himself. I didn't take him to be the jealous type.

"I want to claim you, darlin'. I want everyone to know that you are mine and I am yours."

I don't get a chance to say anything back because he drags the front of my costume down, exposing one of my nipples. He quickly latches on to it and sucks hard.

"Oh my god," I moan, throwing my head back as he moves to the other one.

"You are perfect, Aspen. I can't get enough of you. This fucking costume was killing me all night."

"Sorry, not sorry," I say a little breathlessly because I can't think straight when his hands are moving up my thighs. My pussy clenches as I wait for him to reach it.

"You like teasing me, don't you?"

His hand stops at the edge of my underwear as he waits for an answer. "Yes."

With my admission, he pulls my underwear down my legs and throws it in the same direction as my hat. "Now I'm going to show you exactly what you did to me tonight."

He gently pushes me back onto the island and spreads my legs even wider, fully exposing my dripping pussy to him. He parts me with his fingers and barely gives me time to adjust to them sliding inside me before his tongue is on my clit. By now, he knows exactly what I like and what's going to get me there.

My back arches off the counter as he pumps faster inside me. His tongue works in slow circles around me, pushing me toward my climax but not enough to get me over. He's playing with me. Edging me. Pleasuring me without giving me what my body craves.

"Brooks, please!"

He looks up at me from between my legs. "Not yet, darlin'. You'll come when I'm ready for you to come."

I gasp as he licks me again. "Please!"

"You've got to be patient. You tease me, I tease you."

I instantly regret my costume choice for the night. "I didn't mean to."

"It's too late to take it back, darlin'."

He licks me again, and I ache for more. He brings me back to the brink and then pulls away again.

"Brooks," I moan his name. I hear him chuckle over the sound of his belt unbuckling and his zipper coming down.

He grabs my waist and pulls me off the counter before flipping me over and laying me, chest down, on the counter. I barely have time to adjust to my nipples pressing on the cold marble before I feel him behind me. He slides inside easily, pushing himself to the hilt.

"Fuck, Aspen. You take me so well. It's like you were made for me."

He pulls back and then slams back inside me. I grab on to the sides of the counter to steady myself. Brooks and I have slept together more times than I can count at this point, but this is the first time it's not in his bed. This feels urgent, like he couldn't wait to have me. That turns me on even more than him filling me over and over again.

His cock hits me deep inside again and again. It feels like I'm no longer in control of my body. Brooks adds to his control by grabbing a fistful of my curls and pulling my hair back. It's so erotic that my pussy clenches him tight.

He hisses. "Is this ok?"

"God, yes."

He fucks me hard and fast until I'm sure I can't take a single second more without exploding. Then he stops completely. I whimper as he releases my hair, and I lie back down on the counter to catch my breath. My eyes are watering, my body is covered in sweat, and I need to finish, but Brooks isn't ready for that yet.

"Do you want to come, Aspen?"

"Yes, please!"

He wraps his arm around my waist, finding my swollen clit between my legs. He presses on it with his rough fingertips.

"We're gonna come together, ok?"

I nod against the counter.

"Answer me, darlin'."

"Yes. Ok. Just please let me come."

He chuckles at my desperation as he starts moving inside me again. He thrusts and plays with my clit, quickly bringing me back to the brink.

"Not yet, Aspen. Not yet."

"I can't stop it!"

"Yes, you can."

He picks up his pace as I squeeze around him. "Almost there, darlin'. You're doing so damn good."

He thrusts a few more times and I explode with joy when he tells me, "Come, Aspen."

My body listens in an instant. Pleasure washes over me, and I nearly cry from how good it feels to finally finish. Brooks is gripping my hips as he's frozen behind me, pumping his release in me.

"I—" Brooks starts but stops himself, leaving me to wonder what he was about to say. "You are perfect, Aspen. Perfect for me."

My body feels like Jell-O as Brooks pulls out, and I feel his release travel down my leg. Brooks gently picks me up off the counter and gathers me into his arms, only putting me down so he can start a bath for me. I step into the bubbles once the tub is full, and I expect Brooks to leave me there, but he doesn't. He sits on the floor next to me the entire time I soak and helps me wash my body once I'm ready.

I know that I am head over heels in love with Brooks Calloway: the one man I shouldn't want. Now I just have to hope that he doesn't break my heart like his son did.

CHAPTER 33
Brooks

THIS IS THE WEEK.

I've scheduled a lunch with Zach in a few days to tell him about my feelings for Aspen. I can't possibly put this off any longer. He deserves to know the truth, and it's unfair to Aspen to keep asking her to keep this between us. She's right, it makes it feel like we're some dirty little secret. She deserves so much more than that.

I let her know this morning that Zach agreed to lunch on Wednesday and that I'll be telling him then. She tried to hide her excitement, but I could tell she wanted to smile. It felt like a punch to the gut knowing how much this means to her. The bare minimum, and I've been putting it off.

I'm stuck in a lose-lose situation. I know Zach will never forgive me for this. And I also know that I'll lose Aspen if I don't tell him. Since I've already crossed a line with Aspen, there's no going back at this point. I've made my bed, now I have to lie in it.

There's a knock on my office door, and Aspen pokes her head in.

"You busy?" she asks.

"Never too busy for you."

She smiles and walks in, closing the door behind her.

"Everything ok?" I ask as she walks toward me. She's in black leggings paired with a long-sleeve Moonlight Ranch shirt, since it's starting to get cooler during the days. Her curls are extra bouncy today, and she's never looked more like mine. Maybe because I know I'm in love with her, or maybe because I know we're about to come out to everyone about our relationship, but she is mine, and I'm way too excited about it.

"Yeah, I just missed you," she says, sitting down on the corner of my desk. She missed me even after I just saw her a few hours ago wrapped up in my sheets. How the fuck did I get so lucky?

"Come here." I slide my chair back and gesture for her to sit on my lap.

She smiles and doesn't hesitate to straddle me. I grab onto her hips to get her as close to me as I can. She leans down to kiss me. Not just any kiss. She slides her tongue across my bottom lip, begging me to open for her. I know what this kind of kiss means. My girl is horny, and I know exactly what she needs from me.

She rocks her hips against me as I trail my hands under her shirt and up her back. She lets out a tiny moan when she feels the friction from my jeans rubbing her through her thin leggings.

I pull her shirt off and toss it haphazardly to the side.

"God, your tits are amazing," I tell her, trailing kisses across her chest. She giggles as my scruff rubs against her skin.

My hands reach around her to unhook her bra when the world stops. The door to my office opens, and my heart drops to my stomach when I hear, "Hey Dad, have you seen —" A pause while my son realizes what he walked in on. "Aspen?"

Aspen pulls away from me quickly and hops off my lap. In the blink of an eye, she's grabbing her discarded shirt and pulling it back over her head.

"I, uh, hey Zach. What're you doing here?" she asks. She cringes as she says it. I think we both hope he didn't see anything, but there's no way he didn't see his ex-girlfriend straddling my lap, topless.

I know better than to be messing around with her in my office, especially without double-checking that the door was locked, but Aspen makes me lose my mind. I can never seem to think straight when I'm around her.

"What am I doing here? What are you doing in *here*?" It's then that I realize he's holding a bouquet, and I just know he was coming here to try to get back together with her... again.

"I work here," Aspen answers.

"And your job description involves making out with my dad on his lap?"

The three of us stand there frozen for an uncomfortably long time before Zach shouts, "What the fuck?"

"Zach, I—" Aspen starts to explain, but I know this needs to come from me, not her.

"Aspen, honey, can you give us a minute?"

She looks over at me, and I give her a little nod to let her know that it's going to be ok. She sighs and quickly walks out of my office, keeping her eyes on the ground. Zach's eyes stay glued to her until the door is firmly shut behind her, and then I only see pure anger when he looks back at me.

"Zach, I've been meaning to talk to you about this."

His eyebrows shoot up. "Oh? You've been meaning to tell me you're fucking my girlfriend behind my back?"

"She's not your girlfriend anymore." It's the wrong thing to say, and I know it the moment it leaves my mouth.

"You knew how I felt about her! You knew I wanted to get back together with her. You knew I still loved her. All this time I've been confiding in you, and you've been sleeping with her?"

"I haven't been sleeping with her the whole time," I clarify.

He rolls his eyes. "You're really going to try to make that point right now? You're doing it now, so does it really matter?"

"Yes, it matters because neither of us was planning on this happening. I was really trying to help her when you left her with no place to go. You're the one who brought her to a town where she knew no one and then cheated on her. I gave her a job because *you* asked me to. I gave her a place to stay because she didn't feel comfortable staying with you anymore."

"Oh, so it's my fault she fell into your bed? How could

you possibly go from helping her to sleeping with her? Huh? How does that work?"

"I tried to stay away from her, but…"

"You couldn't? Yeah, that's great. This is so fucking awesome." He kicks the side of my desk with his boot. I'd tell him to calm down, but I'd rather have him take this out on me than her. If he needs to get his anger out, he can do it here.

"I was going to talk to you about it this week. That's why I made lunch plans with you."

"You thought telling me this in a public place would be a good idea? I mean, what were you expecting here? That I'd be ok with this? That we could all be one big happy family? After I told you how much I wanted her back, you took her right out from under me."

"I didn't take her, Zach. She doesn't feel the same way about you anymore. She made a choice to move on."

"Yeah, well, you made a choice too. I hope you're fucking happy. Mom was right. You only care about yourself."

He slams the bouquet into the trash can in the corner of my office and stomps out without a second look back at me. I knew he would be mad. I knew he wouldn't understand. But I guess a small part of me hoped he would hear me out.

And of course, his mother has never said one good thing about me. I'm sure I'll hear from her the moment he runs home and tells her what happened.

I lean back in my chair and drag my hands down my face. How did I get here? How did I let myself fall for Aspen when I knew it would rip me away from my son?

Fuck. I need to get out of here.

———

I spend the better part of the afternoon with my horse. Beck asked no questions when I stormed into the stables and silently tacked her up and left. I rode through my favorite trail on the ranch and spent some time by a small creek that I used to ride to when I was younger and needed a break from my parents.

I didn't gain any more clarity, but I do feel more sure about my decision.

I love Zach. He's my son, and that will never change. But I've given so much of myself to other people over the years, I think I forgot how it feels to be happy.

I worked hard at the ranch to continue on my family's legacy in Blue Haven. Despite what Zach and his mother think, I didn't take over the ranch for myself. Moonlight Ranch has been in my family for almost a century, and I'll be damned if it goes under because of me. My parents worked hard to keep this place going, and they trusted me to continue it. I take pride in that.

Also, despite what Zach and Lacey think, I did the best I could to be the dad I always hoped I would be. But Lacey made it extra difficult by whispering terrible things about me to Zach. I never had a chance to have the family I've always dreamed of.

I give everything I can to the ranch and Blue Haven. I fund every town event I can. I employ as many people from town as I possibly can. I've always put the people of Blue Haven before myself.

The one thing I want for myself is Aspen. Every scenario I run through my head, she's always my end game. She's only been in my life for a few months, but I already know that I can't imagine a life without her. I feel truly happy around her. She's given me purpose again after I felt lost for so long.

Which is why I'm frustrated when I get home and don't see her. I should've found her as soon as Zach left my office, but I needed a minute to digest everything that had happened. I didn't want to take out my frustration on her, and I know I always think better outdoors.

I pull out my phone and don't see any missed calls or texts from her. There are a few missed calls from Harper and a text from Lacey telling me what a scumbag I am. I'll ignore that one for now. I've got bigger things to worry about.

I call Aspen, but it goes straight to voicemail. I walk back to my room to change out of riding clothes and notice all of her stuff is gone. Her phone charger is gone from by the bed, along with the vanilla lip balm that she puts on every night before she goes to sleep. Her Kindle is missing.

In the bathroom, her face wash, curl cream, and toothbrush: all gone.

What is going on?

My heart is racing at this point. Did she leave? After everything?

I call her again. Nothing.

I finally scroll to Harper's contact and call her.

"Hey," she answers quickly.

"Hey, have you seen Aspen by any chance?"

She sighs into the phone. That can't be a good sign.

"What?" I ask.

"I'm guessing things didn't go well?"

"That's putting it lightly."

"Listen, I was at the front desk with Aspen when Zach came out of your office. He said some pretty terrible things to her. She was very upset. And then she came to find you, and your office was empty." Fuck. "I tried to reassure her, but she kept saying she needed to go."

"Do you know where she is?"

"Not exactly, but I would check with Jazz. Are you ok, Brooks? It sounded pretty heated. I've never seen Zach so angry before."

"I'm fine," I lie. "But I've got to go. Thanks," I say quickly and hang up before she can try to deep dive into all my issues. The only thing I need to do right now is to find Aspen.

I quickly find Jasmine's contact in my phone and call. She takes so long to answer that I'm certain it's going to go to voicemail. She finally picks up my call, but I can barely hear her.

"Hello?" she whispers.

"Jasmine. It's Brooks."

"Yeah, I know." Right. I'm sure she has my contact info.

"Right. Uh, have you seen Aspen?"

"Yes."

I pause and wait for her to provide more information, but she doesn't.

"Can you tell me where she is?"

She sighs. I'm getting tired of people sighing at me tonight.

"She asked me not to."

"Why? What is going on?"

There's rustling through the phone, and I can hear Jasmine walking, which gives me a sneaking suspicion that Aspen might be hiding out wherever Jasmine is.

"Listen, I think she just needs a little bit of time. She's upset about what Zach said, but she also feels terrible about coming between you two. She just needs to think."

"No, she doesn't. There's nothing to think about. She belongs with me!"

"I know that and you know that, but our girl needs a minute to breathe, ok? I'll keep an eye on her tonight and text you where she is in the morning."

"Jasmine, no. I need to talk to her now."

"I can't let you do that."

"Jasmine!"

"Talk to you in the morning, bossman."

She hangs up, and I have the sudden urge to throw my stupid phone against the wall, but I stop myself because then I wouldn't get the stupid text I have to wait for.

How am I supposed to get through tonight without her?

CHAPTER 34

Aspen

I CAN TELL my eyes are swollen before even looking at them. I spent most of the night crying, which is annoying because I promised myself I wouldn't cry over a man ever again, but here we are.

Jazz let me stay at her place last night, and by 'let' I mean she practically forced me to. She followed me to Brooks's house, helped me get my things, and made me come straight to her house.

My original plan was to leave Blue Haven immediately. I let myself get too comfortable and think that this was finally going to be the place I call home. I should've known it was too good to be true.

When Zach screamed at me in the lobby of Moonlight Ranch, it was a harsh reminder that I don't belong here. This is his town. Not mine. Yes, he uprooted my life and then fucked me over, but he has the history here. People are always going to be on his side. Besides the few friends I've made, I'm by myself. I'm always by myself. I need to stop thinking that that will ever change. Maybe this is the universe's way of telling me I don't deserve happiness.

My heart feels so heavy. I feel so alone.

"There she is," Jazz says as she walks into her room with a coffee cup. "I was worried you were gonna sleep all day."

She hands me the cup, and I take a sip.

"What time is it?" My voice sounds so groggy.

"Almost eleven."

Oh my god. I never sleep that long. I guess I needed it after last night.

"How are you feeling this morning?" She sits next to me on her bed.

"Like shit," I admit.

"Are you still thinking about leaving?"

"I feel like I have to, Jazz."

"You don't. You can't leave me!" she whines, which makes me smile. I hate that I've finally made a friend and now I'm going to have to leave her. But she'll be fine. Everyone is always fine when I leave. I'm always the one who isn't fine.

"I don't belong here. All I'm doing is pissing off Zach and ruining Brooks's life."

"First of all, fuck Zach. He deserves to be pissed off. Everything that is happening to him is his own damn fault. Second of all, I highly doubt that Brooks thinks you're ruining his life. The man has been calling and texting me all morning. And third of all, stay for me. We can grow old together. Get lots of cats and yell at kids for running through our yard."

I can't help but laugh at that because I can totally picture it. The two of us in rocking chairs on a front porch, gossiping about everyone in town. That would certainly be fun. But knowing I was so close to Brooks… I don't think I could do it.

"Why don't you come with me?" I ask her even though I have no idea where I'm going. Maybe I'll go back to Florida, or maybe I'll find a new place. Start over all on my own. I've done it before. I'm sure I can do it again.

She gives me a pointed look. "You don't even know where you're going. And I like it here in Blue Haven. My family is here. You're my family too now, so you belong here."

I sigh. "I don't know…"

"Listen. Don't be mad, but Brooks is in the living room."

"What!"

"He really wants to talk to you, and I think you should hear him out."

"Jazz, I told you, I can't hurt him any more than I already have."

"And you think leaving him without any explanation won't hurt him?" I hang my head. She's right. Of course, she's right. "That's what I thought. So hear him out. If you still want to leave after you talk to him, then I'll help you pack."

My friend, who is always happy, looks so sad right now. I hate that it's because of me.

"Alright," I respond softly. It's not that I don't want to see Brooks, but seeing him again—seeing the hurt in his eyes—is going to make it so much harder to leave.

"Here. Let's just…" She starts patting down my hair, and I realize I must look like I just rolled out of bed because I did. "Ok, that's a little better. Gotta make sure you still look hot. I've got a stake in this game."

I laugh as she leaves the room. My heart feels like it's going to beat through my chest as I listen to Brooks's heavy footsteps come down the hall toward Jazz's room.

He knocks gently before slowly pushing the door open. I stay seated on the bed, but I can't take my eyes off him. Even with dark circles under his eyes, he's still the most handsome man I've ever seen. He's in a dark henley and my favorite pair of jeans. Instead of his cowboy boots, he's opted for his work boots. The ones he always leaves by his front door in case he has to leave quickly. The fact that he's wearing them today makes me wonder if he ran out of his house the second Jazz told him where I was, but I shake the thought from my head. I have to be strong. I can't ruin this man's life any more than I already have.

"Hey." He stays on the other side of the bedroom, which I appreciate since this is already going to be hard enough. Being close to him would be too much, but my fingers twitch with the need to touch him.

"Hi."

He swallows like he's nervous. "You wanna tell me what's going on?"

My eyes sting from the threat of tears. He sounds so defeated. "I-I can't do this, Brooks. I can't ruin your life. You don't deserve that. I have to leave Blue Haven."

"Darlin', the only thing that's gonna ruin my life is if you don't come home with me."

Home. I thought I finally had one…

"I don't have a home. I thought maybe… but all I've done is cause trouble. Zach is never going to forgive us. This whole town is going to hate me." I hate the way my voice shakes, but there's no sense in hiding how upset I am. "So, I'm going to go. That will be easier for everyone. It'll be easier for you to repair your relationship with Zach if I'm not here. You can just tell him I was a mistake."

Brooks crosses the room and kneels down in front of me. "Aspen, those words would never come out of my mouth. You are not a mistake, and you never will be. Yeah, Zach is pissed. He has every right to be. But that's not your fault. It's mine. I made this choice because I wanted it. I want you.

"Of course, I'm going to try to earn his forgiveness, but at the end of the day, our relationship was strained before I ever knew you. He's never wanted me in his life, and this gives him the perfect excuse to cut me out. It hurts like hell, but it always felt like fighting a losing battle with him."

God, I hate that Zach has made him feel like this. In the short time that I've known Brooks, all he's wanted was a relationship with his son. I know he'd be such a good dad if he were just given a chance.

"You make me so happy, Aspen. You've done nothing but bring absolute joy to my life, and I refuse to let you walk away without a fight. I love you, Aspen. I want it all with you: the ranch, the house, the marriage, the babies. You are my future. Please don't leave."

I can barely see him through the tears in my eyes. This man loves me? He's choosing a future with me? It's like he saw inside my soul and knew exactly what my biggest wish was and is doing everything he can to make it come true.

"No one has ever chosen me before," I murmur.

He grabs one of my hands and interlaces our fingers. He's shaking, which makes me cry even harder.

"I do. I choose you, Aspen. Every single day, I choose you."

"Are you sure?" I manage to ask between sobs.

He smiles and nods. "I've never been so sure. When I got home last night and all your stuff was gone, it felt like the wind got knocked out of me. I always thought it was silly when people would say they found their other half, but that's what this feels like to me. You complete me. You make me whole. You make me excited about life again. I don't want to do this without you."

"Me either," I admit.

"Then stay, Aspen. Let's build our life together. Please."

He squeezes my hand tighter while I think of what to say. I want to stay. I want it more than anything, but it feels impossible. "Everyone is going to hate me."

"That's not true!" Jazz shouts from the hallway. Should've known she'd be eavesdropping.

"It's not true," Brooks echoes her. "And who gives a fuck what anyone thinks? I don't. Not anymore. Please stay, Aspen. Stay with me. Let me love you like you deserve to be loved."

My heart and my brain are fighting. I want to stay so badly, but I'm terrified of getting hurt again. It's a big risk to stay here with Brooks. But is it a risk I'm willing to take?

My head starts nodding before I even decide what to say, and I manage to choke out, "Ok."

I'm in his arms in a split second. He lifts me up, and I wrap my legs around him. He kisses my tear-stained lips and keeps saying he loves me over and over again. I barely get a chance to tell him I love him too in between kisses.

"Alright, alright. Let's simmer down," Jazz calls out as she walks in with her eyes covered. "I love you both, but I do not need this to go any further in my bedroom."

Brooks chuckles and gently lowers me to the ground. "Let's get you home."

I wipe my eyes and start to gather my things.

"Well, I'm glad this all worked out. At least between the two of you," Jazz says while she helps me grab my stuff. I didn't do much unpacking. Just my toothbrush, toothpaste. The basics. "And Aspen, I can promise you that more people will be on your side than Zach's. No offense, Brooks."

"None taken."

"But he's lived here his entire life. He grew up with these people. I'm an outsider."

"Yeah, but I can assure you that Zach hasn't always been the most upstanding citizen, and I know for a fact that a lot of people are mad that he didn't want to continue on with Moonlight. In my humble, and usually correct, opinion, I think most people will be happy to see Brooks get a second chance. Especially if y'all are serious about those babies you mentioned a few minutes ago."

My cheeks heat as I glance over at Brooks, who is watching me as he leans against the doorframe, his hands tucked into his jeans and looking absolutely delicious. Yeah, I think I'd definitely be interested in having his babies. And by the look in Brooks's eyes? I'd say he's interested, too.

"Alright. Enough with the googly eyes. And when people find out about what Zach said to you yesterday? They are not gonna be happy."

I've been trying not to think about the awful things Zach screamed at me as he stomped out of Brooks's office. I'd never felt more embarrassed in my life. Everyone in the lobby and the restaurant turned to look at me. Harper and Jazz quickly got me out of there, but I couldn't stop hearing the words replaying over and over again in my head.

Slut.

Whore.

Fucking bitch.

You name it, Zach yelled it.

It hurt more than I care to admit. Up until that point, I was hoping he'd handle it better than that. I should've known that was wishful thinking. Obviously, I knew he'd be mad. I even understand his anger. But shouting at me in my place of work in front of people I don't even know? That was unexpected.

At least it's out there now. He knows, which means everyone else will know soon enough.

Brooks grabs my bags. "Come on. Let's get you home."

I hug Jazz and thank her for letting me stay the night. She waves me off and tells me I'm welcome anytime.

As we're walking out of the house, Brooks tells me, "We'll talk about what Zach said to you later." He takes my bags and throws them in his truck.

"I'll follow you," I say, pointing to my car parked on the curb.

"No, ma'am. I'm not letting you out of my sight today. You'll ride with me, and we'll come get your car later on."

He opens the door, and I don't hesitate to climb in and let him take me home.

CHAPTER 35
Brooks

THIS MORNING IS a complete one-eighty from yesterday. Instead of my stomach being in knots, I'm calm and relaxed. Most importantly, I'm not alone. I pull Aspen closer to me, grateful that she's here. The past forty-eight hours were a nightmare, but having her back with me is the outcome I was hoping for.

She wiggles in my arms.

"Good morning, beautiful."

She grunts in response. She's never been a morning person.

I nudge my nose against her cheek. "I'm gonna make you pancakes. You want blueberry or chocolate chip?"

"Chocolate," she mumbles into the pillow.

"Coming up." I give her a quick kiss before I slide out of bed, leaving her cocooned in our blankets.

I put on a pot of coffee and look out toward the ranch. The sun is rising over the mountains, indicating a new day and a new future for me. For most of my life, I thought I'd end up here alone. That I'd have no one to share this with. But now, it feels like my life is starting all over again. I've done the hard work, and now I finally get to enjoy it. And with the woman of my dreams.

I get to work on the pancakes, cooking them slowly so they get nice and fluffy and also so Aspen gets a little bit longer to sleep.

When I'm flipping the last one, she saunters into the kitchen with a yawn. I turn to look at her and can't help but smile. Her curls are a mess. I didn't go easy on her last night. And she's wearing one of my Moonlight Ranch sweatshirts. It comes down to her upper thighs, giving me a nice view of her long legs.

She makes herself a cup of coffee while I plate up our breakfast.

"If you keep making me breakfast like this, I'm going to get used to it."

"Good," I tell her, taking the seat next to her at the island. "I want you to get used to it. My woman gets whatever she wants."

I've barely cut into my first pancake when there's a pounding knock on the front door.

I look at Aspen. "You expecting anyone?"

She shakes her head, and I let out an annoyed exhale. An intrusion this early in the morning is never good.

But I can, with full certainty, say I was not expecting to see Lacey standing on the other side of the door.

"Lacey. What are you doing here? Is Zach ok?"

Her face twists into a look of pure disgust. "Is Zach ok?" she mockingly repeats. "No, he is not ok. He just found out his father is dating his ex-girlfriend."

I sigh. I wish Zach would talk to me about this instead of siccing his mother on me. I guess I should've known she would try other means of contacting me when I didn't respond to her texts or calls. But in my defense, I've been busy. Lacey was last on my list.

"Tell me it's not true, Brooks. Tell me he's mistaken."

"He's not mistaken," I admit. "Aspen and I are together."

She looks at me like she has no idea who I am, and really, she doesn't. She's always seemed to think she had some sort of weird claim over me since we have a child together. But whatever claim she had ended the moment we broke up.

"Have you lost your mind?" she asks.

"Not that I'm aware of."

"She's the same age as your son." Technically, she's two years older than Zach, but now doesn't feel like the time to bring that up. Plus, it's none of her business.

"Yes, I know how old she is."

Her eyes widen when she realizes that I don't care. "So, you're choosing her over your own son then?"

Just like Lacey to jump to conclusions. "No. Of course not. But Zach has pushed me away at every possible turn over the years. Because of you, I assume." She rolls her eyes. "He wants nothing to do with me, and as much as that kills me, I can't keep fighting a losing battle. I didn't mean to fall in love with Aspen. It just happened, and I'm tired of putting my happiness aside for everyone else when no one else seems to care about me.

"I understand Zach isn't happy right now. I don't expect him to be ok with this. But I'm hoping that one day he'll realize that Aspen and I are together for us and not to hurt him."

Lacey shakes her head. She's certainly not the one I want to be explaining myself to. "You're a pathetic excuse for a father."

Those words always sting, but I can't act like they're not kind of true. Especially at this moment. "Yeah, well, neither of you ever gave me a damn chance."

She huffs a laugh and tries to look over my shoulder to where Aspen is sitting, but I shift slightly, blocking her view. "Have a nice life with your little whore."

"Hey! You watch your fucking mouth, Lacey. Now I see where Zach gets it from."

I couldn't believe the things Aspen told me he'd said to her. I should've followed him out of my office that day. I could've gotten her away from that quicker. I should've known he would go to her next.

"At least I've given him a loving home and plenty of support," Lacey tells me, as if that's any consolation.

"Yeah, keep telling yourself that, Lace. The kid has no respect for anyone except himself."

"Oh, please. Don't try to turn this around on me. You're the one that fucked up here."

"I'm willing to own up to my mistakes. You're the one who can't look past your own ego to see that our son is not the little saint you wanted him to be. Now, if we're done here, my breakfast is getting cold."

She opens her mouth to say something else, but I shut the door before I have a chance to hear it. Out of everyone in Blue Haven, Lacey is the last person whose opinion I care about. I've stayed silent about how she's treated me over the years, but I'm done trying to be the nice guy.

I walk into the kitchen and sit back down next to Aspen. I focus directly on my food, because as much as I don't want to admit it, Lacey's words got to me. I do feel like I've failed Zach as a father. And while I know it's not entirely my fault, I feel like maybe I could've tried harder. Maybe I should've made him spend his weekends with me even when he didn't want to. Maybe I shouldn't have given him as much freedom as I did. I really thought that as he got older, he'd come around and want to spend time with me. Hindsight is twenty-twenty, I guess.

Aspen rubs my back and asks softly, "You ok?"

I take a deep breath. "Yeah. Just not how I wanted this morning to go."

"I imagine we might have a few more mornings like that once people find out about us."

I put my hand on her leg. "Well, whatever happens, we'll get through it together."

"And you know you're not a bad father, right?"

"I don't know. Kinda feels like it sometimes."

"You were way too young when you had Zach. I think you did the best you could at the time. And there's only so much you can do for someone who constantly pushes you away."

The tension relaxes in my shoulders. Of course, I already knew what she's saying, but it feels nice to hear it from someone else. Especially from her, since she got Zach's perspective too.

"Thank you, darlin'." I lean over and give her a gentle kiss on her lips. "Now eat your pancakes. We're going riding in a bit."

She smiles and picks up her fork.

———

The stables are busy today. Beck is gearing up for a morning trail ride with three families when we finally get there. I texted him earlier to make sure he left mine and Aspen's horses in their stalls. He wasn't happy about it, but he agreed anyway.

He waves at us when my UTV pulls up. I grab Aspen's hand as we walk toward him, and I catch his eyes falling to our hands. A small smile tugs at his lips.

"Well, look who it is," he says in greeting.

"Hey, Beck."

"Mornin', Ms. Aspen. I take it to mean you two are official now?" he asks.

I pull Aspen toward me and kiss her. "Yep."

"Ok, a simple yes or no woulda been fine," he teases. "Get out of here before I have to be witness to anything else."

We both laugh, and I start to lead Aspen over to our horses, but she stops.

"Beck?" she says.

"Hm?"

"Thanks for not judging us. I know you and Brooks probably don't talk about your feelings much, but I want you to know that we both appreciate how supportive you've been. I'm so glad Brooks has such good friends."

"I appreciate you saying that. You're part of the family now, too, Aspen. You ever need anything, you know where to find me."

She nods and then turns back to me. Her eyes are beaming with happiness, and I know in this moment that I've made the right choice.

Aspen is my family. She's my partner. No one else has ever felt right because I was waiting for her. It doesn't matter how we got here. All that matters is that we're here now.

We ride out on the trail. It's a little bit longer than the ones we normally go on, but it's one of my favorites. And I know we'll be alone for most of the ride.

Aspen's horse trots behind mine through the trees. The mornings are cold now, but it's one of my favorite seasons on the ranch. I love the sound of hooves on crunchy leaves and the wind through the tree branches. I inhale the cold air. Yes, fall is a season of change, and that's exactly what I'm going through right now.

We reach a point on the trail where I jump down and tie our horses up. Aspen and I walk the rest of the way up to the top of the hill. This spot overlooks the entire ranch.

"This is it, darlin'. This is our life. Are you ready for that?"

She looks over at me, her smile brightening her entire face. "I've been ready, Brooks."

I pull her into my arms.

"Thank you for giving me a home and a family, Brooks. This is everything I've ever wanted."

"You're everything I've ever wanted, darlin'. Thank you for staying."

CHAPTER 36

Aspen

"SO, basing it on this hot dog, how big is Broo—" Jazz starts to ask, while holding up a hot dog we're prepping for the grill.

I hold up my hand and shake my head. "No. Do not finish that sentence."

"Oh, come on! Just hold your hand around to show me."

"No way!"

Her shoulders slump, and she throws the hot dog back on the plate. "You're no fun."

"I know. I know."

Brooks chooses this moment to walk in from the back door. "Ladies, is the meat ready for the grill?"

"Oh, the meat is definitely ready," Jazz declares.

I laugh, but Brooks looks unamused. That's what he gets for inviting all of the ranch staff over for a cookout. Apparently, it's something his parents used to do, and he continued it for a little while until it got too overwhelming for him with everything else he had to handle.

Last week, we were sitting outside at sunset, and he started telling me about it. He has so many great memories from these cookouts. I could see by the dreamy smile on his face that he missed them. I immediately suggested we do it again. We decided to do a potluck to make it a little easier. He'd grill burgers and dogs while everyone else brought their favorite sides or desserts.

He was worried no one would come. Honestly, I would've called it a success even if it was just the two of us, Jazz, Harper, and Beck. But it turns out, people at Moonlight Ranch do actually like Brooks (I don't know why he's surprised by this), and now we have a full house of employees sharing stories and food out back.

Brooks has been beaming all night. This is just what he needed after everything we've been through the past few weeks.

Brooks rolls his eyes at Jazz, which makes us both laugh. "Can you bring it out here, please?"

"Yes, sir!" Jazz grabs the plates of burgers and hot dogs we prepped and heads outside while I finish cleaning up in the kitchen.

I'm not even alone for two minutes when someone says my name. I look over my shoulder to see Harper taking a seat at the kitchen island.

"Hey, Harper. Having fun?" I ask.

"Yeah, I'm so glad Brooks decided to start these up again."

"I know. It's great having everyone here together. I hope it's not too cold, though." The Calloways used to do this during the spring, but Brooks didn't want to wait. So we bought some portable heaters and made sure to have a nice big fire going outside.

"I think everyone is super comfortable."

I nod in relief.

"You know I don't think I've told you this, but I'm really happy you and Brooks are together."

"Really?" So far, it seems like all our relationship has done is cause issues.

"Yeah. I've never seen Brooks this happy. I think he's been going through the motions for so long, and everything has always been about the ranch. But then you walked in, and his face lit up again. He came alive. He's genuinely happy for the first time in a long time."

"Thanks for saying that, Harper. That means a lot coming from you."

She smiles and nods. "So, how has he been holding up with the whole Zach situation?"

I sigh. "It hasn't been great. I think he's at the point now where he's trying to give Zach some space. He's texted him a few times but hasn't gotten anything back."

"It's probably going to take some time."

I nod in agreement. "I just… I just hope we didn't make the wrong decision."

"About what?"

"Us being together. I hate that I'm the reason they had a falling out."

"Aspen, honey, this has been a long time coming. Zach has been looking for an excuse to cut Brooks out of his life for awhile. All you did was help speed that up a little. I know Brooks wants that relationship with him, but it was never gonna happen. Zach made up his mind years ago, and all he's done is drag Brooks along. I hate to say it, but I'm glad this happened. I'm glad Brooks is finally thinking about himself."

"I know. I kind of agree, but I know Brooks is hurting."

"I'm sure, but hopefully he'll get over it eventually. What about you? Have you heard from Zach since his little outburst? I still can't believe he said those things to you."

I shake my head. "No, I haven't. I'm sure he's blocked me, which is fine. I have nothing to say to him."

It still hurts when I think about the way he yelled at me that day. I understand his anger, but I don't think he needed to express it like that in front of everyone. I didn't do that to him when he cheated on me. I calmly removed myself from the situation. With Brooks's help, but still. I didn't berate him in front of everyone he knows.

"Good. If he does start bothering you, let me or Beck know. We'll handle it."

My body instantly relaxes. I know that she truly means that, too. I never thought I would have people who actually cared about me in the way the people at Moonlight Ranch do. If you had told me earlier this year that I was going to fall in love with a small town in northern Georgia and never want to leave, I wouldn't have believed you. But now, I can't picture myself anywhere else.

This is home.

These people are my family.

This is everything I've ever wanted.

"Thanks, Harper."

"No need to thank me. We look out for our family around here."

I nod. "Yeah, I'm starting to see that."

"Come on, let's get back to the party."

The two of us walk out back and see Jazz and Brooks bickering by the grill. Beck is playing catch with his daughter. We've set out chairs and tables, and everyone is sipping on a drink while they chat. The best part is the sun getting ready to set. The late autumn chill has set in, making the bonfire the perfect centerpiece for the night.

"Hey, darlin', come here," Brooks calls when he spots me.

I excuse myself from Harper's side and head toward him.

"Did you need me to grab you anything?" I ask.

"Nope. Just need a kiss from my woman."

Jazz makes a gagging noise before she walks off. I smile and lean in to kiss Brooks. His hand wraps around my waist, pulling me in closer before he kisses me.

Every time we kiss, it's like a sense of calm washes over me. I have no doubt that this is the man I'm supposed to be with. We had an unconventional start, but that's not going to stop us from having the most amazing ending.

"I love you," I murmur as I pull back.

"I love you, too," he says before giving me another quick kiss. "And I wanted to say thank you for planning all this. This place and these people mean a lot to me, and I'm so grateful that you've accepted all of this into your life."

"We're a team now, right? That's how it works."

He swallows down the emotion I see forming in his

eyes. "Yeah, I just… I guess I never thought I'd have all this. And now I do." He gestures to the backyard filled with people. "My life feels right all of a sudden. And that's because of you, Aspen."

"And you make me feel like I belong. I've never felt more content than I do right now. And that's because of *you*."

He kisses me again, but it's interrupted by a small voice and someone poking Brooks's leg.

"Excuse me, Mr. Brooks."

We look down to see Beck's daughter, Jade.

"Hey, Jadey. What can I do for you?"

I take a step back so he can focus his attention on the little girl who can't be any older than five.

"I'm hungry," she explains.

We both laugh.

"Me too. What do you want, a hot dog or a hamburger?"

"Hot dog, please!"

"Coming right up."

Brooks finishes grilling the meat, and I help him get it all set up before everyone digs in. The two of us stand by the back door, sipping spiked apple cider while everyone fills their plates. This year has been such a season of change for me, and I can't help but be grateful for everything I have. My life feels like the perfect example of everything happens for a reason. If I'd had a good family life, I never would've moved to Atlanta. I never would've met Zach. Which means I never would've moved to Blue Haven and met the love of my life.

All the pain, all the heartbreak. It was all worth it to bring me to this moment with my new family. The family I chose for myself.

"Hey, lovebirds! Come eat!" Jazz yells at us.

Brooks and I smile at each other before we make a plate and situate ourselves between our friends.

I guess happily ever afters really do exist.

Epilogue

Aspen

ONE YEAR *later*

"I hear congratulations are in order." I look up from the table at Melvin's to see Mayor Cunningham staring down at me with a huge smile on his face.

"Thank you so much!"

He grabs my left hand to inspect the ring on my finger. I can't blame him. I've been admiring it for days. I don't think I could've picked out a more perfect ring if I got it myself.

Brooks proposed to me this past weekend. He woke me up early to go on a ride, which is not unusual for him. He likes to get a ride in first thing in the morning and knows I like to go with him. It's so relaxing to wake up surrounded by nature.

We went on one of our favorite trails that has the best view of the sunrise this time of year. He got down on one knee just as the sun was rising. It had been a complete surprise to me.

I later found out that Jazz, Harper, *and* Beck all knew it was going to happen, and all three of them managed to keep it a secret from me, which is pretty impressive.

"So, when is the big day?" Mayor Cunningham asks.

"Oh…" Brooks and I haven't even talked about it. I've been on such a high from the proposal, wedding details have been the furthest from my mind.

"Why're you askin'?" Brooks asks from across the table. "You trying to make it a town event?"

Mayor Cunningham rolls his eyes. "Of course not. I'm just curious. And I wanted to let you both know, I'm also an ordained minister if you happen to be looking for one."

"Oh, really?" I ask with raised eyebrows, surprised to hear this little fact about him.

"Yes, ma'am. Did it for my cousin's wedding a few years ago. I've done a few other weddings since then, too. And for you two? I'd do it at no cost. Just something to think about."

Brooks chuckles, but I look at Eli and sincerely thank him. What a sweet thing to offer us. "I appreciate that. We'll definitely keep that in mind once we start planning."

"Good. Good. Well, if either of you ever needs anything, you know where to find me. Enjoy the rest of your day."

"Thank you. You too!"

He tips his head and then walks away from our table.

Brooks leans forward and asks, "You are not seriously considering having Eli marry us, are you?"

I shrug. "Why not?" I've never once thought about who would marry us, but it doesn't seem like a terrible idea to have someone who knows us do it. Over the last year, I've worked with Eli a lot through the ranch. Mostly because Brooks doesn't want to, but also because I genuinely like him. He's always been very nice to us, and I love that he always has the town's best interest in mind. After all, this town is my home now. I want to make sure it's in good hands.

"First of all, it's Eli…" Brooks suggests, like that explains anything.

I roll my eyes. "He's a nice guy. Plus, it'd be free, and he'd more than likely be willing to come out to the ranch to marry us."

Brooks looks at me curiously. "You wanna get married at the ranch?"

"Oh, well, I assumed you'd want to do it there."

"But what do you want?" he asks.

I've never really pictured my actual wedding day. Sure, I wanted to get married and have the babies and the life. But that was all after the ceremony. I was never one of those girls who looked through wedding magazines and scrapbooked every dream. I don't have any Pinterest boards of centerpieces and extravagant bouquets. I simply wanted the family that came along with the wedding.

"It doesn't really matter to me," I answer honestly.

"Really? I assumed you'd want some fancy ballroom or something."

I laugh thinking about gathering Blue Haven residents in a fancy ballroom like the one at the hotel I used to work at in Atlanta. Yeah. No. That's not happening. "The only thing I care about is that you're at the end of the aisle."

He smiles and grabs my hand. "There's no question about that. I guess the ranch it is."

"It makes sense, too. The ranch is where we fell in love. It's where we'll live out our future together. Might as well make it official there."

"How are you this perfect?" he asks.

"Yeah, remember that next time you get mad at me for leaving the fence unlocked."

He sighs. "I wasn't mad. Just… frustrated."

I laugh. He was definitely mad but tried to pretend that he wasn't after he spent hours riding around the ranch trying to find the horses that got out. "Right."

He shakes his head and scoots out of the booth. We head outside and toward his truck when I remember that I needed to get something in town.

"Hey, I need to run to the drug store really quick."

"Alright. I need to go to the bank. Meet back here in ten?"

"Yep!"

He gives me a quick kiss before we go our separate ways.

Luckily, the drugstore is mostly empty, and thankfully, Brenda is not at the cash register today. I just know she'd have a field day telling the whole town what I'm about to buy. I grab a small basket and throw some random lotion, gum, and a tube of mascara in before I make my way to the aisle I really need.

Family planning.

I quickly find the pregnancy tests, but why do there have to be so many different brands? This morning I realized I'm two weeks late. At first, I freaked out, but then I realized that Brooks is going to be so excited if I am pregnant. I want to make sure it's true before I tell him, though.

I finally pick the one that actually says if you're pregnant or not, because I don't want to have to stress about decoding the lines.

I throw the box in my basket and try to hide it as best as I can with the other items. I'm about to go check out when someone says my name, and I stop in my tracks. It's been awhile since I've heard that voice.

I turn around slowly. "Hi."

I've seen Zach a few times over the last year, and while he's never happy to see me, the anger has faded a little each time. We never really talk, but I know he graduated from the police academy and was hired by the county. I also know he's started dating someone new. He's moving on, and I'm so happy for him even if he's not happy for me.

"How are you?" Zach asks. He looks uncomfortable talking to me, and I get it. However, it's also hard to forget those two years when we were inseparable.

"I'm good. How about you?"

He nods. "Yeah, I'm good too. I, uh, heard about the engagement."

I wince a little, preparing myself for the worst. Brooks told me that he texted Zach before he proposed, just so he wouldn't hear it from someone else. Brooks has done a lot of one-sided texting with Zach over the last year. He understands why Zach won't talk to him, but I know it still hurts.

"Oh. Yeah." We both glance down at my ring.

"I'm happy for you," he says, and it sounds like he might actually mean that.

My eyebrows rise in surprise. "Really?"

"Yeah, I mean, don't sign me up to be best man or anything, but I'm glad that you're happy." He reluctantly adds, "I'm glad my dad is happy, too."

"Thank you, Zach. That really means a lot."

"But just so you know, I will not be calling you my stepmom."

I laugh. "I would never expect you to."

"So, are, uh, other congratulations in order?" he asks and tilts his head to my basket and the box of pregnancy tests.

My face instantly heats. "Oh, well, I'm not sure yet."

He gives me a friendly smile, one I haven't seen in a long time. "Don't worry. Your secret is safe with me."

I exhale my worry. I know I'm not his favorite person, but I trust that he won't tell anyone. "Thank you."

"You know. It's kinda funny," he says, laughing to himself.

"What is?"

"How things ended up. When I brought you here to Blue Haven, I remember being so worried that you were going to hate it here. But look at you. You've made this place your home all without me. Maybe it was fate that I brought you here so that you could end up with him."

I nod slowly. This is not something I ever thought I'd hear Zach say, and it makes my heart so happy. "Yeah, maybe."

"Well, anyways, do you need anything else? I'll walk you out."

"Oh, no. Just need to pay."

He gestures for me to lead the way to the cashier. We both pay for our items and walk outside together to find Brooks leaning against his tailgate, waiting for me.

He stands when he sees Zach walking next to me, but I shake my head at him. I know he would jump at the chance to talk to Zach, but I don't think Zach is ready for that. Not yet, anyway.

"I'm not over it yet," Zach says suddenly. "But I'm getting there."

"I understand. We appreciate that you're trying."

"Maybe… maybe I'll try harder. I mean, I wouldn't want to miss out on my future little brother or sister."

I look up at him. "I would love that, Zach."

He smiles and nods. "I'll see you around, Aspen."

"See ya around."

I watch him walk away in the other direction before I meet Brooks at his truck. He helps me inside and starts driving home before he asks, "So what was that about?"

"I think that was him trying to be understanding."

"Really? You think he might come around?" The hope in Brooks's voice breaks my heart.

When Brooks looks back toward the road, I put my hand on my stomach. "Yeah, I think he might."

Maybe if I really am pregnant, this baby will bring our family back together.

I look over at Brooks and see a small smile pulling on his lips as he drives. He's excited about the possibility even without knowing about the baby.

An hour later, when I've gotten three positive pregnancy tests in a row, Brooks cries into my shoulder and tells me how happy he is and how much he loves me. Moving to Blue Haven was the best decision I've ever made, even if it was for the wrong Calloway man.

The End

Thank you for reading Broken Boundaries! I hope you enjoyed Brooks and Aspen's story. Reviews are so important to Indie Authors. I'd love for you to leave an honest review on your favorite platform.

As a thank you for signing up for my newsletter, you'll receive a FREE ebook of my grumpy sunshine romance: Fragile Heart.

Newsletter sign up

Book 2 of the Moonlight Ranch is coming late 2026. Be on the lookout for Crossed Lines: Beck's story!

Crossed Lines

Acknowledgments

Thank you to my best friends who consistently support me even after 15 books. I'm the luckiest girl in the world to have such amazing friends.

Thank you to my husband for helping me when I wanted to give up writing this book. You pushed me when I needed it. I love you.

Thank you to both my editor and cover designer for being absolutely fantastic to work with every single time.

And to every single person reading this. Thank you for giving my work a chance. You guys give me the strength to keep going.

About the Author

D.C. Kile lives in Georgia with her husband and two kids #TwinMom. If she's not writing steamy romance, she's probably reading it. She also enjoys cooking, drinking coffee out of really large coffee cups, and daydreaming about future vacations.

D.C. Kile would love to hear from readers, so be sure to follow along on social media. She can be found on Instagram, TikTok, and Facebook @AuthorDCKile.

Be the first to know about new releases. Sign up to D.C. Kile's newsletter for the latest updates:
Newsletter sign up

Also by D.C. Kile

UNDERWOOD FARMS SERIES

Out of Place

Here with You

It's Our Turn

TORTURED HEARTS SERIES

The Penalty

The Breakdown

The Fall

Other titles can be found here at authordckile.com/books/

www.ingramcontent.com/pod-product-compliance
Lightning Source LLC
Chambersburg PA
CBHW071729150726
47998CB00005B/1563